Deep Analysis: Frightening Conclusion

Deep Analysis: Frightening Conclusion

Aaron Kaplan

Copyright © 2009 by Aaron Kaplan.

Library of Congress Control Number: 2009905598
ISBN: Hardcover   978-1-4415-4432-2
               Softcover   978-1-4415-4431-5

All rights reserved. No part of this book may be reproduced or transmitted in any form or by any means, electronic or mechanical, including photocopying, recording, or by any information storage and retrieval system, without permission in writing from the copyright owner.

This is a work of investigative reporting and the author's own analysis, and opinion. Names, Characters, places and incidents are the product of the author's research performed to the best of his ability using a variety of sources, official and non official, and are not used fictitiously, and any resemblance to any actual persons, living or dead, events, or locales is entirely coincidental.

This book was printed in the United States of America.

To order additional copies of this book, contact:
Xlibris Corporation
1-888-795-4274
www.Xlibris.com
Orders@Xlibris.com

CONTENTS

INTRODUCTION
"God," "god," and Us: the Little People 17

CHAPTER ONE
Roswell, Anunnaki, the Middle East and the Deluge 23

CHAPTER TWO
The Pyramid, Moses's Biggest Secret!..56

CHAPTER THREE
Dying Experts, the Renaissance, and the Search for Energy 67

CHAPTER FOUR
The Modern Age, Hitler and the Bomb 76

CHAPTER FIVE
Adolf Hitler..86

CHAPTER SIX
The South Pole, Antarctica, and Admiral Byrd 95

CHAPTER SEVEN
Operation Highjump, the Black Hole, and Meeting with Aliens 112

CHAPTER EIGHT
Nuclear Bombs Exploding on Our Mainland, Central USA 137

CHAPTER NINE
Back to Roswell, Silicon Valley,
the Death of Countless Microbiologists...145

CONCLUSIONS AND CLARIFICATIONS 161

DOCUMENTS AND NOTES...181

INDEX...203

DEDICATION

I would like to dedicate this book to my beautiful wife Sally, without whose help and inspiration this book would never have been written.

Yes! She inspired me, directed me, told me how to, showed me how to, and on many nights even typed for me, and always said "Go finish the book!" What dedication.

This book is also dedicated to my dear mom Toby, who passed away during the writing of this book, and let me tell you about some real inspiration. She always urged me to do my best. After her death, I started working twenty four/seven, and never felt it.

This book is also dedicated to all those serious researchers and authors who had the fortitude to engage in subjects similar to mine; who in their own ways tried to alert the human race of what is about to come; who have been socially pilloried for their questing activities and beliefs.

I would also like to dedicate this book to all the people, ordinary citizens, who have seen aliens and their crafts and have suffered because of it.

The wheels are in motion—events have began—they can't be stopped!

Like the old saying (joke) goes: It won't be long now!

The predetermined final ending may only be modified, but not eliminated!

FRONT COVER "Egyptian Rocket Goddess".
BY: AUDREY FLACK, SCULPTRESS.

BIOGRAPHY

Audrey Flack holds a graduate degree and an honorary doctorate from Cooper Union in New York City, and a Bachelor of Fine Arts degree from Yale University. She attended New York University's Institute of Fine Arts where she studied the history of art.

She was awarded the St. Gaudens Medal from Cooper Union, and the honorary Albert Dome professorship from Bridgeport University. She is an honorary professor at George Washington University, and is currently a visiting professor at the University of Pennsylvania.

Audrey Flack has taught and lectured extensively both nationally, and internationally.

A pioneer of Photorealism and a nationally recognized painter and sculptor, Ms. Flack's work is in the collections of major museums around the world, including the Metropolitan Museum of Art, The Museum of Modern Art, the Solomon R. Guggenheim Museum, and Whitney Museum of American Art and the National Museum of Art in Canberra, Australia. She was the first photorealist painter to have work purchased by the Museum of Modern Art.

Throughout her career, Ms. Flack's work has been featured in numerous traveling museum exhibitions, including "Twenty-two Realists" (1972) at the Whitney Museum of American Art, New York; "Super Realism" (1975-76) at the Baltimore Museum of Art; "American Painting of the Seventies" (1979) at the Albright-Knox Gallery, Buffalo, NY; Contemporary American Realism" (1981-83) at the Pennsylvania Academy of the Fine Arts, Philadelphia; Toyama Now, 1981" (1981) at the Museum of Modern Art, Tokyo, Japan; and "Making Their Mark: Women Artists Move into the Mainstream"(1989) which traveled to the Cincinnati Art Museum, the New Orleans Museum of Art, the Denver Art Museum and the Pennsylvania Academy of the Fine Arts. Ms. Flack has also held numerous solo exhibitions including at the

Roko Gallery, New York; French & Company, New York; and the Louis K. Meisel Gallery, New York, among others.

A major retrospective of her work organized by the J.B. Speed Art Museum in Louisville, Kentucky has traveled to four museums around the country during 1992-93.

There are numerous books on her work. The most recent being "Breaking the Rules" by Thalia Gouma Peterson, published by the Abrams Publishing Company in New York.

Among her public commissions are a Monumental Gateway to the city of Rock Hill, South Carolina, consisting of four twenty-foot high bronze figures on granite pedestals, and Islandia, a nine-foot high bronze sculpture for the New York City technical college in Brooklyn New York.

Audrey Flack lives and works in New York City and Long Island.

A Bevy of Goddesses
By Laurie S. Hurwitz
American Artist, September 1991

"I've always collected sculptures and I've always put sculptures in my paintings, just as Cezanne put them in his still lifes," says the artist. "Making sculpture attracted me because of its substantiality. Our society is fragmented, empty, and falling apart, so I wanted to make solid objects, things that people could literally hold on to, things that wouldn't fly away or disintegrate." Her first sculpture, made in 1981, depicts a seated cherub clasping a shield over his heart and nearly fits into the palm of your hand, not unlike a votive object.

Then came a series of progressively larger images embodying female strength, ranging from a black medicine woman and a sun goddess to mythological deities such as Athena and Diana. These works culminated in Civitas, a group of four, thirteen foot high bronze goddesses that preside over a section of the parkway in Rock Hill, South Carolina. Together, the various figures Flack has depicted during the past ten years comprise "a virtual temple dedicated to the archetypal female muse in her myriad guises," as art historian Susan P. Casteras writes in the catalog to Flack's recent solo show, "A Pantheon of female Deities," at Manhattan's Louis K. Meisel Gallery.

Blending the philosophies and legends of various cultures, including Greek, Indian, Chinese, African, American, and prehistoric, many of the figures, such as the medicine woman, are healers; others are images of women beginning to assert their own power. Egyptian Rocket Goddess, which the artist says is about "breaking free," has a determined facial expression and a frontal physical stance that, with arms extended and head thrust out, literally pushes forward. Combining ancient and modern imagery, the taut Egyptian Rocket Goddess has snakes wrapped around her arms, a traditional sign of female power and fertility dating back to a sculpted Minoan snake goddess from 1600 B.C.; her drapery and head-dress are adorned with the sleek, contemporary image of a rocket.

EMAIL: LOU@MEISELS.COM
Audrey Flack <audreyflack@hotmail.com>

ALL SEEING EYE

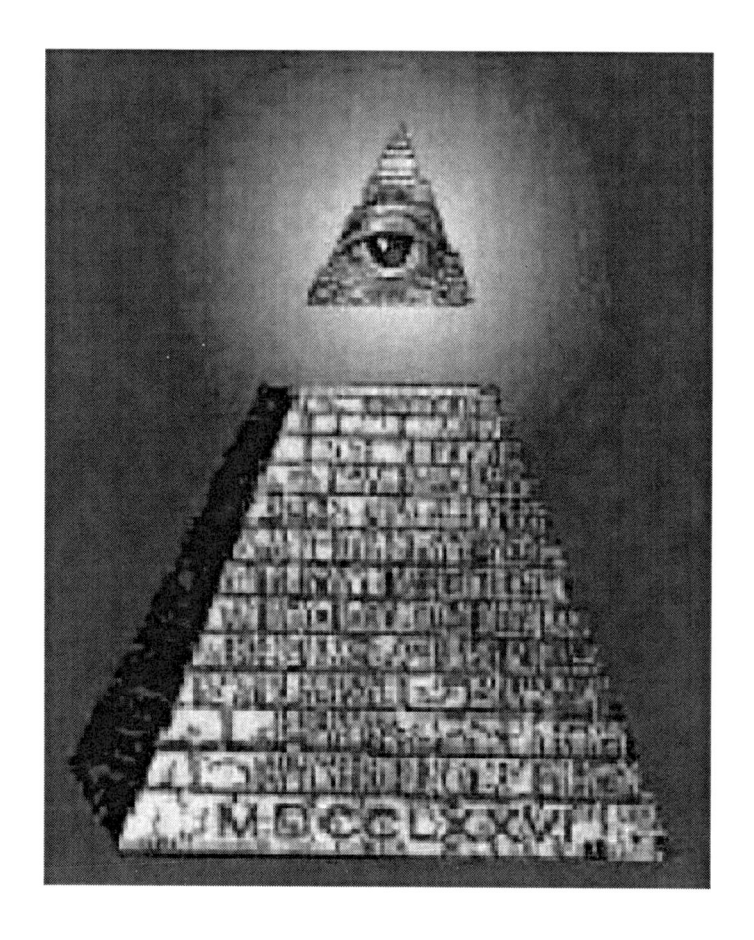

From Egypt we find The Great American Seal
Masonic **"THE SEEING EYE"**

ABOUT THE AUTHOR

I attended and graduated from Samuel James Tilden High School in Brooklyn, New York, in June of 1964. I continued my education and graduated from the College of Aeronautics, class of September of 1967, near LA-GUARDIA Airport, Flushing, New York. I was employed for over thirty-five years in the Aerospace/Aircraft Industry civilian and military projects. Work performed on all types of aircraft, including designing major parts for Jet Engines, including the rights to a patent received from Pratt and Whitney, Jet Engines Mfg. in Hartford, Connecticut. I have also been employed by such other companies such as Fairchild Republic, Grumman Aircraft, Sikorsky Helicopters. I also worked for EDO Corp., involving submarines, and Electro Visual Engineering, involving flight simulators (the newest 3-D type).

The work that I performed included designing modifications on all type of aircraft, military and civilian. These projects also involved designing new aircraft and analyzing major problems and, yes, finding solutions!

I have also a great deal of knowledge of the Hebrew language—reading, writing, and speaking. This is due to one main reason: I was raised in Israel as a youngster from the age of two to fourteen. I was born in Berlin, Germany, in 1946.

I also used to fly private aircraft and drove race cars at the race track, including once in a while the Midnight Drag Race scene.

So at this point all in all, I believe that I am pretty well rounded to do this type of research: analyze and arrive at the correct conclusion!

So please go on and enjoy some new and exciting findings and frightening conclusions!

And the reason to enjoy this book? I will not leave you hanging with a maybe, possible, perhaps, or no answer at all. In this book I am giving you the exact answer, as I see it and as it is—just the facts!

Nepal

7,000 B.C.—The Lolladoff plate, discovered in Nepal, appears to show a hovering disk-shaped object in the center and a small being, portraying an alien resembling an alien gray, beside it. The circular pattern is reminiscent of the spiraling movement of consciousness—Golden Ratio—of creation.

INTRODUCTION

"God," "god," and Us: the Little People

We all heard of the crash at Roswell, and most of us heard and read regarding the subject of alien abductions in one form or another. For many of us who attended Bible study or religious schools, we learned of the fallen angels, which sometimes are referred to as the "Nefilim." We learned about Noah's ark, Moses and his brother, and spokesman, Aaron, and the pyramids. And in the twentieth century, we all know about the two atomic bombs, one that was dropped over Hiroshima and the other dropped over Nagasaki in Japan at the end of World War II.

But until you read in simple English, without using any fancy math formulas to confuse you, until you read this book, you'll never know the truth, the plain truth as it occurred, and now as I see it, after I interpreted certain records, including some parts of the Bible that allegedly may be—I repeat, *may* be—incomplete, due to missing information that we must now be aware of and need to know.

To write this book, I researched many sources of information; read the works of such great writers such as Zecharia Sitchin, Michael Tsarion, Glenn Kimball, Lynn Marzulli, Patric Heron, and more; reviewed all the records available to me from other numerous books and many Internet sites, television shows; and from listening to many very popular midnight radio talk shows.

I analyzed all the information that I saw, read, and heard, filtering all that through a special filter, my brain, and have incorporated only the most truthful, factual, and meaningful information to form the comprehensive and cohesive conclusions summarized in writing this book.

When making a critical decision or in gathering any type of information, you must do it without bias or prejudice. The information from the Democratic side and from the Republican side; from the Left and from the Right; information from the Bible, the Old Testament and the New Testament, and any other religious sources; all newspapers; television and radio; and all other information from any other source available. After you have gathered all this information, you will need to filter it! How? Again, by using your brain.

Yes, your brain that you were born with and use every day to make all types of decisions and use to survive, the brain that God gave you!

Speaking of "God," for the sake of my readers, this book is not intended to be a religious book; it is not intended to be used by any religion to promote or demote the name of "God." "God" with capital "G" or little "g" in this book is used strictly as a scientific method to identify, if possible, a certain form or *Entity* in charge or in command of a situation occurring at the time of happening. For the purpose of my reader, it may be the same "God" or "god" that exists today or that existed in the past of old, or may not.

As you read, you'll notice that I, the author, will repeat myself more than once; it is not by chance, it's by design. It's to make sure that the information and ideas that I gathered get through to you, the readers, in full clarity!

So please remember, I wrote this book not to promote or demote any religion, any religious figure in any shape or form, including when mentioning the word "God" or "god"! All the information written here is in the best of my ability to bring you information that other writers cannot find or are unwilling to accept as truth, afraid to bring forward certain conclusions that may make mankind aware of what is really going on right in front of their eyes and all around them.

During a war, a major war or a minor war, or just any military conflict, in order for one side or another to win, they must gather *intelligence* information to be considered without prejudice. In other words, you can't think or make decisions by thinking with your heart. If you think with your heart before making a critical decision, you'll wind up in defeat or in a concentration camp.

The information that I reference in my book is available to all. In some instances, I read the Old Testament and the New Testament and found new information and data never heard of before. As strange or as controversial as this seems, it is known that for whatever the reason is, some writers, news reporters, or television/radio announcers are refusing to actually write or tell the truth; it could be because of possible career difficulties or fear of bodily harm.

Not afraid of exposing the truth is the writer-researcher Zecharia Sitchin and one of the very few individuals in the world who is an expert in the Sumerian language. By basically understanding the Sumerian language and not being mislead by other researchers' statements, Sitchin came to great and very accurate conclusions as outlined in his first book, *The 12th Planet.*

In his first book the 12 th Planet, and the many books that followed in this series, he talks about the alien race the "Anunnaki" and their flying machines, or as we know them by now as "UFO'S or flying saucers!

I believe the UFO'S, or so called flying saucers, have been visiting here a lot longer than we've been here.

There is no doubt in my mind that this is true. The only reason people are starting to talk about it is because now-a-days we have cam-corders that can show the evidence instead of having to depict it on a wall, in a cave.

Today's modern UFO'S and Alien Contacts being reported have a strong similarity to the Ancient descriptions of the "Anunnaki's" Android Beings. When we look at the descriptions of our modern "gray alien", we can clearly see that they do not look like us, or the Anunnaki. Rather, they look like the ancient humanoid depictions of Figurines. The majority of Abduction cases usually have a similar story to them in that the Aliens abducting them will perform medical examination and sometimes experiments having to do with human reproduction.

The Sumerians had amazing knowledge of the solar system, and of their GODS coming down to Earth. They also tell of another being that they described in our terms as "Android Beings". The Sumerians tell us that the Anunnaki had "helpers" that often performed such tasks as flying their craft, or helping with miscellaneous needs. The Sumerians directly explain that these "Helpers" were not alive, but acted as living entities.

Not only did they make figurines of the visitors, they also wrote down in Cuneiform text (on stone) what took place during the encounters with these "Android Beings". There are many stories where Emissaries of GOD helped out in one way or another.

Is it possible that the Grays were created by the Anunnaki as "Watchers" to oversee their experiments here on earth? If the Anunnaki are the GODS spoken about in all ancient texts and even the Modern Bible, then it is possible that they could have also created an "Android Race" aside from creating humans.

Maintaining the idea that the Anunnaki really do exist on Nibiru (Planet X), or now known as the 12th Planet, and they created man using Genetic Engineering thousands of years ago, then it makes sense that they would have quite an interest in us, especially now, quite an interest. We might be one of their grandest experiments. A very special breeding experiment, for more than one reason.

As per Sumerian tablets and seals that were found, one of the original reasons could very well have been to mine for gold, that was used on their own planet Nibiru to create and build protective domes around their cities.

What if they also performed the same experiments on other species OFF the planet Earth. If the Anunnaki exist, then there are also MANY other races on other planets as well. This would only be logical. Maybe the Anunnaki also used a mix between the known "ZETAS" or "GRAYS" and created an Android race to serve the Anunnaki.

If you are wondering whether I am connecting the dots the correct way, then let me tell you.

I am not an astronomer, however, please remember the name "ZETA". It's going to come up later on in this book in a very unique and mind boggling situation, in a worldwide famous abduction case!

Lately however, according to my research, it is becoming more and more evident that these so called alien abductions are being performed by a certain group of the Anunnaki, or as we may call them the Fallen Angels, who have been banished from the rest of the universe and imprisoned here on earth, by their own kind. The last time they tried to escape was circa 12,500 B.C. about 1000 years prior to Noha's flood (the Deluge). This subject will be covered in full detail in the next few chapters.

These abductions in very recent times, are having more and more mounting evidence of a very sinister, diabolical and frightening reason for us the human race.

When we analyze the descriptions of Aliens from people who claim to have been abducted, most of the aliens are described as being small gray beings that have large eyes, a bulbous head, and act almost "Android" like accompanied at times by Tall Blonds.

We have to think real hard, open our minds, and just wonder about something. There are a lot of theories about UFO's and some contend that they are unmanned others manned. One of the arguments against UFO's being manned is the distance that a craft would have to travel to get here. This being based on the premise that we haven't found life forms in our own solar system so another intelligent species would have to come from out there somewhere. The designs haven't changed too much in our recorded history so we have to wonder, either they don't need to: they may have reached the best design that their civilization is able to make or they can't. If UFO's are one shot missions they can't change them because they weren't designed to be changed. No ability to get back to their own world to upgrade. Which might explain why they supposedly sometimes crash.

This is the most common theory among some of us humans, but what if this is not the reason for the UFO crashes, and what if most of these UFO'S do not arrive here from out of space, and what if they arrive from inner space, our Earth!

I am no Zecharia Sitchin, not even close by a long shot, but I do understand the Hebrew language. This has enabled me to discover certain information conveyed in the Bible regarding major events that I believe are missing, and that changed the written past, due to possible error, or willfully omitted, in order to mislead mankind as to what our dear future may bring.

During the Iraq war, there were many news briefings. As we can remember, there were many comments that pertained to the safety of our troops, the progress of the war, and the equipment used, including comments about our troops not having armored SUVs, no ammo, no ice cream, etc. Some complaints, of course, were very legitimate. But it came to a point one day during the news briefing given by Secretary of Defense, Donald Rumsfeld, that the questions being asked were so out of line, that he turned directly toward the audience and the newspeople and said, "You are not news reporters, you're newsroom bred news reporters." He was so right!

After reading this book, you'll see the amazing, but direct correlation between

- the crash at Roswell;
- the Fallen Angels and/or the Nefilim;
- DNA and genetics;
- Noah's Ark and the Deluge;
- alien abductions;
- the famous seeing eye on the dollar bill;
- the nuclear bomb;
- the Internet;
- and finally, the mysterious deaths, recently, of hundreds of microbiologists.

I wrote before of Zecharia Sitchin. There is another author researcher, Michael Tsarion, whose work is very similar to Zecharia Sitchin, although Tsarion's work is taken from a slightly different perspective, a different angle, especially regarding two events that took place approximately 55,000 years ago, and again in the year 11,500 BC! Also, now in the present, I have analyzed some of the numbers and data from both Sitchin and Tsarion to reach certain new and terrifying conclusions conveyed in this book.

One final note before I present this story: You must remember and keep in mind that the aliens to whom I will be referring are super-shape-shifters, able to transform in an instant. It's scary.

CHAPTER ONE

Roswell, Anunnaki, the Middle East and the Deluge

The first public sighting by civilians of UFO's flying or crashing did not occur at Roswell. On June 24, 1947, at approximately 3:00 p.m. (PST), Kenneth Arnold was flying on a business trip at an altitude of 9,200 feet. He observed 9 flying objects, "flying saucers," in formation near Mount Rainier, Washington. At the time, this was taken as a new exciting sighting, very innocent it made most magazines of good taste and lots of talk. Then suddenly, out of the blue, on July 3, 1947, only about ten days later, we have the famous crash at Roswell. A crash of a Disc! A flying saucer crashed!

Did anybody in reality try to ever make a possible connection between the sighting by Kenneth Arnold on June 24, 1947, and the crash at Roswell on July 3, 1947? Not that we know of! Why did the Disc crash at Roswell? There was talk of other crashes, not too far away from Roswell, in the town of Corona, and a few more in the New Mexico countryside.

As soon as the crash happened, the Air Force sent Major Jesse A. Marcel to investigate. Major Marcel was an Officer, but not a regular officer—he was an Intelligence Officer who had served with the 509th Division, part of the Roswell Army Air Force Base. At that time, it was where the nation's only known nuclear bombs, fifteen of them, were stored, including the only planes to fly them—the B-29s. Yes, remember the atomic bombing of Hiroshima and Nagasaki? The crew was trained and came from the 509th division at Roswell Army Air Force Base.

Now to become an Intelligence Officer, and not just any Intelligence Officer but the one stationed in a nuclear air force base, the only one in the country at the time, he must have been a very highly trained person, trained to observe and detect anything unusual, and I mean *anything* at a split second observe and identify. So when Major Marcel went out to the crash site, at first glance he said that he saw a Disc; then to my mind, he saw a *Disc*. He did not see a Square. He did not see a triangle nor a pink elephant. He did not see a flying Macy's Parade balloon. He saw a *Disc*! It's over; Case Closed.

The military immediately enforced one of the greatest cover-ups of any event ever thrust upon the general public. All of the information that followed in the future after this event is simple government bull! Whitewashing, propaganda, to delude you.

And did you ever notice currently that whenever an important sighting occurs, a sighting of a UFO, flying saucer, flying triangle, right away or following soon after, we see on television a talk show host with a UFO expert, and what do they bring up again? Yep, Roswell! They are always diverting our attention from the real thing. We have to look forward toward the future and away from the past, Roswell. It is like the person or scientific investigator that is walking in the deep woods looking for Bigfoot. After spending days and days in the woods, getting close to something, he sees Bigfoot and, like a fool, follows it! But where does this individual wind up? Nowhere, just all alone in the woods. Bigfoot is always gone. Now I'll bet you, if that investigator would have retraced Bigfoot's tracks, he may have discovered the truth, something of utmost importance—it looks to me more and more as if Bigfoot is being employed to divert attention as needed away from what is really going on.

But before we leave the subject of Roswell, an important note: Remember what I have just told you about Kenneth Arnold's sighting, the 509th Bomb Group of the 8th Air Force from Roswell Air Force Army Base, providing the air crew for the nuclear bombing mission of Hiroshima and Nagasaki and the crash at Roswell. I'll be returning to this topic with some frightening conclusions later on.

* * *

We are going to return in a big way to the Roswell incident shortly in this major story. But first, you have to realize that to understand fully what is going on here and how I reached my startling conclusion on exactly—yes, exactly—what took place in Roswell on July 3, 1947, we will have to do a little time travel to our ancient past.

In 1968, a very controversial Swiss author named Erich von Daniken published a book called *Chariots of the Gods*. In this book, and in twenty-six other books that he wrote since then, von Daniken presents evidence for extraterrestrial influences on early human culture.

Von Daniken is one of the key figures responsible for popularizing the paleocontact and ancient-astronaut hypotheses. Von Daniken, while building on previous works by other authors, claims that intelligent extraterrestrial life exists and has entered our local solar system in the past, and that evidence and actual proof is abundant. He also claims that human evolution may have been manipulated through means of genetic engineering by extraterrestrial beings.

Yes, even then, von Daniken believed that humankind had been generated through the use of "genetic engineering." We have no reason to believe that our ancient ancestors' memories were so much worse than our own that they could not remember these alien visitations well enough to preserve an accurate account of their presence. There is little evidence to support this notion that ancient myths and religious stories are the distorted and imperfect recollections recorded by elder priests about ancient astronauts. The evidence—that prehistoric or "primitive" people were (and still are) quite intelligent and resourceful—is overwhelmingly to the contrary.

Speaking about nondistorted and perfect recollections regarding ancient astronauts, guess who came along with the so-called the Real McCoy of books. Zecharia Sitchin! Why do I call it the Real McCoy? Well, Sitchin's lifelong interest in the archeology of the Middle East culminated in a book that was published in 1976 called *The 12th Planet*.

This book, appearing at the height of the ancient-astronaut controversy, culminated with claims by Erich von Daniken that he had discovered evidence of the presence of UFOs and extraterrestrials in the artifacts from various ancient languages, proposed a new option concerning ancient history, and lifted the debate to a new level. While the debate generated by von Daniken was largely resolved, Sitchin's hypothesis survived and has continued to be the subject of a series of books through not only the 1990s, but also until this day with the possibility of some very heavy government pressure applied here (I shall explain later, but by government pressure, I mean they wanted to keep him muzzled up).

Zecharia Sitchin was born in Baku, Azerbaijan, and was raised in Israel. There he picked up the knowledge of modern and ancient Hebrew, learned the Old and the New Testament, and studied the history and archeology of the Near East and other seminal and European languages; but his real specialty was to study the ancient Sumerian language.

Sitchin became one of the very few people in the world who mastered the old, ancient Sumerian language and became an expert in interpretation of Sumerian cosmology, and this special skill enabled him to reach some of the following fantastic and very realistic conclusions.

And by the way, these fantastic so-called conclusions, it seems, are now becoming reality, one by one. In other words, his data, the conclusions Sitchin wrote about, especially with regard to a special, mysterious so-called missing planet, are coming into reality to the amazement of the so-called expert world governments and world leaders (the puppets)! By the way, have you seen the world's top astronomers' faces lately? Don't worry, we will return to this question later.

Of course, the real so-called world leaders, the real *puppet masters*, know all about that subject. They have known it all along from the ancient past to our present situation. They must have known it for millennia. After all, they are our makers and our keepers—oh yes! They also must know some hard facts regarding our very near future. Could our demise be part of this near future? We'll see as we follow this story.

* * *

Now remember, by Sitchin's own admission, he used and still uses almost exclusively the Sumerian texts, Sumerian tablets, and the Old Testament as a parallel source to do his research and reach his conclusions. By the way, as a major footnote, during the war in Iraq, many more Sumerian cylinders and tablets have been discovered, and I believe that the U.S. government is using Zecharia Sitchin with his skills as an interpreter.

By staying on the path of directly studying the Sumerian language and records, he can focus more on records of actual events that happened in the past, without being distracted or mislead by other sources who may have used diluted information all throughout the centuries. According to Sitchin's own interpretation of Sumerian records dealing in cosmology, there is an undiscovered planet out there that follows a long, elliptical orbit, that permits it to reach our inner solar system roughly every 3,600 years. This planet is called "Nibiru." Other scientists and researchers who have "viewed" this planet via the Infrared Telescope (IRAS) have called it other names, "Planet X," or as Sitchin labels it, the "Twelfth Planet."

According to Sitchin, one of planet Nibiru's moons collided with a planet located between Jupiter and Mars, which the Sumerians called "Tiamat," splitting the heavenly body in two. Tiamat, as outlined in the Sumerian text "Enuma Elish," is also the name of a Sumerian goddess. On a second pass, Nibiru itself struck Tiamat. One part of Tiamat remained a planet, while the second part became the asteroid belt and comets. Later in history, another Nibiru moon struck Tiamat once more, pushing the planet into a new orbit. According to Sitchin, that planet is what is known today as planet Earth.

According to Sitchin, when the collision supposedly occurred between Tiamat and Nibiru, the planet Tiamat, along with the other planets nearby revolving around the sun such as Mars and Jupiter, had the same orbit, going counterclockwise. But when Nibiru came by close enough for a direct collision, Nibiru was traveling in an opposite orbit, going clockwise. So at the moment of impact with two planets heading toward each other at hyperspeeds, like a head-on collision between two freight trains, the resulting catastrophe force was multiplied.

* * *

The *Nefilim*, a Hebrew word mentioned from the Old Testament in Genesis, refers to the entities known as the *Anunnaki* in Sumerian myth. According to Sitchin, these Anunnaki are also the citizens and original inhabitants of Nibiru, having evolved on Nibiru some forty-five million years ahead of equal developments on the planet Earth.

Now since the planet Nibiru has such a large elliptical orbit that transports it very far from the sun, the question arises how can the Anunnaki survive the long cold winters? With all their years of experience, the Anunnaki managed to built a form of giant canopies around their cities using supersmall microscopic particles of gold, which may have been one of the reasons originally for them staying here, on earth, to mine gold!

Sitchin claims that the planet Nibiru also keeps warm by heat generated from radioactive decay and a thick atmosphere while it travels through the cold and darkness of dead space.

The Anunnaki are a very advanced "Humanlike"* extraterrestrial race. Sitchin claims that they first arrived on Earth about 450,000 years ago, looking for minerals, especially gold, which they found and mined in Africa. These beings became known as "gods" (yes, with a little "g"). Now I want to be very careful here; these beings, the Anunnaki, the "gods," have the ability to shape-shift! Just keep this in mind.

These "gods" were the rank-and-file warriors of the colonial expedition to Earth from the planet Nibiru. The Anunnaki genetically engineered *Homo sapiens* as slave labor to mine gold in the African gold mines. The Anunnaki achieved this by crossing extraterrestrial genes with those of *Homo erectus*, and this process may have been done in stages through the years. After the Anunnaki set up human kingship, the human race thrived as a civilization in Sumer in Mesopotamia. This civilization was set up under the guidance of these "gods"; however, later, a war developed between factions of the extraterrestrials. In this conflict, nuclear weapons were used. The fallout from these weapons destroyed the whole area including the city of "Ur" around 2000 BC.

A short while ago, I mentioned the name "Enuma Elish"—what is it? I'll try to explain and, in a few words, clarify the meaning. "Enuma

---

* They are able to shape-shift at an instant!

Elish" is the epic of Creation. The information was gathered from about seven tablets and contains a thousand lines. It was recorded in Old Babylonian texts. Its texts contain links to analysis of Biblical parallels; most of its contents were written no later than during the reign of King Nebuchadnezzar in the twelfth century BCE.

* * *

I just brought to you a very special theory and conclusion from Zecharia Sitchin's interpretation of universal and our own world's events that took place roughly until the flood of Noah at the end of a mini ice age, some 13,500 years ago. (No, be very careful here. I am not stating that the end of the ice age was the only cause for the flood. Read on.)

Now according to Zecharia Sitchin, and by now also other experts, it seems that whenever the orbit of planet Nibiru is due to bring it near planet Earth, bad things happen. Many world governments, including our own, did read and do read the works of Sitchin, and they realize that the next contact between Earth and the Twelfth Planet, Nibiru, is just around the corner. Is it by the year 2012? (Yes, by the date of December 21, 2012).

Zecharia Sitchin's book *The 12th Planet* at the time of its introduction contained over twenty years of research regarding ancient aliens and genetic manipulation. Now if we believe in Sitchin, if we trust his translation abilities, then we must be prepared for the imminent return of an alien race, the Anunnaki—the race who created us, this alien race that visited us last some 3,600 years ago.

On the day of their return, their leader may be going by the famous name given him by the Mayans in South America: "Quetzalcoatl," "the great white god." (Or could the leader be going by the name: Enki, or Enlil, or Yahweh, Adonai, Ashem. Who knows?) However, the return date could be any day now. And that is the real reason why world governments may be running scared! They are running scared for the simple reason that they are fully aware, realizing that upon their return, the aliens may be looking for their favorite people. Could those be the Chosen People? I will discuss this subject later on at length since it has a direct link to our biological past and our future. Yes, I said biological; it may or may not be of a religious nature.

Zecharia Sitchin was born in 1922. He is about eighty-eight years old. An eighty-eight-year-old man, Zecharia Sitchin is possibly and allegedly being brought up on charges by the U.S. government. These are only rumors. I have no idea what the actual charges are, if any. All I know from watching a few sites on YouTube and other Internet sites is that the U.S. government wants especially to shut him up. They are allegedly demanding that he keep his mouth shut regarding the Twelfth Planet. Not only that, they are also demanding that he must surrender all data. Yes, I said *all* his data and notes regarding the Twelfth Planet.

It looks like the U.S. government is running scared because of what Sitchin allegedly might know. If I am not mistaken, I believe that some reporter spoke to Sitchin's wife a few years ago, and she told him that if people knew what her husband knew about the planet Nibiru (or Planet X, the Twelfth Planet) and its inhabitants, they would be terrified. (Trust me, if that is the case, then our government knows all about it, and they are not telling.)

* * *

Now that I have conveyed the findings of one great research writer Zecharia Sitchin, who gave us his views on our ancient past and our so-called makers, it is time for another view and sort of a jump forward to another time period in history, to examine Michael Tsarion's findings regarding events around 55,000 years ago. In around the year 2000, Tsarion wrote a book called *Atlantis, Alien Visitation, and Genetic Manipulation*. This book also spoke about the planet Tiamat, the planet Nibiru, the Twelfth Planet, the war of the gods, etc., but here comes a difference of opinion.

Michael Tsarion claims that the Nefilim or what he refers to as "Fallen Angels" arrived on the planet Earth only 55,000 years ago. He states that they arrived here by default. This race of beings, a race of aliens, numbering about two hundred, were pursued throughout the galaxy by another group of aliens who originated from the same race and happened to be their superiors. They all supposedly originated on the planet Nibiru. This is correct; they are all of the same race, the Anunnaki. Now the question arises: Why are they being pursued by their so-called superiors?

The answer is both complicated and yet simple. It seems that this group of two hundred renegades, who were being chased, were a group of scientists. A group of scientists who specialized in DNA and/or genetic manipulation. Simply said, they were creating life when and where needed, either doing it as ordered or on the "QT." These entities are superexperts at this endeavor, seemingly performing this work since time began.

It is possible that these beings not only could be skilled shape-shifters, but they could also originally appear to us as partially see-through spirits. The only reason why I am using the word "spirits" is that it could be that their planet Nibiru has a field around it that may be keeping it in existence in a different dimension. While these beings have the ability to move in and out from one dimension to another, most of us humans can't detect or identify them. Just remember the movie called *They Live* with the ex-wrestler, actor Roddy Piper, where the good guys had to use special eyeglasses to detect the true form of the alien.

* * *

Even though the pursued group of renegade Nibiru scientists were from the same race as their pursuing Superiors, these Superiors were much more powerful and possessed some awesome and powerful weapons in their arsenal in order to protect and control the galaxies. They were all creating life, from the first stage to the last!

ILL. "A"

CAP. 1. בראשית א

GENESIS CAP. 1. 2. ב א

וַיֹּאמֶר אֱלֹהִים יִשְׁרְצוּ הַמַּיִם שֶׁרֶץ נֶפֶשׁ חַיָּה וְעוֹף יְעוֹפֵף
עַל־הָאָרֶץ עַל־פְּנֵי רְקִיעַ הַשָּׁמָיִם: וַיִּבְרָא אֱלֹהִים אֶת־ 21
הַתַּנִּינִם הַגְּדֹלִים וְאֵת כָּל־נֶפֶשׁ הַחַיָּה ׀ הָרֹמֶשֶׂת אֲשֶׁר
שָׁרְצוּ הַמַּיִם לְמִינֵהֶם וְאֵת כָּל־עוֹף כָּנָף לְמִינֵהוּ וַיַּרְא
אֱלֹהִים כִּי־טוֹב: וַיְבָרֶךְ אֹתָם אֱלֹהִים לֵאמֹר פְּרוּ וּרְבוּ 22
וּמִלְאוּ אֶת־הַמַּיִם בַּיַּמִּים וְהָעוֹף יִרֶב בָּאָרֶץ: וַיְהִי־עֶרֶב 23
וַיְהִי־בֹקֶר יוֹם חֲמִישִׁי: פ

ATANEENEEM AGDOLEEM

Illustration A

Deep Analysis: Frightening Conclusion

In Genesis chapter 1, we read the following:

- In the beginning God created the heavens and the Earth.
- The Earth was without form and void.
- Then God said, "Let there be Light" (first day).
- Then God said, "Let there be a firmament in the midst of the waters."
- Then God made the firmament.
- And God called the firmament Heaven (second day).
- And then God created Land, Earth, Water, Seas, Grass, Seeds, Fruit, Trees, Light, Large Light (Sun), Small Light (Moon), living creatures, birds, Great Sea Creatures,* cattle and creeping things, beasts of earth, and last but not least, and so God created man in his own image, male and female.

Okay, folks, this is a prime example of Terraforming. From the first step to the so-called last step; Creation of man and woman, human life!

Apparently, this group of scientists has been terraforming planets for eons. They must have done something wrong. "Big time," in order to be pursued throughout the galaxy with a vengeance. Now let's examine what they could have done wrong.

Could they have had sex with females on other planets when they were not allowed to do so?

Could they have had sex with human women on earth who got pregnant and gave birth to giants, on at least one or two earlier engagements?

Could they have created dinosaurs that lived next to humankind? Humans who should not and could not exist with dinosaurs in the same playing field?

The reason for me saying dinosaurs is as follows: In the Bible, the New Testament has a different translation from the Old Testament. In the New Testament, Genesis 1, verse 21 says, "Great Sea Creatures." In the Old Testament, Genesis 1, verse 21, it says, "Ataneeneem

---

* "Great Sea Creatures." This term was taken from the New Testament.

Agdoleem" (See illustration A). In the Hebrew language, that means very large alligators or crocodiles, or large dinosaurs with scales. ("Ataneeneem" means Alligators, or Crocodiles; "Agdoleem" means large, very large, giant.)

And again, they could have slept with the daughters of man and/or performed human genetic and DNA experiments counter to their Superiors' orders.

By the way, a few years ago, a footprint of a human being, a very modern man, was found next to a dinosaur's footprints! (See documents and notes).

* * *

In the book of Genesis, it also says that when the Nefilim landed on earth, there were giants in the earth. But what exactly is meant by this statement? And how is that possible?

This could possibly mean that this group of two hundred alien renegades had pulled this stunt before. How? Simple! On a previous trip to Earth, the scientists had impregnated human women once before.

And now again, the entities were (and still are) super DNA and genetic experts. Their function seems to be to fly through the universe, locate planets that had been terraformed, and be able to sustain life, or planets that already have life existing on them and lift its so-called human life to a new and higher state.

Their leader's name is "Lucifer." This was his name in the past, and that is still his name today. How can I prove it? It may be easier than you think, and here is just one way how I can prove it.

The answer is given in the famous "Fatima Prophecy"; however, the answer may be also hidden in another part of the prophecy for which you were not allowed to be aware: This was actually an occurrence, a so-called religious happening, which became known worldwide, with the direct involvement of the Vatican. On May 13, 1917, three children in Fatima, Portugal-Lucia, age ten; Francisco, age eight; and Jacinta, age seven—saw and heard something. At first, the whole village and the children saw a vision of the sun dancing and moving erratically in the sky. I, the author, personally would put a simple $5 bet that what they witnessed was a sighting of a flying saucer.

Yes, a flying saucer in the year 1917, how about it? A very short time afterward, the dancing sun came lower and lower; and an apparition appeared, a female, a vision of the Virgin Mary. Now again, I must stress for the importance of this story, three little girls (females) saw an apparition, a vision of the Virgin Mary, also female.

These three girls were shown and given three prophesies by that apparition; the first two had to do with the rise and fall of Communism in Russia, an assassination attempt of Pope John Paul II, and the global prosecution of the Church. But there was one secret left to tell. The third secret is the one that was kept away from the public for many years by the Vatican, and even now, the story is being released step by step as to not alarm the public.

The third prophecy had to do with an approaching comet or planet. This wouldn't by any chance possibly be the planet Nibiru, planet X, or the Twelfth Planet, would it? In 1984, Pope John Paul II made a comment regarding the third prophecy by saying, "The destruction that will come upon the world will be so great, it need not be told, for the reason it may cause terror and panic now." Pope John also mentioned massive tidal waves and fires.

There is evidence now that the Vatican is secretly working with NASA to prevent this global catastrophe that is on its way to Earth from deep space. I believe that movies like *Deep Impact* and *Armageddon* were made to condition us and prepare us, the human race, for what's to come. There are secret rumors that NASA is now practicing to destroy small planets in space using so-called "Bunker Buster" nuclear warheads! Give me a break! This firepower may contain enough juice to blow up a large comet, but a planet, maybe the size of Nibiru? (By the way, did anybody ever think that the occupants of Nibiru may just decide to shoot back?)

Surprise, surprise! Would it not be funny if some of those nuclear warheads that came from Soviet Russia after the collapse of the old "Soviet Union" found themselves on one of these weapons heading into deep space? Do you remember the movie *Meteor* with Sean Connery, or am I dreaming?

Later on in this book, you will read how possibly and allegedly our elders stopped the same planet, halted or diverted planet Nibiru about 3,600 years ago. Read on for the new and exciting revelation!

* * *

And now for a shocker, the fourth prophecy. Yes, a fourth prophecy. I, the author, am going out on a limb here and raising the stakes! The Fourth Prophecy that I refer to is more in a form of a statement; a revelation to the world on who is who, and who may really still be in charge. The following information was kept so secret that even in the Vatican, behind closed doors, it was not spoken of.

It is a name that I mentioned earlier, "*Lucifer.*" Before I go on, just remember what I said in the beginning of this book, "No religious affiliation at all," only scientific.

Now it seems that beside what the three little girls saw and heard that day at Fatima, at the same time, hiding behind a bush in the field was a little boy. Yes, a boy (male), and he also saw an apparition, a vision—a figure of a man (also a male). And that vision spoke to the boy and voiced a very short statement: "You are all my children. You are the children of Lucifer."

Now how about this blockbuster! Just imagine what steps the church took in the past and is taking in the present to keep this underwraps under the rug or even deeper. If this ever came out to the public in a real big way, the name *Lucifer* could be immediately tied to all of our deep past, who we are, who made us, who manufactured us and so on, and what would happen to religion from that point on. Who knows! Because it may not have far to go as it is. I don't think that the folks at the Vatican are sleeping well at night! Yes, they know what's coming. The Church of Peace knows. Do you?

* * *

Did I just use the words "Church of Peace"? Is this the same Church of Peace that

- a. during the Spanish Inquisition killed and tortured tens of thousands of Jews while trying to convert them to Christianity?
- b. under many convents in the world especially in Europe and America lie skeletons of thousands of babies born to nuns?

c. stood by basically, mostly in silence, as millions of Jews and other minorities were being gassed in concentration camps in Europe?
d. stood by with sealed lips, while at the same time U.S. president FDR ordered a ship full of Jews away from an American port back to Germany to be gassed? (Yes, your favorite president, FDR! Well, how about that, fellow "Jewish Democrats"?)
e. stood idly by after WWII as Jews were being chased, shot, and killed by the English nation (the English Mandate) to prevent them from entering Palestine, now Israel, and again forced to live in camps in Cypress and other places.
f. allowed for years child abuse by their priests and nuns.
g. That allowed in the open, relations between priests and little boys. (Hi, Pope!)

I think I'll stop here on this topic of the great Church of Peace. Oh yes, did you, church leaders, see something interesting with your eyes through the lens of your telescopes as of late? Is something coming your way? Seen in your own observatories? Is it a very large mysterious planet perhaps?

* * *

Now back to Lucifer, who it seems was and still is the leader of the Nefilim, Fallen Angels, those two hundred renegades who escaped and were banished to remain here on planet Earth.

As this group of aliens was running away, the first action they took was to land on a planet called Tiamat, which originally was the Twelfth Planet before it disappeared. How? Let's see. As this group of two hundred aliens was hiding on Tiamat, they built and set up a make-believe base, a decoy to appear as if they were stationed there. And remember, Tiamat was mostly a water planet.

Now before I continue, another reminder: I am deliberately using viewpoints from different sources in order to blend them and pave the way toward a correct pathway to reach my conclusions. I reviewed the works of Zecharia Sitchin. and now I shall incorporate some viewpoints of Michael Tsarion and others.

As soon as the group of two hundred renegades set up the dummy camp, they split the scene fast; they got off the planet Tiamat immediately! Meanwhile, their superiors, their pursuers, totally destroyed/blew up the planet Tiamat, thinking that the two hundred renegades were hiding there.

Now as a sideshow, if you asked me who were the good guys or the bad guys, the pursuers or the renegades, I could not tell you as of yet. However, I do know that in order to destroy a planet like Tiamat, you'd need a superweapon! Once in a while, you hear of an ancient weapon called the "Spear of Destiny," and the "Tablets of Destinies." They are mentioned by quite a few authors and mentioned more than once in the Sumerian texts. (See conclusions and clarifications.)

There is a Sumerian cylinder seal existing in which Zecharia Sitchin is trying to explain that the Twelfth Planet, Marduk, shooting his lightning at Tiamat. To my understanding, however, Sitchin used that to illustrate that planet Nibiru (and or its satellites) collided physically with the planet Tiamat. Did Sitchin really mean to say that? Or is he having second thoughts?

* * *

Now that same cylinder seal can be interpreted in a different way. It can be used as evidence for the theory that a superpowerful weapon was used to destroy Tiamat. It actually shows a figure aiming a weapon and shooting lightning at the planet Tiamat. This took place roughly 55,000 years ago. (See illustration D)

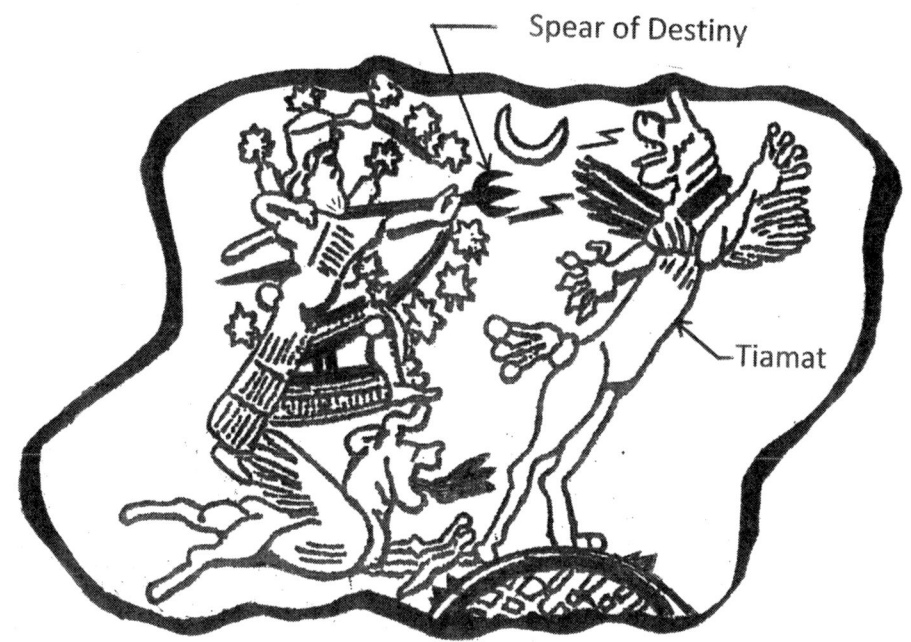

ILL. "D" "SUMERIAN CYLINDER SEAL"
Weapon used to destroy Tiamat: Spear of Destiny

Illustration D

This weapon could have been "the spear of destiny." Now when the planet Tiamat blew up, totally destroyed, all of its water contents, Landmass, fish, livestock, whatever, had to be displaced somewhere. Yes, it went into space. It became the Asteroid Belt. At times, we hear stories of people from all over the world, working during the day or at nighttime, and suddenly out of nowhere, things fall from the sky and drop on their heads. Fish, frogs, toads, etc. We used to call them crazy people, but maybe not.

As the planet Tiamat was destroyed, and it was a water planet, most of its waters with all its contents live fish, frogs, etc., were thrown into space by the explosion, also land, soil, rocks, etc. Yes, as I stated earlier, it formed the Asteroid Belt.

The temperatures in space in our vicinity between our planets range from -250 to -400 degrees Fahrenheit.

In these cold temperatures of deep space, water turns immediately to sort of supercold dry ice crystals with its contents of livestock, fish, etc., preserved forever. Very similar to our lakes freezing in the winter, and in the spring and summer, magically, all life in the water returns to normal.

Maybe if the next time this happens, we will have to try to lock down the exact spot where it happened, and the time of day, we may see something startling. We may find out that at that instant, the Earth by its orbital path came closest to the Asteroid Belt, and that the Earth's magnetic forces attracted something from it. Something that remained in the cold, void of deep space for thousands of years, something from the remains of the destruction of the planet Tiamat.

Yes, when the planet Tiamat exploded, its contents, landmass, and waters became what is known today as the Asteroid Belt. So now the explanation may become very simple. Every time our Earth's orbit brings it to its nearest point of the Asteroid Belt, the Earth's magnetic forces will act and pull in whatever they can.

And if you can visualize that action, then you can visualize and understand the following. This main action caused the first flood on planet Earth approximately 55,000 years ago. All the waters from planet Tiamat went into the so-called Asteroid Belt, frozen in super-large-size chunks. And on the next time around when Earth's orbit came close enough, all of this frozen water mass that was attracted by Earth's magnetic field got pulled to the Earth in a form of an enormous superflood, or known as the first deluge, and thus formed most of the great oceans.

* * *

Now let's take a little break and ask ourselves the following questions: What exactly are we doing in Iraq? What are we doing there now? Well, in the beginning, after the main war activities had stopped, soldiers were spotted running into museums, antique shops, and government buildings' vaults. Running around like chickens without heads? Not exactly!

Speaking about vaults, it seems that our troops came fully prepared with "keys" to these vaults, keys made far in advance. Yes! Somebody knew exactly where these vaults were to be found, their contents, and also the exact method of entry. Now all these soldiers, American soldiers (no French soldiers, please), running around from museum to museum, were carrying containers and filling them with Artifacts. Which artifacts? Well, artifacts that may have been needed to complete the assembling of the real WMD weapons that you may not have been allowed to know about.

WMDs may not necessarily be what we have been led to believe, such as: poison gas, nerve gas, nuclear parts, etc. They may be parts of a totally different nature; parts to complete assemblies of old ancient weapons of mass destruction, weapons that have not been around for thousands of years. Weapons so powerful that they may have no equal. Or they may have been looking for what we call "Star Gates" that create doorways to other worlds, other dimension, or other times.

I'll bet you didn't learn about all of that from your old school teacher or your local newspapers, etc.

So when our Leader, President Bush, said that we were looking for WMDs, he was right on. Yes! The only question remaining then is, What kind? Ancient ones?

During our Iraq war, we heard very often the phrase "Order out of Chaos." But do you really know what was meant by that during the

Iraq war, in Iraq! Let me explain. When you are looking for something very important in a strange place with enemies all around, you have to create a diversion. You have to create chaos, in order for the local yokels to keep busy with their own problems so that they would be diverted and not see what you're doing or what you're looking for.

This is the main reason why we did not choose members of Saddam Hussein's old Republican Guard to take part in the new army. They knew too much. So now we formed a new army, fresh, with no ties to the old guard. A new, fresh young army. Remember the phrase: "See nothing! Hear nothing! Say nothing!"

There are many things that we found in Iraq, especially in the area of old Babylon. We have built massive structures in Iraq, in Babylon, and in the deep deserts. We looked for actual Star Gates and searched for burial sites of the old Nefilim and/or their descendants. I understand that we have found both!

We also found some alien bodies cryogenically frozen at certain deep sites. Rumors are that their bodies are still alive; however, that no human can get too close to them. These preserved entities seem to omit some sort of mental vibrations, and if you get too close, these vibrations will shatter your brain from as far as fifty feet away.

To meet certain military objectives in this area of the world, rest assured that we have built above and below ground gigantic airfields with endless storage facilities equipped with weapons that most of the world has never seen or heard of. So, no! We are not getting out of Iraq anytime soon, at least not "all" the troops.

The Defense Department last year issued decks of playing cards to our troops in Iraq. Do you remember the old playing cards with the pictures of Saddam Hussein, his sons, and all his ministers? Well, these are not them. The new playing cards display Ancient Artifacts, the reason given that the cards are training aids to help the service members understand the archaeological significance of their deployed locations. You, folks, don't really believe that, do you? It looks like the real reason may be that our special branch of government is looking for certain artifacts to complete something spectacular that we found. It could be an ancient scientific tool or part of a certain ancient military program, and of course, I can never leave out the words "Star

Gates" or "Time Gates." And now for a little treat. Guess who was the alleged person who helped design the special playing cards for our troops in Iraq. Rumors are that the person was Zecharia Sitchin. That means that he is now somehow, in one form or another, working for Uncle Sam.

Before the Iraq war broke out, the French were warned by the United States not to help the Iraqis with any secret ancient so-called diggings or rebuilding projects of major artifact finds and to stay away from certain archeological sites. The French did not listen. It also seems that Saddam Hussein's two sons knew too much; they knew secrets regarding certain ancient secret projects that they were trying to bring back into existence, to resurrect certain gates, weapons. Well, the sons were killed off immediately! I wonder why.

Right after the end of the war, we heard of some Buddha temples with giant tall columns being blown up in the Iraqi desert. Who would want to blow them up? Bin Laden? Taliban? Our own Black Ops?

The answer may be found in my next section regarding Napoleon Bonaparte. It seems that the world's most powerful nations always find ways to discover certain artifacts, which they require; and when the right time comes to locate something controversial and important, it is "never done intentionally," it's always "By Accident."

* * *

Napoleon Bonaparte was one of the most successful French leaders ever, including one of the best military leaders until the Battle of Waterloo where he and his armies suffered a decisive defeat. In 1798, Napoleon Bonaparte was on what was called an Egyptian expedition. On this expedition, he had 197 scientists, mathematicians, language specialists, etc. All of that talent? For what purpose?

Officially, you see, Napoleon's expedition was not sent to find anything. However, during the Battle of the Pyramids that took place against the Egyptian army called *Mamelukes*, Napoleon's soldiers found something while building a fort. They found the famous "Rosetta Stone" by accident. (As they were just digging? What a coincidence!)

Napoleon Bonaparte's army had all these experts with them, digging everywhere and nowhere, and found the Rosetta Stone "*by accident?*" What are the chances? Or did all these scientists know where to dig? The "Rosetta Stone" was found in El Rashid, which means "Rosetta." Immediately after the find, Napoleon sent an emissary to France and the Vatican with the news.

A few days later, an answer came back from the Vatican. I have no idea what the answer was, but a short time later, Napoleon sent in a cannon division to the site of the Sphinx. The nose and face of the Sphinx were destroyed by cannon fire. This action seems to resemble the action of the destruction of the Buddha's temples in the Iraqi desert.

The Rosetta Stone is a text written by a group of priests in Egypt to honor the Egyptian pharaoh. It lists all of the things that the pharaoh has done that are good for the priests and the people of Egypt. The "Rosetta Stone" was carved in 196 BC. It was written in three scripts being used in Egypt. The first was hieroglyphic, the second demotic, and the third Greek. Rumors are that some information in the Rosetta Stone pertained to the identity of the original face of the Sphinx. That would allow mankind to pin down the exact day the Sphinx may have been built. It looks like somebody didn't want this to happen, someone in very high places. (See illustration H.)

Just what are the Church, Vatican, certain world governments, and leaders trying to hide from us? It can only be two things: Who we are, and where we came from!

Napoleon Bonaparte died on May 5, 1821. He died on the island of Saint Helena in the middle of the Atlantic Ocean. I guess that the Church and the King of France did not want Napoleon to talk or be spoken to. He knew too much.

* * *

We shall now return to our old friends, the Nefilim, the two hundred renegades. At this point, the real fun begins! After the pursuers (bosses or big gods) destroyed the planet Tiamat, they were very careful and suspicious. They knew who they were dealing with, beings of their own kind. And just in case, they thought that if the renegades were able to survive the exploding planet and did manage to escape to Earth, then they had to take some type of new countermeasures in order to prevent an escape by this group of two hundred from Earth. For one reason or another, they wanted these two hundred renegade Nefilim quarantined and banished from the universe!

In order to accomplish this task, they, the pursuers, imposed a "Gamma G" Barrier, an invisible shield, very similar to an energy plasma charge around the Earth. (See illustration F)

The Moon may be in existence not as long as some experts would like you to believe; it may have come into existence not long ago. It may be artificial, and it also may be hollow!

The center of the power plant of this invisible barrier or belt is based on the Moon. The distance of the Moon is approximately 250,000 miles from the Earth, and therefore, so is the barrier. This must not be confused with the Van Allen Belt.

Due to the fact that this group's specialty was DNA, genetics, etc., their Superiors created this barrier to search, sense, and destroy the two hundred's DNA and genetic structure. Yes, this barrier will destroy its target by honing in on the subject's internal DNA structure!

This group that landed on Earth was named the Nefilim, a Hebrew word meaning "The Ones Who Fell Down to Earth." It also can translate to as "The Ones Who Were Cast Down to Earth" or "The Fallen Angels."

Now as I mentioned earlier about the possibility of the Moon being hollow, the author-researcher Richard C. Hoagland has also mentioned a very similar theory regarding the Moon being hollow in one of his books. When our astronauts were on the Moon, on more than one mission, they tried to drill into the Moon's surface. At first, they only found three to five inches of fine dust. Strange for the Moon to have been there for so long and only gather so little dust; it is indeed very strange. Also, if you watched the videos from when our astronauts walked and jumped on the Moon, there were no dust uprisings from the surface. What, no real dust? Is the gravity of the Moon's surface so much higher than we were led to believe? Didn't we all learn in our best and top schools that the gravity of the Moon is only one-sixth that of the earth?

When our astronauts' drills went through the dust and tried to drill through the hard surface of the Moon, they could not. The superdrills they had could not drill through the Moon's surface (crust) as if it was made of steel! Also, when they experimented with sound waves and very hard manual test vibrations, the Moon kept vibrating for a long time and was sounding like a hollow bell!

Did you ever ask yourself the big question, Why didn't our astronauts return to the moon? There is a possibility that while our astronauts have been there, they may have seen things, structures that should not have been there! The occupants living there may have told our astronauts, "Do not return!" However, there may be another reason. It could simply be their bloodline. There is certain evidence floating around that suggests that most of the astronauts that have actually landed on the moon have all held these so-called titles of being thirty-second, or thirty-third degree Masons. At the same time, they may have had a very special blood type, or shall I say bloodline, that may have been modified for this special mission. A blood type that allowed them to walk on the moon and not be stopped by this esoteric "Gamma G" Barrier! Yes, they may have been walking human/alien experiment test-tube subjects! When they returned to Earth, they did not look too good and almost never spoke of what they saw or found on the moon. All we heard was, "Everything was Great, Beautiful!" (No more questions, please!)

* * *

Just remember, when the Nefilim came to Earth, it was written in Genesis that there were giants on the Earth. Now the only time we hear of "Giants" being born, is in the Hebrew word "Geeboreem." That word is used in the Book of Genesis (in the Old Testament) as a code word for the direct offsprings or descendents of the Nefilim. Genesis says that the babies born to the women of Earth who had sexual relations with the Nefilim were too large for natural human child birth, and as a result, many women had died giving birth to these "Geeboreem." When the Nefilim returned this second time around, they realized immediately why this happened, and they

"Shed their Skins to be with the women of Earth because they were beautiful."

Now the term "Shed Their Skins" means to change their appearances physically, anatomically, and cosmetically. The question that arises is which method the Nefilim used to accomplish this? One method is to shape-shift to any appearance at will, and I don't think that they can hold this exact shape indefinitely. And the second method is to completely revise their DNA/gene structure to physically and anatomically fit Earthling women. I am sure they chose the latter. Now this choice is probably the main and most likely reason why they are in trouble and cannot leave this planet Earth. In the modern Hebrew language used today, the word "Geeboreem" means *heroes* or *the brave ones*. However, in the book of Genesis, it was meant exactly as written above, giants!

So it seems that everyday life/work was rolling along for these Nefilim from 55,000 years ago through 13,500 year ago in a place called "Atlantis." This is where they set their new home base, an area, not a city. This territory, which our group chose as their home base, until this day is unknown. We have heard of many experts with many different opinions of where it may have been, but the true location is still very elusive. Just imagine, this group of two hundred original Nefilim are trapped on planet Earth. They know it. They are kept at bay in their own Hell, trying to find a way out and off this planet before the next approaching catastrophe.

These problems and other family feuds could have been the reason for the famous War of the Gods that the author Sitchin references.

Before this war started, the Gods knew what would happen with the oceans on Earth. The flood would destroy "everything in the flesh," mankind and animals only. Now remember, the alien entities were not of the flesh. They were (and still are) in "Spirit Form" and thus cannot die except by their own natural ways, which at this point, we do not exactly know. (The words of warning used by "God" to Noah: That everything in the flesh shall perish!)

There is a possibility that in extreme cases, these entities can do one more thing. Their own world/planet may exist in a different dimension than ours, so that in our atmosphere on our planet's plane of existence, they may look like spirits, allowing these entities to change their appearance by shape-shifting, physically changing their outer structure by a forced action that looks like what we call "possession" (I will discuss this very hot topic later in my story).

* * *

Noah was very friendly with one of the "gods," so this "god" commanded Noah to build an ark and also instructed him exactly how to build it. In the Old Testament, Genesis, chapter 6, verse 19-20, Noah was told to bring his family and the animals, two of each kind (one male, one female). Suddenly, in chapter 7, verse 2-3, God tells Noah, "Because you are a real righteous man, you may bring seven pure animals and two unpure animals." However, when it came time to board, the Old Testament says they boarded "two by two," with no mention of the "seven" boarding. In other words, the seven pure of anything alive.

Did "pure" mean humans or animals without any alien contamination, i.e., with no alien DNA/genes, etc., no cross-breeding? Or did extra animals (cows/sheep), seven of each, of "pure" nature entered through a back door. (Dead on ice? And/or used not only for food but also for DNA experiments? And had to be pure?) Just remember, in animal mutilation cases, in the past and today, they have mostly been performed on cattle, sheep, and horses.

Let us soon see why there might have been another sinister reason for this action by the gods who were going to be left behind.

It seems that in order to assure the survival of a certain sought after type of "DNA/gene" pool before the flood, a "god" (that could have been one of the entities from the two hundred renegades, or could have been one friendly god from outside of this group!) had told Noah to build an ark so strong that it would be able to survive a superstorm and accommodate some of the human race and animals for future life. Could it also have been for future DNA research. Now was the ark actually a giant DNA lab, or was it just to preserve the pure human race and its pure DNA? Did it have a dual mission?

Now after the flood, or deluge, known as Noah's Flood and actually the second flood occurring approximately 13,500 years ago, "God" promised Noah eternal life as a gift for his help with the ark. Noah lived to 950 years. The gods, a short time earlier, cut the life span of a human earthling to 120 years.

* * *

Now during this second flood, Noah's flood, something went wrong on earth, to the humans, and to the alien gods. Something came up that they could not conceive could happen! At the same time as Nibiru approached the Earth on its visit every 3,600 years, all the godlike aliens would escape to Nibiru except the banned 200, so a war broke out.

This war was set off between the two hundred renegades being left behind and some of their supporters, and the ones that were leaving. During this "War of the Gods," some very powerful weapons were used: (**a**) Atomic bombs, (**b**) Fusion Weapons, (**c**) Electromagnetic weapons, and others that affected the magnetic field of the Earth. And the effect of all that? A resulting polar shift and also the ice melting due to the end of a mini ice age, the melting of the ice sheets in Antarctica that was occurring at that time. All that caused the Earth to lose its balance and tilt. Water gushed around from every direction.

Now we do know that the Nefilim knew that the flood might happen but did not expect a major catastrophic disaster. Their home base in Atlantis sunk. They lost everything, spaceships, manufacturing facilities, major equipments, and most important, an energy source to fuel their spaceships. Now these aliens,* Nefilim, Anunnaki, Nibiruites, whatever they are, now have to rebuild all they lost from scratch, from nothing; remember, nothing around, no industry, just people, farms, horses, cattle, etc.

Yes, they have to rebuild everything that they had lost. However, they know that it must be done before a fatal deadline coming in

---

* These aliens knew that this great flood was going to arrive, so they sequestered themselves in very deep specially built caves, designed to withstand and block out large volumes of water. But what they didn't expect was the ferocity of the waters caused by natural and other outside factors.

2012. From now on, their back is against the wall like a trapped rat in a corner—watch out! They must survive no matter what. Whether the cost will be in dollars or in human lives. Yes, the alien-"gods" must survive!

The Nefilim, the "gods," knew that their normal life span here on Earth was about 1,000-1,200 years without outside help. Since they were *the* experts in genetics, the chances are that they chose that some of them would go into "deep freeze" to be resurrected at a proper time in the future, prior to 2012, December 21.

But where would these deep-freeze locations be? Where are they now? I say, just follow the movement of our super-armed forces; yes, the good old U.S. Army!

* * *

I mentioned Iraq before. But did anybody ever remember or hear about Operation Urgent Fury in 1983? Does Grenada ring a bell? We invaded Grenada on October 25, 1983, to rescue the government from a possible "Cuban" takeover. Good move! This operation was created with lightning speed, superfast action, with many thousands of American and foreign students watching from their college dorms. Guess who the commander of the invasion was. The one and only Deputy Commander General Norman Schwarzkopf!

Now listen to this. Only three weeks before the invasion, a body washed ashore on a nearby beach. The body was discovered by a local farmer or fisherman. The body had a very strange one-piece jumpsuit made of a strange material, but this entity was almost seven and a half feet tall, had reddish blond long hair, six fingers on each hand, and six toes on each foot.

Is the time near? Is someone or something being resurrected on cue? Does the word "Cryogenics" ring a bell? Like Richard C. Hoagland says, "I don't believe in coincidences."

INANNA. The Babylonian Goddess.
Could she also be Ishtar?

* * *

Let's go back to Iraq. In 2003, a German scientist found a tomb, a grave in Iraq, in a city called "Uruk" (about 300 kilometers south of Baghdad and 150 kilometers north of Basra). The tomb of Gilgamesh. We all know about the epics of Gilgamesh. Gilgamesh was said to be partly divine. He ruled in the first dynasty of Uruk for 126 years around 2700 BC. His father was Lugai Banda. His mother was Ninsun or Rimat Ninsun. She was a "goddess" directly tied to the Nefilim. So Gilgamesh was half god (alien) and half human.

Gilgamesh had two lovers; maybe? One was Ishtar, and the other Inanna—it seems that these two names belong to the same woman; she was using a different name in each part of the country. Something is going on here. Ishtar was on a spaceship leaving Earth at the start of the flood (deluge) around 11,500 BC. As per Sitchin in his book *The 12th Planet*, she was crying because all the people on Earth were going to die by drowning. Now Gilgamesh lived and ruled around 2,700 BC. Either Ishtar was also a frequent time traveler, high flyer, or a "Supergoddess," or maybe all of the above.

Based on these facts, now we may understand why in many alien "abduction cases," the pretty woman in the center of the spaceship calls herself Ishtar. Keep this in mind.

* * *

In the epic of Gilgamesh, it says that the Gods created Gilgamesh's double—he was cloned. If he was cloned, then which one is in the grave at Uruk? It makes no difference, just think, to recreate an original half Nefilim, a god, is a great feat on its own! Remember the movie *Jurassic Park*? I am sure that our experimental departments and our military special forces have this situation at bay.

Just remember in Genesis, chapter 10, verse 8, it mentioned a boy named Nimrod. Nimrod is the great grandson of Noah. And as he grew up, he started to become a giant in the land. The word "Geebor" in the Old Testament of Genesis means that he may have begun to become a giant, a direct offspring of the Nefilim, a direct descendent of the Fallen Angels. He could also be the Egyptian god, Osiris or Gilgamesh. Some scientists say that Gilgamesh and Nimrod may be the same person.

I understand from outside and independent sources that a short time ago, around the area of Gilgamesh's tomb in Uruk, large helicopters were observed taking something away. Now I wonder what we are really doing in Iraq. Just what is going on in our secret underground military labs?

Now many experts on Space/UFO studies have been asked the following question: How many alien races do you think are on planet Earth? Answers range between twenty and one hundred—we hear about the giants, Nordic, reptilians, grays, goblins, etc. But in almost all of the abduction cases, we see the grays. They are supposedly everywhere! Oval-shape head, large eyes, skinny long fingers, skinny bodies. They seem to handle all of the actual physical work, i.e. actual abductions, including going through walls and performing all of the medical experiments. Now the medical experiments are all done almost the same way, same procedure, same instruments being used, and at the end and afterward, the abductees are given the same exact message: "To better mankind" or "to help their dying race" or "to stop testing atomic bombs."

So here is the sixty-four-thousand-dollar question: From all of the many alien races that are supposedly here, why do all of these alien races "outsource" the physical work to the same subcontractors? The grays! Not on your life! I am wondering why until this day, the great writers and experts could not figure this one out.

Yes! You heard about this from me first! One of the biggest secrets that nobody else bothered to connect!

These grays were likely created eons ago by the ancient Nefilim.

Now there are also rumors that between the late 1940s and the 1960s, some treaties were signed between our presidents and some alien race or races. Or if this story is true, could they have signed the treaty with our old friends, the *Nefilim*, the *Fallen Angels*? Since they are shape-shifters, they can manifest to be or look like anything they want in an instant! Watch out! It seems that another country had signed a major treaty with the same aliens back in 1936. Which country? Nazi Germany. We shall soon see why!

* * *

Now back to the question: What can Lucifer and his two hundred Nefilims do in order to get off this planet?

First, they must protect themselves from known dangers, lessons from the past: (**1**) the passing of Nibiru every 3,600 years; (**2**) Atomic bombs—two different aspects; (**3**) something that they know that takes place every 26,550 years—Galactic alignment, the next date, December 21, 2012; (**4**) entering black axiom also known as dark matter in our galaxy; and (**5**) the Sun, which by now is currently known among astronomers and scientists that it's losing over 200 percent of its gravity force, and that percentage is increasing with each passing day. Sunspots are disappearing! This will allow the sun's deadly superflares of gamma rays to reach, scorch, and burn the Earth. We may expect this in four to five years max! So either way we look, we are fried!

For Nibiru, these aliens seem to possess the knowledge of some of the most powerful weapons in the universe and the knowledge how to build them and use them.

The pyramid at Giza, just what is its purpose? If your car is stuck on the road, well, then you must get it to a safe place, but how? Push it, pull it, by hand, or by a tow truck? The same can be done with planets. In a car, you must always know in advance the location of these strong safe points, such as front or rear bumper, etc. Therefore, could the pyramid also be a tool to keep the Earth vibrating at a certain correct rhythm? The pyramid could be a superweapon! It could also be used to push or pull the Earth or the reverse; this action could be applied to an approaching body from outer space, an approaching planet. For full explanation, keep on reading!

To meet all of these requirements, we need a power source that is unimaginable. The pyramid was built on the center landmass of the Earth and the Earth's main Vortex center. If you would want to push or pull the Earth or stabilize it, this is the exact location you would choose, and somebody did! When?

Some say that the pyramid was first built in 46,000 BC, and then reconstructed around 28,000 BC, and again in 10,500 BC and in 9,500 BC. Some experts say that the pyramid at Giza was built some 13,500 years ago, just after Noah's flood. This would only coincide with one of the last two reconstruction dates (of 10,500 BC and 9,500 BC).

It was also constructed right next to the Nile River. For drinking water, or for a totally different purpose? A very special secret divine purpose. There are boat basins next to the pyramid—that means, that water was there at the time! For our purpose, we will pay attention to the King's Chamber, the underground chamber, the pit, and last but not least, the multifunction ventilator shafts. All those mentioned are still existing there today!

The most important part of this puzzle is the seems-to-be missing so-called golden upper part of the pyramid, the upper tip portion, which was said to be made out of gold. And let's not forget the copper conduits found all over the pyramid's shafts and the King's Chamber. There seems to be heavy copper lines embedded in the walls of the King's Chamber that are leading to the upper tip.

Did we all forget the little motorized Radio Shack-type Moonraker vehicle that ventured inside the pyramid? Just watch the video courtesy of Dr. Zahi Hawass.

CHAPTER TWO

The Pyramid, Moses's Biggest Secret!

What was the pyramid, and what is the pyramid today? I believe it is a giant Spark Plug or an Igniter. Well, how did I come to that conclusion? It's simple. If you follow the embedded copper lines in the walls and all the copper conduits from the King's Chamber to the top of the pyramid, with the knowledge of the missing "Golden" tip . . . Now we have a Spark Plug. But what about the power source? I understand that Heavy salt deposits have been found embedded in the lower walls of the King's Chamber with a small amount of fish skeletons, That means that not only some sea water was there, but also that small fish were forced up there!

And speaking of the King's Chamber, let's not forget the famous "Coffer" that was made of solid black granite. And the coffer's famous size and measurements that are almost identical to the very famous Ark of the Covenant. What is it? And where did it come from? The Ark of the Covenant is a kit, a powerhouse kit! It is capable of producing power beyond imagination!

The Ark of the Covenant is by itself a sort of a very powerful capacitor. God instructed Moses to build it with special Acacia wood in the center and overlay it with gold all-around (Exodus 25:23-24) perfect insulation. And now its size: length, 2½ cubits; width, 1½ cubit; and height, 1 ½ cubits (45" long x 27" wide x 27" tall) (Exodus 25:10).

The Ark was meant to store **(1)** some sort of radioactive meteorites, **(2)** the Ten Commandments, **(3)** Aaron's Rod, and some say **(4)** a sample of the Manna (a food that the Israelites were fed by God from UFOs via some sort of porthole. (The Rod is said to be short and cylindrical, and its staff is about three feet long.)

To make all stories short, it is the opinion of most scholars, theologians, and hardware experts, including a theory, that its design came from a very old alien race. That this Ark when teamed up with the Rod becomes an unbeatable weapon, tool, and/or a lifelong food supply source that transfers its powers through a porthole from another dimension of time and space.

Now what were some of the major events or miracles that we know of when the Ark of the Covenant was used?

1. The parting of the Red Sea
2. The Walls of Jericho with Joshua
3. Crossing the Jordan River
4. To feed the Israelites in the desert

Now the major events or miracles that we know of when the "Rod" was used were the following:

1. The pharaoh's palace with the snake tricks.
2. Parting of the Red Sea when the Israelites crossed.
3. To provide drinking water for the Israelites at the end of their desert journey when Moses hit the rock.
4. To defeat the Amalek when they entered Canaan (Exodus 17:9-10). When Moses raised his hands with the rod, the Israelites were winning. When Moses lowered his hands with the Rod, the Israelites were losing.
5. Hold It! Hold It! There is one more, "The Biggest Story Never Told"!

* * *

ILL. "C"

EXODUS CAP. 16. 17. טו יז

CAP. XVII. יז

יז

וַיִּסְעוּ כָּל־עֲדַת בְּנֵי־יִשְׂרָאֵל מִמִּדְבַּר־סִין לְמַסְעֵיהֶם עַל־ א
פִּי יְהֹוָה וַיַּחֲנוּ בִּרְפִידִים וְאֵין מַיִם לִשְׁתֹּת הָעָם: וַיָּרֶב 2
הָעָם עִם־מֹשֶׁה וַיֹּאמְרוּ תְּנוּ־לָנוּ מַיִם וְנִשְׁתֶּה וַיֹּאמֶר לָהֶם
מֹשֶׁה מַה־תְּרִיבוּן עִמָּדִי מַה־תְּנַסּוּן אֶת־יְהֹוָה: וַיִּצְמָא שָׁם 3
הָעָם לַמַּיִם וַיָּלֶן הָעָם עַל־מֹשֶׁה וַיֹּאמֶר לָמָּה זֶּה הֶעֱלִיתָנוּ
מִמִּצְרַיִם לְהָמִית אֹתִי וְאֶת־בָּנַי וְאֶת־מִקְנַי בַּצָּמָא: וַיִּצְעַק 4
מֹשֶׁה אֶל־יְהֹוָה לֵאמֹר מָה אֶעֱשֶׂה לָעָם הַזֶּה עוֹד מְעַט
וּסְקָלֻנִי: וַיֹּאמֶר יְהֹוָה אֶל־מֹשֶׁה עֲבֹר לִפְנֵי הָעָם וְקַח 5
אִתְּךָ מִזִּקְנֵי יִשְׂרָאֵל וּמַטְּךָ אֲשֶׁר הִכִּיתָ בּוֹ אֶת־הַיְאֹר קַח

כידך

⟵ HAYEOR

Illustration C here

Lo and behold, now for the untold story, the major "Clue" and incident in our story that ties in the Ark of the Covenant, Moses and Aaron's Rod, the pyramids, Nibiru, the Twelfth Planet, and the year 2012 is written in a simple sentence in Exodus, chapter 17, verse 5. As I mentioned earlier, at the end of a forty-year journey through the desert, just before entering the land of Canaan, the Israelites ran out of water. So Moses went and spoke to God out of desperation for help.

Here is what God said in Exodus, chapter 17, verse 5, "Go on before the People, and take with you some Elders of Israel. Also take in your hand your Rod with which you struck the river and go." In verse 6, "Behold, I will stand before you there on the rock in Horeb and you shall strike the rock and water will come out of it that the people may drink. And Moses did so in the sight of the Elders of Israel."

The Clue: In the English translation of the New Testament, the word "River" is used. In the Old Testament, in Hebrew, this word "River" is called "Hayeor." It is the part of the Nile River where Moses was found floating in a small basket by the Pharaoh's daughter right around the pharaoh's palaces. And it also happened to be the same body of water running next to the great pyramid at the time. In Exodus 2:3, the woman put the child in the small ark and laid it in the reeds by the river's bank (in reality it is part of the river Nile near the pharaoh's palace called the Hayeor or Yeor). (See illustration C.)

Why the English translation says only "river" but the Hebrew says "hayeor," I can't guess, only I do not believe in coincidences. Because this would tend to imply that Moses and Aaron were part of a very important mission before the Israelites left Egypt, a mission that could be astronomical, reaching beyond worldly and biblical proportions. "The Biggest Story Never Told!"

DEC 21, 2012, IN THE VERY NEAR FUTURE, THE FINAL ATTEMPT TO STOP NIBIRU! THE LAST TIME THIS WAS DONE SUCCESSFULLY, WAS CIRCA 1597 BC, BY MOSES.

* * *

A story: A mission that was never told, never spoken of. Why? Here it comes. The connection between the Pyramids, the Ark of the Covenant, and 2012. The Ten Plagues: We all heard of the ten plagues that hit Egypt before the Exodus began. Here they are in exact order of occurrence: (**1**) blood, (**2**) frogs, (**3**)lice, (**4**) flies, (**5**) disease to livestock, (**6**) boils, (**7**) hail, (**8**) locusts, (**9**) three days of darkness, and (**10**) death of the firstborn.

Now just remember, from previous actions, the Ark of the Covenant with the aid of the Rod has no limits, and even the Rod by itself with the movements of Moses or Aaron could move or create the movements of large, enormous volume of water. Also, from the pyramid's inner construction, it looks like it was built to withstand some enormous inside water pressure.

In addition, just before the period of the ten plagues, an ark was placed in its correct and preconstructed location within the coffer inside the King's Chamber, within the great pyramid, with all its connections and proper attachments in place, just waiting for the moment of action.

And now came the moment of truth, after Moses received forty years of training in the Midian Desert on how to handle and command the Rod.

And as God commanded Moses on the bank of the "Yeor", Moses raised the rod!

Blood. Following the Rod having been waved in a command motion, the Ark of the Covenant started to gather an enormous amount of power, power that came from another dimension through a porthole. Suddenly a "Power Beam" of tremendous strength streamed out from the upper Golden tip of the pyramid and headed into space, toward an incoming object, toward another planet, Nibiru, the Twelfth Planet and/or its satellites. Portholes to the universe and other dimensions were now newly created; however, at the same time, the Ark of the Covenant began to turn red-hot! Just like a racing engine at full throttle!

Outside by a portion of the Nile near the banks of the river, called the banks of the Yeor, the power rod was waved once more. Suddenly, a tremendous amount of water started to move upward from below the Great Pyramid of Giza to the King's Chamber containing the Ark of the Covenant. Through an opening at the lower part of Pyramid's base, the waters started to move through the shafts toward the upper parts of the pyramid and the King's Chamber. Through the pit, through the subterranean chamber, the well shaft, the descending passage, up and up.

With the rush of the supervoluminous amount of water, thousands of gallons per minute or faster, a great air pressure was created at the upper levels of the pyramid within the King's Chamber. And the location of relief valves? Yes, the air shafts! (See illustration B.)

The rushing incoming waters entered in from the living river, bringing in with them anything that was living in the water, for example, small fish, large fish, frogs, etc. As the waters were gushing and rushing back out, they were boiling hot, turning red from the blood of all living things passing through. The river below turned red and stunk from all the blood.

Frogs. The bloody waters reached the shores around. The frogs could not survive in this hot bloody stew. They had to escape to deeper grounds, thus invading people's homes and so on. Does a possibility of a bad Three-Mile Island scenario sound feasible to you? (Just a note. Einstein once said, If you stop hearing or seeing frogs, or if the bees disappear, watch out!)

Lice and Flies. Have you ever been at certain beaches at low tide? Well, just imagine the sight and smell of the beaches there with that rotting and bloody mess of stewed fish and meat, very attractive conditions for lice and flies.

Disease on Livestock. The livestock got sick and diseased from the surrounding environment.

Boils. All that electricity in the air created rain, instant acid rain, probably also mixed with bubbles full of smoke. When that dirty mixture hit the skin, it caused boils from the infections.

Hail. And then arrived the hail. In Exodus, "Moses stretched his Rod out toward heaven and the Lord sent thunder and hail and fire darted to the ground, and the Lord rained hail on the land of Egypt. So there was hail and fire mingled with the hail" (Exodus 9:23-24).

These symptoms were very similar to what happens during a super-lightning electrical storm.

Locusts. Just imagine the magnitude of the lightning's electrical energy beam coming out of the tip of the pyramid. Apparently, at the last stages of this operation, the smoke and smell disturbed the nesting grounds of the locusts, and they started their annual migration instinctively a little early; but this time, in very large masses, the whole flock, out of fear from danger.

Darkness. My guess is that to produce this energy beam that was meant to deflect a planet the size at Nibiru, it was needed to be made a little more powerful at the end or during the last three days of the operation, and that caused the skies to darken with heavy dust and soot flying everywhere.

Death of the Firstborn. This could be interpreted in many different ways, so let's just leave that to Theological and Biblical experts.

This megaoperation must have succeeded. Why? Ever since then, there have been no major world floods like Noah's flood (The Deluge) and no planetary collisions with Earth. For that reason, we now have a full historical record of our planet in almost every detail for the last few thousand years.

* * *

Now I, the author, must explain a few touchy points regarding the Ark of the Covenant, the Rod, and how Moses and his brother Aaron got to this point. It is sort of a Catch-22 situation: We all know that God gave Moses and the Israelites instructions how to build the Ark of the Covenant after the Ten Plagues' incidents, and after they left Egypt, on the way to freedom.

Remember, a previously constructed Ark of the Covenant was already in place in or on the coffer inside the King's Chamber within the Great Pyramid built by a previous leader and/or group for that special day every 3,600 years. It looks like God knew exactly when he would need Moses and the Israelites to move out of Egypt and give them a new Ark of the Covenant along with the Rod until the next round 3,600 years down the road. Yes, God freed the Israelites and in return, they made a vow, a covenant with God to keep and guard the Ark of the Covenant at all cost until called upon by God.

The Ark of the Covenant has since had some very long and mysterious journeys throughout its almost 3,600-year history. The big question now is, Where is the Ark of the Covenant today?

Israel, the nation, was born, created on May 14, 1948, about 61 years ago. Who remembers Operation Solomon on May 24-25, 1991? In a period of 36 hours, about 14,500 Ethiopian Jews were flown from Ethiopia to Israel in 34 El Al jumbo jets and Hercules C-130s. A modern Exodus! The author is usually not a betting man, but is willing to lay odds that the Ark of the Covenant found its way to Israel on one of these planes. Just a small note, especially to the small cute little fellow that is in charge of Iran: "By now, if Israel has the Ark, they also know how to use it!"

* * *

Now back to Moses, born circa 1527 BC. Moses spent the first forty years of his life at the Pharaoh's palaces. This is after the Pharaoh's daughter first found Moses floating in the Nile River's banks in the special area called "Yeor." Close to the age of forty, Moses killed an Egyptian guard in circa 1487 BC and, as a result, had to flee the area.

Moses fled to the land of Midian, a desert. He spent forty years there, at the beginning as a sheepherder. One day while attending his flock, he came upon the so-called famous "Burning Bush," and at that instant, he heard God's voice speaking to him from within the Bush. When God spoke to Moses, God made a statement that God knew Moses's forefathers and that through Moses, God would keep his promise and lead the Israelites to the Promised Land. And then God introduced Moses to the magic Rod and its powers. During those forty years in the Midian desert, Moses likely benefitted from many training sessions by God that instructed him on how to use the Ark of the Covenant and the Rod. Those training sessions would later result in opening and exposing the great powers of the universe.

At this point in time, I, the author, believe that unknown to Moses, a previously constructed Ark was already in its place inside the Great Pyramid. An ark that was built way in the past, roughly 3600 years earlier (circa 5047 BC), by a previous generation after the last pass of the planet Nibiru. What did God mean by "He knew his forefathers Abraham, Isaac, Jacob"? Were they all possible abductees? Could it be because of their special DNA or bloodline? Were Moses and Aaron watched also to make sure they survived and stuck around for their special and trusty mission? A futuristic mission of unprecedented proportions.

God instructed Moses to leave Midian back toward the Pharaoh's palaces just a very short time before the big event of the Ten Plagues. This could not be a coincidence! And the last thing that God instructed, "You must stop here in the same exact location on your way out of Egypt with all the Israelites." God knew Moses would succeed! And what would God give Moses as a reward? Yes, the Ark of the Covenant, the second Ark of the Covenant of his generation. The "Ark of the Covenant" described in Exodus.

If this is correct, then it means that something was wrong with the beginning of the story of Exodus as described in the King James Version. Wrong translation? Revised information? Missing information? Or even the omission of the complete story or missing chapters or certain verses? This last possibility would have to have been done deliberately in both the Old and New Testaments.

Could the allegedly missing information be contained in the mysterious, not released, very famous Dead Sea Scrolls? Or hidden somewhere deep down below in the Vatican's famous secret library, with other worldly secrets?

It seems that back in the old days of the AD 1500s, if you did not like the new version of the Bible, the King James Bible, you may have become sort of beheaded. Like it or lump it! This King James, who was he and what was he? And what about Queen Elizabeth I?

* * *

Let's go back and mention the Reptilians. Some experts, including Zecharia Sitchin and Michael Tsarion, say that the Nefilim look just like us. But just in case, what if they don't look like us? Remember, the Nefilim are super-shape-shifters, so what if they are also part Reptilian?

In the early 1990s an ex-NASA scientist, Alex Collier, was involved in exopolitics, Earth transformation. He claimed to be a Contactee with some Nordic-looking humans from the constellation of Andromeda and claimed to have had a number of contact experiences. He spoke of many alien races who were all benevolent. But when it came to the Reptilians, he warned people to watch out; and if they saw one, especially with a long tail (Higher Ranked), to get out of its way fast before it shape-shifted or after. This definitely would make them a malevolent race.

During one of Alex Collier's interviews all the way back in 1994, he claimed that in the last 25 years, 31,712 children were missing from the United States. Also, in the last five years alone, that in Westchester County, New York, only, some 3,000-plus children went missing.

In 1991, a book came out called *Silent Invasion* written by Ellen Crystall. In this book, she specialized in an area of Upstate New York near Stewart Airport, a former Air Force Base, right off Route 84 and 17K. Stewart Airport used to have a very large amount of cargo aircraft including the giant C-5As. Some of the locals, including farmers, said that during many nights, they saw large trucks coming from the direction of Stewart Airport to or through Pine Bush and heard cries of cattle and/or other animals. In addition, some military personnel were seen accompanying these trucks. The people believed that somewhere in the area of Pine Bush, New York, there was a very large underground opening, leading to what. Or where?

Note, it's also written in the Bible that the Nefilim and/or their descendants, the Geeboreem, liked the smell and taste of human flesh (in BBQ form), especially children's. Are we talking about Cannibalism?

CHAPTER THREE

Dying Experts, the Renaissance, and the Search for Energy

And now about Queen Elizabeth and British Royalty. Back in October 1997, Princess Diana died in a very mysterious car accident. There were stories about love and pregnancy. Rubbish. What you didn't know or hear much about is that just a few months earlier, Princess Diana, in public, during a few press interviews, said of the whole Royal family: "They are all a bunch of Freakin' Lizards, all of them." A bunch of lizards! She declared this in public on numerous occasions. If you are doubtful, just watch the videotapes! However by making these statements, she just about accused the Royal Family of being reptilians. She signed her own death wish!

Now the famous John E. Mack. John Mack was a professor and psychiatrist at Harvard University Medical School. He was very much involved with alien-abduction cases in very close contact with abductees, similar to a character in the made-for-TV movie/miniseries, *Intruders*. Then at a later point, he started to concentrate on the Reptilians, and you can see his taped interviews on YouTube. Mack must have been getting very close to discovering something big in the last few months of his life regarding the Reptilians.

A few months later, he met his "accidental" death in London, England. He stepped off the sidewalk and was hit by a drunk driver. Now what did we say earlier about coincidences?

And just one more example. U.S. geologist Gene Shoemaker who became very famous with his work on comet Shoemaker-Levy 9 that collided with the planet Jupiter. Shoemaker was always studying the impacts of comets on the moon. He also trained astronauts on how to explore on the moon, what to look for as far as geology. One of Professor Shoemaker's last projects in 1994 was called "Project Clementine." The purpose of this project was to find water at the moon's lunar poles.

Shoemaker must have stumbled across something during his research. Did he uncover some evidence that there is an invisible barrier originating there? Did he find out that the moon is hollow? Did he find out about hidden underground waters, or did he find out that the gravity of the moon is much stronger than we were told?

* * *

In school, we were taught that the gravity on the moon's surface is one-sixth that of Earth's gravity. Dr. Werner von Braun gave an interview to the *New York Times* magazine after the liftoff of Apollo 11 on July 16, 1969. He was asked about the moon's gravity and answered that the distance from the moon, or the "point of parity," is forty-three thousand miles from the moon's surface. To explain the point of parity in simple English, this is an imaginary point that exists in space between the moon and the Earth, where the Moon's gravity is equal to that of Earth. If von Braun is correct regarding the point of parity, then the gravity on the moon's surface must be much higher than the one-sixth we were always led to believe because a gravity that is one-sixth that of Earth would calculate to a point of parity much farther away from the moon than von Braun stated. (By the way, von Braun, after giving that answer, was demoted and lost his position.).

Is that the reason why when our astronauts walked or jumped on the Moon's surface, there was no dust to be seen?

Could Shoemaker have theorized an artificial water supply on the Moon that could also be used for stability (stabilizing the moon, if it's hollow, against vibrations?), therefore making the Moon artificial? Shoemaker was killed instantly from a car crash in Australia that took place on the afternoon of July 8, 1997, when his car collided head-on with another vehicle on an unpaved road in the Tanami desert.

Again, do we believe in coincidences? *Nyet*, hell no! A lonely unpaved road in the Australian desert? Head-on? Maybe it is time for a new scriptwriter!

* * *

Queen Elizabeth I, born on September 7, 1533, was she Human? Alien? Nefilim? Reptilian? Part of each? Who knows? Perhaps the investigator, author, David Ike, knows! Elizabeth was known as the "Virgin Queen!" Does the word "Virgin Mary" sound familiar? For the purpose of our topic or subject matter being discussed here, according to some scholars and researchers, the word "virgin" goes back to a certain special bloodline that some say came from the descendants of a serpent race. With its famous DNA symbol, the spiral snake. This bloodline it is believed goes back to the original fallen angels, the Nefilim or serpent people, and all that interbreeding must be accomplished and performed within the enclosed group. Is this what they mean by the phrase "Royal Bloodline?"

By now our old friends, the original two hundred fallen angels, the Nefilim and/or their descendants, are very, very concerned. They have been here for thousands of years and have not succeeded in finding a way off this planet earth, no escape route! All of that can be blamed on weather, polar shifts, and wars among their own kind, which is the same saying as the phrase "War between the Gods," and also, of course, the main possibility, and/or the actual main reason for all that is the Gamma-G barrier that was put in place to prevent this group from escaping the Earth's envelope beyond the moon. They are quarantined here on planet Earth!

It appears that by the mid-1500s (AD) the Nefilim (the two hundred renegades) have succeeded in bringing mankind to a certain level of education to be in shape and or in a certain mental state, helping them rebuild their loses from the Atlantis/deluge catastrophe.

It is by then that they discovered that they and their flying machines (Flying saucers) could not penetrate this so-called invisible Gamma-G Barrier around the earth. It is at that time that the aliens decided to contact Queen Elizabeth I. Contact was made through their emissaries that were known as the Masons, Freemasons, Illuminati, the Bildenbergs, whatever they called themselves at the time; they are all the puppets of the puppet masters, the original fallen angels.

You must keep in mind that until this day, the same fallen angels, the Nefilim, through the past centuries, by their overwhelming knowledge of weaponry, use of sciences, financial markets, and food supplies, have kept the population at bay! Kept them dumb, in the dark, kept the average person's head in the ground as per an old saying. However, you also must keep in mind that to bring the average person, the human race, up to par, it has to be done in stages.

Do you remember the movie *2001: A Space Odyssey* with the famous black cube, the "Monolith"? At every instance that the black cube appeared, mankind's intelligence increased. He received a mental lift, got smarter, and wiser, advancing forward! Did Arthur C. Clarke know something? Did the black cube or the symbol it stands for appear every 3600 years?

* * *

Queen Elizabeth I, when she was asked for help regarding the Nefilim, she contacted a very close friend, a confidante among government circles, named Sir John Dee.

Sir John Dee was an astronomer, astrologer, an occultist, and black magic expert. He also tried in the last thirty years of his life to communicate with entities from another dimension, which he referred to as "Angels." He did that by learning a strange language called "Enochian," which the Angels use.

Dee also opened a portal to the fifth dimension. It is said that Sir John Dee succeeded in contacting another race in that dimension. He discussed with them the problem that the Nefilim were having, and they agreed to help. (These so-called angels could possibly be existing in multidimensions.)

Before I go on, a few more words about Dee. According to Leo Zagami—a Vatican insider who, until only recently, was a high-level member of the Italian Illuminati and a thirty-third degree Mason—Sir John Dee was working for Queen Elizabeth's intelligence service. He was the original so-called "007" secret agent, and he worked for the Western Illuminati.

The entities in this fifth dimension told Dee that the only way these beings can escape the invisible chain/barrier around the Earth is through the use of pure matter. That pure matter that they were referring to has to do with nuclear energy (in a different form) and afterward the heavy use of silicon will be required, and as a last step, they mentioned the use of DNA. (I will explain this later since the specialty of our old friends, the fallen angels, was, is, and will be the DNA/Gene field). Does the word "Microbiology" sound familiar to your ears?

These entities also said to Sir John Dee that in order to create pure matter, they will have to do things in reverse. First is to create nuclear energy, and only then to extract pure matter from it. (This last one must be done through a very special process, still I believe unknown to mankind today.)

We all know by now what that refers to: the atomic bomb! This bomb must have been very familiar to our old friends, the Nefilim.

* * *

Sir John Dee passed along this information to Queen Elizabeth I and down to the Nefilim. The Nefilim knew that the human race right now in the time period of AD 1500 was not fully ready knowledgewise or industrially to proceed with such an advanced task.

The 1500s was the period where the famous name "the Renaissance" was introduced. In this period we developed, created, professors, superastronomers, scientists, researchers, advanced medicine, colleges, universities, and great learning centers.

All this knowledge will now have to come into use in the Manufacturing field, to actually build and manufacture badly needed critical parts, and also to develop super-energy sources and fuels to totally rebuild, repair, and replenish fuel supplies, in order to have the physical capacity to break down the existing Esoteric Gamma-G barrier around the earth.

Yes! Again as far as this two hundred Nefilim group trapped here on earth is concerned, this barrier must come down, or else! As I mentioned earlier, the Nefilim themselves in the flesh, in suspended animation, or their bloodline descendants are now cornered almost like rats!

The main reasons for that being are the following:

1. The approach and/or the passing of Nibiru that is very soon due, at every 3,600 year orbit.
2. Atomic bombs that may be used the wrong way in massive and large quantities.
3. The Galactic alignment that may be causing strange and dangerous gravity effects here on earth.
4. Black axiom also known as Black matter, some scientists call it Dark Energy. (This last one is as if the Earth is entering a giant sand blaster, carwash like, except a mixture of grained steel, sand, etc., is being used—no survivors). Oh yes, all that fine action is due roughly on December 21, 2012, including entering a full Galactic alignment.
5. And finally, the always unexpected, the sun's super-Gamma rays that could fry the Earth at an instant. As I mentioned earlier the gravity of the sun is now roughly 200 percent lower than a couple of years ago.

* * *

Now I am going to mention one more item or topic, which might be terrifying this group. This may sound like science fiction and far-fetched, but pay attention! Do we all remember the movie *Star Trek IV: The Voyage Home*? this movie takes place on Earth's twenty-third century. A probe comes to Earth and threatens total destruction. It was emanating a strange sound. It was waiting for something, for a reply, from a whale, a humpback whale. A reply in a form of a whale emitting original sonar sounds. So in order to save the Earth from the alien probe, Captain Kirk and his crew go back in time to retrieve the only thing that could communicate with the humpback whale, another humpback whale from the past, from the twentieth century, because now in the twenty-third century, the humpback whales have been hunted to extinction. After the whale was retrieved and brought to the future of the twenty-third century and deposited into the open oceans, it started to emit sounds to verify that yes, the whales are alive and well. The space probe picked up the signals, completed its mission, and went back on its way peacefully!

And the moral of this story is? It is possible that our old friend, the so-called Nefilim, are aware of one more deadly possibility that will be facing them with the approach and the return of planet Nibiru, the Twelfth Planet.

* * *

The leaders, the rulers, the kings of the Nefilim, the ones that live on and occupy the planet Nibiru, are on their way here, on their next pass (2012). The names of some of them were known as Enki, Enlil, and one more famous name known in Central America, the super white God "Quetzalcoatl"! Now this white God promised, gave his word: "I shall return!" And it's my guess that this will happen on the next pass, when? You got it, 2012! (See conclusions and clarifications.)

* * *

Hot note: Before I continue with the main topic, just to refresh your memory, remember that these Gods had the ability and the sophistication fifty-five thousand years ago to chase their own people through many galaxies and planets and find them. They are possibly millions of years ahead of us in technology, etc. Therefore, they must possess methods of identifying and locating anything alive from distances very far way. They can tell what type of being you are, your race, creed, color. They can sense all that by using their unique DNA/gene technology.

Now when the Gods return, they may be looking for a certain group of people, their favorite people, the people that they have created and tried to save, these people and their bloodline descendants; and it's very possible that if, or when they find out that another group of people tried to cause them harm and death. Watch Out! (Could they possibly be the chosen people? The ones that God called "am segula"?) Again, there may not be a hiding place for the guilty!

After reading all of that, do you think that there is even a far-fetched chance that this could have been one of the reasons of the creation of the state of Israel?

* * *

Is it also possible that this is another secret that Zecharia Sitchin knows of? About Nibiru the Twelfth Planet and the possibility that an army of giants will appear here very soon? Just looking? Looking for what or for whom? (And is this another reason why the world governments, the Vatican, and the White House are so concerned? Is this why Zecharia Sitchin is being kept muzzled up by Uncle Sam?)

I mentioned previously the movie *2001: A Space Odyssey*, by Arthur C. Clarke, and the movie *Star Trek: The Voyage Home* by Gene Roddenberry, a very good and close friend of Arthur C. Clarke. The subjects that these two writers wrote about and brought out to the public are enormous, and I wonder what else they knew. Also, do you remember the ending of the movie *2010*? Didn't we see two suns? At present time, in reality, are we not very soon going to see two suns in the sky? Our own sun, plus Nibiru? Just ask the owners of some observatories that are located in Antarctica, Arizona, and Australia. And who are their owners? Oh yes, the Vatican!

* * *

At this point, I must mention something very important regarding the date, December 21, 2012. About one year ago, on a very well-known radio show *Coast to Coast*, the guest that was on was a person named Major Ed Dames, a very well-known Remote Viewer. Many people, institutions, here and abroad, have learned of his skills and have learned to trust his answers. On that one night among the many questions asked of him was posed one question. Specifically, "What do you see beyond December 21, 2012?" His answer at first was very sad. He used a very low-key voice as if he had a tear in his eye, and he answered, "I see nothing but darkness . . . nothing, only pitch-black!" This answer came out of him very slowly, and in a very somber voice, he continued to say that he decided to join his longtime girlfriend at her living place somewhere in the mountains in the Ukraine, Russia. Now here comes the second part. A few months later, the same Remote Viewer, Ed Dames, appeared on the same show again, and during the questioning, he was asked the same question, as if he was never asked the question before, and here is the answer he gave this time (I am going to exaggerate here because the answer this time was a whitewash, here it comes): When the sun goes around the moon and Aquarius meets with Scorpio, and so on and so on and so on. In other words, it is obvious that somebody got to him and ordered him to zip it!

If you remember earlier in my story, I was talking about the crashed flying saucer, and what Major Jesse A. Marcel saw at first sight, or at first eye contact! Well, therefore, I believe what Major Ed Dames said the first time during his first interview as is the true answer, not the above fabrication!

CHAPTER FOUR

The Modern Age, Hitler and the Bomb

As a result of educating the masses and heavy advancement in the sciences and progress in the military industrial complex with supertransportation on the ground and in the air, we are now ready with all our resources, human and mechanical, to produce the long-awaited super energy weapon, the "atomic bomb."

We are all familiar with the two atomic bombs dropped on Japan, one on Hiroshima and one on Nagasaki, but what most of us don't know is how in reality the building of this superweapon came about.

Soon after Hitler came to power in 1933, he was immediately introduced to the secrets and the powers of a possible super atomic weapon and its potential. From teenagehood, Hitler was always mystified by the occult, black magic, and control, which was introduced to him.

As soon as he understood the long term-potential of the atomic bomb, he immediately ordered the go-ahead of the project with full speed, including building reactors, extraction of uranium-235, and the building of major facilities to produce Heavy Water, including a secret sight later in Norway.

The Germans were working on a Nazi atomic bomb from 1939-1945. On March 4, 1945, the Germans exploded an atomic bomb in Thuringia, Germany. That bomb contained uranium-235; the bomb destroyed an area of about 500 square meters (it may have meant 500 meters rad). That blast killed several hundred prisoners of war and concentration camp inmates, etc. From documents found in later archives, it was established that this bomb used a Gun-type trigger!

These documents were found in Russian and German archives, especially in documents that were uncovered after the fall of the Soviet Union (released by the old guard, the KGB).

Until the year 2005, the average person on the street if he or she had done some basic research might have come upon some information regarding that one explosion on March 4, 1945. However, some very deep, yes, extra deep, digging will have to be done to uncover the following: On March 14, 2005, and again on June 1, 2005, the BBC News in a news article wrote that documents and drawings were found regarding a Nazi mininuke that was similar to the one *used on March 4th, 1945 in Thuringia, Germany. It was an actual tactical nuclear weapon.*

Tests were also carried out on the Baltic Sea, which is located in Northern Europe, between mainland Europe and the coast of Sweden, which borders with Norway, near Rugen Island.

And yes, Norway, isn't that the country in which all the many nuclear experiments and production of Heavy Water were taking place?

The two (2) explosions on the Baltic Sea were also found and verified in a secret Russian memo that was sent from a Russian Spy to Stalin. The memo said, "I saw two huge blinding explosions on the night of March 3, 1945."

In 2005, according to a Berlin historian Rainer Karish in his book named *Hitler's Bomb* (in German), he reveals evidence that Nazi Germany had tested crude nuclear weapons on Rugen Island on October 12, 1944, and near Ohrdruf, Thuringia, on March 4, 1945. This second bomb could have been an actual "Thermonuclear Hybrid" bomb. That bomb was using shaped charges of the Gun-type trigger, very advanced! This second test at Thuringia is said to be documented on film and is in Soviet KGB files.

So if this is true, then the United States was not the first nation to introduce atomic weapons to the world!

Just a memo: in a letter from Albert Einstein written in 1939, he urged President Roosevelt to start developing a nuclear program that would lead to developing a nuclear weapon.

Then in late 1941, the United States established a secret program, which came to be known as the "Manhattan Project," to develop an atomic bomb.

It seems that for one reason or another, back in 1920s, the German education system was very advanced, especially in the fields such as medicine and the sciences. When I mention the name "sciences," I am referring mainly to Nuclear Fusion. In Germany, you always find the best science teachers and professors.

Now Dr. J. Robert Oppenheimer was born in America, educated in America, but even here we have a connection to Germany, their sciences and their knowledge.

Dr. J. Robert Oppenheimer studied in the University of Gottingen in the years 1926-1928. And he studied under professor Max Born. This is also the institution where he received his Doctoral Degree. (Dr. Oppenheimer was born on April 22, 1904, and died on February 18, 1967.)

As we know now from our major involvement in WWII, Germany had the most advanced weapons, on the ground, on the high seas, and in the air. They accomplished all that by having super manufacturing and precision machinery facilities early on in WWII. (I wonder if the special treaty that Germany signed back in the year 1936 with the so-called aliens had something to do with this success.)

All that said and done, the Americans, finally in July 16, 1945, introduced a completed atomic bomb, the American atomic bomb. The first test of the practical atomic bomb received the code name "Trinity." The Trinity bomb was exploded at 5:30 a.m. on the morning of July 16, 1945. It took place at Alamogordo, New Mexico.

The Trinity nuclear bomb used the same "Impulsion"-design trigger that was used later on the bomb that exploded over Nagasaki. That bomb was named the "Fat Man Bomb." This was a plutonium fission source bomb.

Two atomic bombs were dropped over two major cities in Japan, one bomb over the city of Hiroshima and one bomb over the city of Nagasaki.

The first tactical atomic bomb that was dropped over the city of Hiroshima, Japan, was code-named "Little Boy" and used uranium-235 as its fission source. The date of the explosion over Hiroshima was August 6, 1945.

***Hot! for your eyes only! It is now known from unraveled military documents that "Little Boy" was being loaded up in crates from the assembly line to the airfield, toward the famous B-29 Superfortress named "Enola Gay." Yes! The atomic bomb was on its way to the B-29 before—yes, before—the completion of the test at Trinity! Before completion! The flight took off from Tinian Island base in the Pacific.

The Trinity bomb was a plutonium* fission source bomb, using an impulsion-design trigger. However, the bomb on the way to Hiroshima was a uranium-235 fission source bomb, using a Gun-type trigger.

Under the Manhattan Project, the production of uranium-235 proved to be quite difficult, with the existing technology known in the United States at the time. But the production of plutonium was easier, as it was a by-product of specially constructed nuclear reactors, the first of which was delivered to the Manhattan Project and received by Enrico Ferini in 1942.

The two types of fission bomb assembly methods investigated during the Manhattan project were (1) Plutonium bomb, using the Impulsion-type trigger, and (2) Uranium bomb, using a Gun-type trigger. The Gun-type assembly was not tested before it detonated over the city of Hiroshima!

According to the new records just found, all the American experts at that time—during the assembly of "Little Boy," the atomic bomb that was designated to be dropped over Hiroshima—said and warned that because of the complexity of the Uranium-235 design bomb, with the Gun-type trigger, it was deemed necessary to test it before its use in combat!

To their dismay, the warning fell on deaf ears. It seems that orders came from the top (sources and names unknown). Orders to fully assemble the bomb and ship it out to its destination without delay!

What is going on here? How did they know that both bombs, "Little Boy" and "Fat Man" would be successful? Both bombs used different fission sources and using different type of triggers!

---

*   Plutonium is a by-product of a nuclear reactor.

A REALISTIC PICTURE is worth a thousand words:

YES! THIS IS THE PICTURE OF THE ACTUAL U-BOAT IN MY STORY, THAT ARRIVED IN Portsmouth Naval Shipyard.USA, June 1, 1945. *** **HOT FLASH**: Aboard this U-BOAT, There were also supposedly 2 dead Japanese scientists. Or were they just drugged. Question: what were Japanese scientists doing with the NAZIS? With a U-BOAT full of Uranium U-235?

Hallelujah, praise us all. Open your eyes real wide and open your great mind and just think and wonder, and after you go through all that, ask yourself the following question: When did all these people, all these scientists, suddenly become such experts on atomic bombs? After all, isn't it the first atomic bomb that they ever built? Have they ever done this before?

Or, or, is someone or something else feeding them information, during the graveyard shift perhaps?

Yes! Something here is very mysterious! Does it sound like a second program may have existed somewhere, a second similar parallel program, in which only certain top people participated and fed each other or exchanged information among themselves? Of course, it is not possible. But just in case, read on!

On August 6, 1945, "Little Boy" (the uranium fission) atomic bomb exploded over Hiroshima, and three days later on August 9, 1945, "Fat Man" (the plutonium fission) atomic bomb exploded over Nagasaki.

Please read the next few paragraphs as a lead in to what is to come next, the enigma of certain mysterious German submarines and their connection to a top secret American project!

For the bombing of Hiroshima, a B-29 Superfortress named the "Enola Gay" was used. For the bombing of Nagasaki, a B-29 Superfortress named "Bocks Car" was used.

For the test at Trinity, plutonium was used as a fission source. (Were we short on uranium?)

For the bomb "Little Boy" that exploded over Hiroshima, uranium-235 was used as a fission source. Did we have this uranium all along? Or did a special shipment just arrive; and if so, from where?

For the bomb "Fat Man" that exploded over Nagasaki, plutonium was used as a fission source, the same fission source that was used for the test at Trinity!

Flight-line mechanics said later on that they saw scientists on the runway right next to the "Enola Gay" performing some final assembly work on the atomic bomb itself. Wooden and metallic cargo boxes with blacked-out (painted over) words or numbers were seen there right next to the bomb. And all that took place only moments before the flight took off on its mission to drop the bomb over the city of Hiroshima, Japan!

And now fellow readers, I am sure that by this time, you are all wondering what I, the author, have up my sleeve with all of this fine bit of information. Well, read on because some real excitement and intrigue is coming up. Watch out! Pay very careful attention to dates, and sequence of events!

The author of the book *Critical Mass*, Carter Hydrick, wrote that about three weeks after Germany's surrender, on 5-07-1945, and more than a month before final assembly of the first U.S. atomic bombs, marine guards escorted a Nazi submarine, or U-Boat no. U-234, into a New Hampshire naval yard under a great veil of secrecy. For almost three days, the area was totally off-limits.

If all of the data and information are correct pertaining to the German submarine U-234, and so far it seems that it is, then it means that this submarine's mission was vital to the Manhattan Project or, in simpler terms, vital to the final completion of the U.S. atomic bombs. It carried about 560 kg. (Kilograms) of enriched uranium oxide; it also carried uranium slugs and specialty built nuclear triggers to fit a certain prebuilt atomic bomb! Hydrick contends that the Manhattan Project commandeered these materials to complete both the Hiroshima and the Nagasaki bombs.

In 1945, according to a U.S. investigation called "Alsos," it was determined that a German submarine U-234 tried to deliver uranium and other parts to Japan. But after the German capitulation, the submarine surrendered to the United States before reaching Japan!

Bull, this German submarine U-234 and its crew never had any intentions of reaching the shores of Japan. This submarine headed straight for the USA! This all great intercontinental arrangement must have been preplanned by some real super high "entities"—just think, all these submarines, on these very long underwater missions, never shot at, never stopped (the red carpet treatment), and always arriving at the other end with ready prearranged open friendly arms!

So after reading all that, if any of you out there believe this last story of the U.S. investigation called "Alsos," well, then, your brain deserves to be in the sauce!

This submarine brought parts from Germany. These parts were not some tire lug nuts, screws, bolts, or light bulbs. These parts were manufactured in Germany by their top secret factories (and by that I mean that some of the help check in, but don't check out!). These factories are set up to produce parts with super accuracy and precision to fit certain particular assemblies, and in this case "American" assemblies and Parts that must have perfect male-to-female fits. A perfect fit for the American nuclear bombs!

Now. Just ask yourself the following question: If this whole story is true—but only if it's true (cross my heart and wish to die and all that)—then what are the odds that this is all a big coincidence? None! That's right! I don't believe in coincidences!

A major portion of the answer to this question may be found in the movie *Contact* based on Carl Sagan's novel (1997). What? Carl Sagan again? Well, now it must only be a coincidence!

In the movie, after the first superstructure at Cape Canaveral blows up due to sabotage, Elli Arroway (played by Jodie Foster) returns home and finds a message on her computer with a return call address. She calls back, and who is on the other end? None other than her sponsor, a billionaire industrialist S. R. Hadden.

He points to the zoomed giant TV screen and shows her another superstructure, a second one. Its existence was kept top secret; this one built in Hokkaido, Japan.

And what does S. R. Hadden say to Elli Arroway? "The first rule in government spending: why build one, when you can have two at twice the price, only this one can be kept secret, controlled by Americans, built by the Japanese subcontractors, who also happened to be recently acquired wholly owned subsidiaries of Hadden Industries."

Now. Do I really have to explain this? Or is your insight getting brighter?

Well, just for the few of you with the sort of a foggy insight, let's try this: Why build one when you can have two the price of two? Only these two can be kept secret from one another, controlled by the "Seeing Eye" Corp., built by the Americans and Germans, who also happened to be long-time owned subsidiaries of the Nefilim/Seeing Eye Corp.

It seems that all sides were somehow communicating with one another, sharing vital and very critical information, and all that was done toward the accomplishment of the one major goal: to complete the building of the final assembly and finally field test a tactical atomic bomb! A very large and a very powerful Atomic Bomb.

By sharing certain critical information, I didn't mean of course talking to each other those days on the telephone, or even on a one-on-one basis. But through central command, the Seeing Eye Corp.!

Okay. All right. After we exploded these great nuclear weapons at the same instance of these events, a great amount of energy was released into the air!

At this point, our old friends, the Nefilim, must have rejoiced and were patting each other on the back. We have done a fantastic job, and now we will have to convert this energy back into "Matter"! Trust me, this task, our friends, the Nefilim, with millions of years of experience, this, they know how to do!

However, the following may be good news or bad news, depending which side you are on. Our old friends, the Nefilim, were about to repay an old debt, repay a debt to a longtime supporter of the alien agenda.

THE NUCLEAR CALENDAR

DATE	LOCATION	COUNTRY	EVENT
October 12, 1944	Rugen Island	Germany	2 nuclear explosions (type: unknown)
March 3, 1945	Thuringia	Germany	1 nuclear explosion (type: U-235, gun-type trigger)
May 7, 1945	-	-	Germany surrenders
May 17, 1945	-	-	U-234, the ID No. of the German submarine headed toward the USA loaded with nuclear parts
June 1, 1945			The approximate date the German sub, U-234, arrived in New Hampshire, USA
July 16, 1945	Trinity	USA	Trinity test, the world's first known atomic blast (type: plutonium, impulsion-type trigger)
August 6, 1945	Hiroshima	Japan	Name: "Little Boy" (type: U-235, gun-type trigger, first known detonation of an enriched uranium gun-type device known at that time in the USA)
August 9, 1945	Nagasaki	Japan	Name: "Fat Man" (type: Plutonium, impulsion-type trigger)
August 14, 1945			Japan surrenders
January 27, 1951 to 1992	Nevada	USA	928 nuclear explosions (tests) (type: unknown); of those, 828 were underground

CHAPTER FIVE

Adolf Hitler

The purpose of the Potsdam Conference, which was held in Potsdam, Germany, from July 16, to August 2, 1945, was to decide how to administer the defeated Nazi Germany. Among the heads of states to attend were Winston Churchill, Joseph Stalin, and Harry S. Truman. (The French and Polish were not invited.) The other reason for this conference was to discuss Japan's surrender! (By the way, Churchill was replaced by Clement Attlee on July 26,1945.)

It was here where Truman first alluded to Stalin that the Americans had developed the atomic bomb. Stalin smiled at Truman and, in a very soft voice, said to him, "Yes, I have known for some time!"

Former secretary of state Jimmy Byrnes in his book *Frankly Speaking* (as quoted in April 1948 "The Cross and the Flag") while in Potsdam, Germany at the conference of the Big Four, said that "Stalin left his chair, came over and clinked his liquor glass with mine in a very friendly manner. I said to him: Marshall Stalin, what is your theory about the death of Hitler? Stalin replied: "he is not dead, he escaped either to Spain or Argentina."

The big payoff to the German dictator Adolf Hitler, a gift, "give him his life." (This prearrangement was agreed on when Germany signed the treaty with the aliens, the Nefilim, back in 1936.)

In my opinion, the following events could not have succeeded without the knowledge, permission, and authority of the real top superleaders of the world, who oversee our so-called elected officials.

Most people believed at the time the official story that Adolf Hitler committed suicide, and the most common story that became world's favorite was the double suicide of Adolf Hitler together with his mistress Eva Braun.

Now please remember, that just like Saddam Hussein, Hitler had many body doubles, live ones, and dead ones.

The live ones were to replace him at certain risky live appearances, and the dead ones were prepared for an event just like this, to fake Hitler's death. The dead body doubles would have had to be sizewise, anatomically, and dentalwise perfect.

With Hitler's funding and the very "Well-Known" reputation of the German doctors and dentists, this task was very easy for them to accomplish!

I mentioned earlier that there was a great rush to complete "Little Boy" for the atomic drop over Hiroshima. The main official reason at that time was that it would save thousands of American lives!

However, there could have been at least two more reasons. In an earlier conference called the "Yalta Conference," which was held on February 4 to February 11, 1945, in the Black Sea resort of Yalta, Stalin had promised to enter the war against Japan within three months after the defeat of Germany.

American military experts at this point of the atomic bomb program knew that they could win the war against Japan on their own, using our great Air Force once the war against Germany had been won.

Russian troops at this time were threatening to overrun most of Europe at full speed, from east to west.

At this point of the game against Japan, there was no way the Americans would allow Russia to gain entry into the Far East arena!

Also it seems that in the way of our super spies in Japan and the Pacific Islands, we the Americans got wind that the Japanese had developed and built a fleet of super bombers, each powered by six engines, loaded with poison gases or bacteria, and or Bubonic plague ready to attack the American mainland from the pacific side in a very short time. Yes! A massive gas attack on the USA. Millions would Die! (See documents and notes).

From among all of the top world leaders, neither Winston Churchill nor Harry S. Truman, or even Joseph Stalin, was aware of a possible above top secret agreement that existed to allow Adolf Hitler's escape. (This agreement was way above their level on a Need-to-Know Basis. Yes, this was all handled by "The Seeing Eye Corp.")

As to verifying what Joseph Stalin said to former Secretary of State Jimmy Byrnes regarding Hitler being alive. the Gestapo chief Heinrich Mueller, during his interrogation in 1948, told his U.S. interrogators that he arranged Hitler's escape from Berlin together with Eva Braun. They left Berlin on April 22, 1945 (just as the East side of Berlin started to be controlled by arriving Russian troops! and then they flew to Barcelona, Spain, on April 26, 1945).

To my readers, just read the following paragraph because it will clarify major events that will be coming up in this book regarding Hitler's escape and whereabouts.

Heinrich Mueller was telling the truth! After his capture, he was kept in the dark—no outside visitors, except top U.S. interrogators. He had no access to any outside information. Now all of the data and the information that he gave to the Americans checked out perfectly per all of the records found later on regarding aircraft takeoffs and submarine departure dates and arrivals. His information was cross-checked with other interrogations of other German air force, navy, and other field officers. So it seems that in one way or another, Hitler knew that his escape would be completed successfully, including the very special place, the final destination that he was heading to. He also knew that when he got there, that he and his people (fellow Nazis) would be protected by some very powerful sources, very powerful entities, second to none!

*** Hot note: To me, the author, it is now becoming very clear that Hitler was playing a very strange game. It seems that Hitler wanted the Americans to know exactly where he was hiding, and he was sort of baiting them, saying, "Come and get me if you can!" Well, somebody tried just that! Keep on reading!

Also, the suicide story of Hitler was based mainly on concocted testimony of three or four fanatical Nazis. However, that was the best story for public consumption. Peace among the natives!

There never was an identifiable corpse of Adolf Hitler nor of Eva Braun. The Russians found the buried (but unburned) corpse of the double of Adolf Hitler near the bunker.

Let's go on. On April 30, 1945, flight captain Peter Baumgart took Adolf Hitler, his mistress Eva Braun, and some loyal friends by plane from Tempelhof Airport in Berlin, Germany, to Tondern, Denmark. At that time, it was still barely under German control! From Tondern, they took another plane to Kristiansund in Norway, also German controlled. From there, they joined a submarine convoy.

Now we have two (2) different dates of Hitler's escape; which story is true? The one by Gestapo Chief Heinrich Mueller, or the one by Captain Peter Baumgart? Surprise, surprise, they are both true!

How? Just read the following information gathered from certain news sources regarding Berlin Tempelhof Airport.

Designated by the Ministry of Transport on October 8, 1923, Tempelhof was the world's first airport with an underground railway station in 1927.

Soviet forces took Tempelhof Airport at the Battle of Berlin on April 24, 1945, in the closing days of the war in Europe, following a fierce battle with Luftwaffe troops. Tempelhof's German commander, Colonel Rudolf Boettger, refused to carry out orders to blow up the base, choosing instead to kill himself. After he died, the Russian troops attempted to clear the five lower levels of the air base, but the Germans had booby-trapped everything, and too many Russian Soldiers were killed! Due to that disaster, it led the Russian commander to make the following decision: he ordered the flooding with water of all of the lower levels. The lower three levels are still flooded to this day, having never been opened up due to unexploded ordnance. (Colonel Rudolf Boettger knew what he had to do, to save his Fuhrer!)

Now to solve the mystery on how Adolf Hitler escaped.

First, the story of Gestapo chief Heinrich Mueller is correct. That must have been the original plan of the departure date in Berlin and the arrival at Barcelona, Spain. (Spain? Maybe?)

Hitler, Eva Braun, and the gang arrived at Tempelhof Airport just as the Russian troops were arriving. Hitler took refuge deep underground in the vast underground rail system. This gang consisted of some very loyal friends and a few that were specially chosen from among the Luftwaffe troops.

At the Tempelhof Airport's deep underground vast rail system, Hitler found a safe hiding place. After his friends felt that he was secured, they booby-trapped the whole area, making sure that no one gets in to find Hitler, and I mean "no one." Only Hitler and his loyal gang knew the safe way out!

When the opportunity came for escape, they came out through secret openings and jumped into what seems to be a brand-new shiny Arado Ar 234 twin-jet "Blitz Bomber," with a fully converted interior, and that was on April 30, 1945. And here they were on their safe journey to Tondern, Denmark, and to Kristiansund in Norway. By the way, if you have a need to know, the cruising speed of the Arado Ar 234 was about 450 mph. Neat, hey?

In Kristiansund, Norway, they joined a submarine convoy. This convoy was headed toward the North Atlantic!

Four (4) submarines left Norway on their last mission in the last days of the war: (**1**) U-234, (**2**) U-530, (**3**) U-853, and (**4**) U-977.

The U-234 reached USA with her special nuclear cargo on June 1, 1945.

The U-530 was located, and the submarine surrendered.

The U-853 arrived in Argentina on July 10, 1945.

And now, the U-977. It did not leave Norway until May 2, 1945. It was waiting for a very special cargo just as Russian troops were approaching! The submarine left its base on May 2, 1945, and arrived in Argentina on August 10, 1945.

That means the U-Boat U-977 was missing for 3½ months after leaving its base in Norway on May 2, 1945. It was out at sea for 105 days!

No! This submarine, the U-977, did not drop off its precious cargo in Argentina or anywhere else in mainland South America. But much farther south. The drop-off point was Antarctica!

The commander of the U-977 was Oberleutnant Heinz Schreter. He was known among his inside circles to have made a similar trip to Antarctica a few months earlier with much of the same crew! Was that a trial run? A training mission to prepare him for the big one?

The German writer Mattern said that Admiral Doenitz told a graduating class of naval cadets in Kiel in 1944 that the German Navy has still a great role to play in the future. The German Navy knows all hiding places for the navy to take the Fuhrer should the need arise. There he can prepare his last measures in complete quiet.

Until today, more than one hundred submarines of the German fleet are still missing. Among these are many of the highly technological "XX II" class equipped with the so-called "water schnorchel," a special-design and coated schnorkel, enabling submarines, in combination with their new developed engines, to dive for many thousands of miles. A trip to the base (at Antarctica?) without being recognized becomes very possible with this technology.

Adolf Hitler was born on the evening of April 20, 1889. He was born in the small village of Braunau, Austria, just across the border from German Bavaria.

There is a possibility that Adolf Hitler's grandfather was Jewish. His mother Maria Schicklgruber was employed as a cook in the house of a wealthy Jewish family named Frankenberger. It is possible that their nineteen-year-old son got her pregnant.

When Hitler was thirteen years old, his father died in January of 1903.

During WWI, Hitler's passions against foreigners, particularly Slavs, were inflamed and submitted a petition to join the Bavarian army. He narrowly escaped death in battle; eventually, he was awarded two Iron Crosses. He rose to the rank of Lance Corporal.

At that time around 1918, Germany was shook up with Communist-inspired insurrections. At the same time Hitler was recovering from war injuries, he heard that some Jews were leaders of these Communist groups, and this inspired within him the hatred of Jews as well as Communists.

Soon after WWI ended, Hitler was recruited to join a military intelligence unit; and from that point, he rose higher and higher.

In 1921, Hitler became chairman of the National Socialists German Workers' Party!

The original name of this party had been the German Workers' Party. Hitler claimed that the party was controlled by Communists and Jews.

In November of 1923, Hitler, after converting that party to a Nazi Party, tried to revolt against the Bavarian government.

The revolt failed, and he and fellow party members were arrested by the police.

Hitler was convicted and sentenced to five years. He was imprisoned at Landsberg where he served only eight months.

At that time, Hitler started to write *Mein Kampf*. It was an autobiography book filled with glorified inaccuracies, self-serving half-truths.

And of course in *Mein Kampf*, he wrote about any excuse to hate the Jews and Slavs. And he said flat-out that the Jews should be eliminated!

After his release from prison, Hitler decided to seize power. He spoke to scores of mass audiences, calling on all Germans not to yield to Jews and Communists.

In 1924, Hitler promptly reestablished the NSDAP in Munich. (Founded by the Occult Thule in 1917, and Vril in 1919).

In 1932, Hitler ran for president and won 30 percent of the vote. Paul von Hindenburg won! So in January 1933, Hitler decided to enter a coalition government as chancellor.

Upon the death of Hindenburg in August 1934, Hitler was the approved successor; the economy was improving, and Hitler consolidated his position.

The German industrial machine was built up in preparation for war in November 1937. He was positioned strong enough to call his top military aids together at the "Fuhrer Conference" where he outlined his plans against the enemies of Germany! I guess Hitler learned early, or he got some advice from higher places. Because when he made the statement "was preparing for war," maybe in reality what he meant was preparing for "Order Out of Chaos." You can hide many, many things. Sound familiar?

Now what happened in the time between the death of Hindenburg in August 1934, and Hitler's full control of Germany in November 1937?

At this time, let's read about some very interesting things. Things that may be way, way out, out of this world.

Did you wonder why Hitler was suddenly using the words the "Aryan Race" and using it more and more often?

In secret documents, it is said that some time in 1936, the first contact was made in the Black Forest between the Germans and the Extraterrestrials. The entities that they met, the Extraterrestrials, spoke with a slight German accent.

These Extraterrestrials called themselves the "Aryans." In reality, they are nothing but our old friends, the Nefilim, the original two hundred fallen angels. Today, they call themselves the Aryans; tomorrow, who knows? They may come up with a name like the Macaronis, the Spaghettis, Tall Blonds (what?), Short Blonds (whatever!).

It was then in 1936 that the "Aryans" made a deal with the Germans and signed a treaty!

A deal was made to build up, develop, and use the future German industrial complex for one main purpose: toward building an atomic bomb and all of its components.

A deal that couldn't be refused; a deal that was so secret that it would even provide the "Aryans" with specialty spare parts that would be a perfect fit for possible other atomic bombs to be built by other nations! Now I wonder what I meant by that. Could it mean some kind of a joint venture? What?

During the last two years of WWII, many Allied pilots claimed to have seen and were even chased by so-called Foo Fighters.

By the spring of 1945, the Germans knew that the war was lost regardless! The Germans had built quite a few flying saucers named "Veil's Machines," "Haunebu," and some were also called "Flugelrads," etc. Some of the Flugelrads were built by BMW, and some were built under the direct supervision of the Aryans for their own use! It seems that the term Flugelrads were a name given to a flying saucer type that was used exclusively by the aliens, the Aryans. Some of these Flugelrads may have been original saucers salvaged from the deep past, and some may have been rebuilt by the Germans, for the Aryans.

Most of these German flying saucers, could reach enormous speeds of from 4000 kph to over 50,000 kph!

***Be very careful. I will talk about this again and again in this book, so remember, these aliens are acting like Vampires. They don't just come into our countries and take control of civilian and military affairs (even though they could!), they sign a "Treaty" that gives them full and legal power! They are invited in, legally! And once they are in, they'll suck your blood, toes, brains, and your soul—they'll suck you "dry"!

As you may have guessed by now, our basic group of the original two hundred fallen angels are superclever! They have fifty-five thousand to five hundred thousand years of experience ahead of us here on Earth, and about forty-five million (yes, millions) years in the universe!

Was a similar treaty signed at roughly the same time with our ex-presidents—Roosevelt, Truman, and Eisenhower?

You bet! Remember the warning by President Eisenhower in his famous speech: "Beware of the Military Industrial Complex"!

What did he really know?

It seems that no country nor its leaders knew what the other country was doing in regard to certain "Projects," not even the best of allies!

Only certain people at the supersecret, above-the-top top level, the "Puppet Masters"! The inside members of the "Seeing Eye Corp." have complete and full knowledge!

And then again, each country is divided and compartmentalized into little controlled so-called subgovernments and/or industrial areas. Nobody, and I mean nobody, knows what the company or the other guys in similar fields are doing or producing and for what purpose! And it seems those who come too close find themselves in so-called "Mysterious Accidents"!

Before I go any further, I mentioned before, in regard to Hitler's hatred toward the Jews, whether it arose from his mother's past, involvement with Communists, or whatever, it all led to the "Holocaust"!*

For more clarification on that subject, just check out the works of the authors and researchers Jordan Maxwell and Michal Tsarion. And yes! Don't forget what I said earlier about the contents of the movie *Star Trek: The Voyage Home* and Quetzalcoatl, the Great White God!

---

*   See conclusions and clarifications.

CHAPTER SIX

The South Pole, Antarctica, and Admiral Byrd

Apparently the United States and England were watching Antarctica for a very long time, by using private expeditions and numerous spy missions to study the South Pole regions.

However, at the same time similar things were also taking place at the North Pole.

Admiral Byrd claimed to be the first one to fly over the North Pole on May 9, 1926!

In 1926, Byrd took leave from the Navy to organize a privately financed expedition to the Arctic, the North Pole, which was to be based on an island called Spitsbergen in Norway.

The island of Spitsbergen is the largest island of Svalbard Archipelago, located in the Arctic Ocean between Greenland and mainland Norway.

The plans for this expedition included a flight over the North Pole supported by Edsel Ford, John D. Rockefeller Jr., the *New York Times*, and others. It is at that time that Byrd started to suspect that this group belonged to a much higher order.

Byrd and his pilot Floyd Bennett claimed to have reached the North Pole on May 9, 1926. Both men were awarded the Medal of Honor.

However, in later years, scholars have raised questions about the success of the expedition in flying over the North Pole.

We shall see soon why not only was this mission a success, but also what did the Rockefellers know even then.

Later in 1946, there was a UFO (flying saucer) crash at Spitsbergen.

Here is a hot pointer: as soon as the crash at Spitsbergen occurred, in 1946, General James H. Doolittle was sent to Sweden by the Shell

Oil Co. to investigate "Ghost Rockets." What? Can you imagine sending General Doolittle to investigate "Ghost Rockets"?

Somehow, he wound up in Spitsbergen to look over the sight of the supposed flying saucer crash.

*** There are recent documents from the Norwegian Air Force, confirming that a second UFO crash took place later in 1952.

Supposedly aboard this second saucer that crashed there were seven alien crew members. All of the crew members were burnt to death at this second crash in the year 1952. So let's see why Spitsbergen was so hot?

Do we all remember the name Dorothy Kilgallen, the journalist who was found dead in her New York apartment on November 8, 1965? That was right; after her interview with Lee Harvey Oswald's killer, Jack Ruby!

However, while all of the people's minds were focused on the JFK subject, very, very few knew of her real "Gigantic" story, a story never to be told.

Before her death, she told friends that she had information that would break a certain case wide open. She didn't refer only to the JFK assassination. She was also investigating another case with some very high officials in the British Government.

Here is what very few people knew about the journalist Dorothy Kilgallen. She claimed that someone in the upper echelon of the British government informed her that a UFO crashed near Spitsbergen and was under investigation by the British and the American military. Supposedly, this informant was Lord Mountbatten. Ho. No. No. No. Not so fast; you have to hear (read) the rest of the story. She must have known that her time is very, very short. Dorothy Kilgallen knew too much of the truth about the assassination of JFK.

Apparently, when she met with Lord Mountbatten in one of their very close business meetings—and this information, of course, came from one of her very close friends—Dorothy Kilgallen was told that a third craft, a flying saucer, actually crashed in England at the identical time of the crash that took place at Spitsbergen in 1952. Inside the craft that crashed in England, they found some dead occupants; however, what is more fascinating is that they found messages regarding future signs for mankind—Crop Circles. That told of future safe havens from the approaching disaster on December 21, 2012. (I wonder if it mentioned a location for a certain future Seed Bank.)

Another pointer about Spitsbergen: the Svalbard Seed Bank. In the year 2007, the Norwegian government started to build a "Doomsday Seed Bank" in which all species of seeds would be stored and to be used only in case of a major regional or global catastrophe.

Could there be an underground alien base deep under the Svalbard Seed Bank?

Even though the government of Norway owns this facility, guess who controls the facility and the program? The Bill & Melinda Gates Foundation and the Rockefeller Foundation!

Just by reading the above two paragraphs, you know you get a gut feeling that something is wrong! You get a feeling that something big is coming down. By something big, do I mean planet Nibiru?

The Svalbard Seed Bank begins to become very interesting since its establishment took place in the year 2007. Because not since the 1920s was there a similar special project. This project to which I refer is the project of the Rockefeller Foundation and other powerful financial interests to use Eugenics, later on renamed Genetics, to justify the creation of a genetically engineered master race. Hitler and the Nazis called it the "Aryan Master Race."

Byrd, after his flight over the North Pole, somehow made a connection between the Rockefellers, Freemasonry, and the Illuminati. (And this was back in 1926.) But at the same time, he was also a very loyal American.

Now back for a moment to the Svalbard Seed Bank, does somebody like the Rockefellers or the Illuminati, or should we just say they ("Seeing Eye Corp.") expect a natural disaster soon? Maybe in the year 2012? After all, that seed bank was built awful fast, out of nowhere! It was built with extreme urgency and secrecy with many private funds. Again, how do they know that it is approaching?

After his flight over the North Pole, on May 9, 1926, there were some rumors and doubts whether or not Byrd actually flew over the actual North Pole. Byrd had reported seeing some very strange things below his flight path, and at the time, scientists tried to debunk him.

In 1927, he tried to cross the Atlantic by flying nonstop between the United States and France. His chief pilot was Floyd Bennet, but during a practice takeoff with Bennet alone in the controls, the "Fokker Trimotor" airplane, named "America," crashed. While the plane was under repair, Charles Lindbergh won the prize.

Byrd later had more Antarctic Expeditions. He undertook four more expeditions to Antarctica from 1933 to 1935, from 1939 to 1940, 1946 to 1947,* and in 1955 to 1956.

Now as a senior officer in the United States Navy, Byrd performed national defense service during World War II (1941-1945) mostly as a consultant to the USN high commanders.

In 1928, he made his first expedition to the Antarctic. This trip involved two ships and three airplanes. Byrd constructed a base camp called "Little America." It was constructed on the Ross Ice Shelf. There they spent a summer and a winter, on a photographic expedition, and performed Geological Surveys!

On November 29, 1929, Byrd made his famous flight to the South Pole and back. The Expedition returned to North America on June 18, 1930.

On his second Expedition in 1934, Byrd was operating a Meteorological station, named "Advance Base," all alone! However, it was too cold. He was picked up by an airplane that was dispatched from "Base Camp" on October 12, 1934, and flew Byrd back to Little America.

While Byrd was visiting Hamburg, Germany, in late 1938, he was offered an invitation to participate in the 1938-1939 German "Neuschwabenland" Antarctic Expedition; however, he very kindly declined!

*** For your need to know! Here is my personal opinion on why Byrd declined: It is very obvious that in those days, the American and English spies were very much active in the South Pole area, especially in Antarctica; and if you doubt me, just look at the activities of Byrd and his escapades. America knew even then that Nazi Germany was

---

*   (* This was the big one, the one expedition that we will focus on was the one in the year 1946-1947. Operation "Highjump.")

building and constructing a huge secret project under the ice in this area of Neuschwabenland, Antarctica. Yes, America and England knew even then! However, they couldn't admit it to the world for the very simple reason that if they were to admit that, then that would be as if admitting that Nazi Germany had invaded another country or another continent! In simple words, "It's wartime." However, it's unfortunate that the Americans and their allies didn't know the real true story of what went on under the ice of Antarctica! The answers will be coming up! Read on!

I mentioned earlier that the submarine U-977 arrived on shore in Argentina on August 17, 1945.

I am positive that the crew of that submarine was fully interrogated "Plus" some by the American Secret Service. As a matter of fact, some inside military people said that the entire crew told the whole story on their own with no outside pressure or fear. It was as if this is exactly what they were supposed to do. Spill all the beans; tell all!

Now do you think that it was strange, or by coincidence, that right afterward the Americans, the English, the Australians, and even some Russians made the final connection, a very strange connection between Nazi Germany and Antarctica!

And that's how we get to Operation Highjump!

In a normal republic like the USA, a democratic republic, the people maintain control through free elections and through the electronic process.

However, that may have been subverted with the rise of the "Executive" Alien-Military Industrial Government Complex within the United States, which is controlled by an Alien—Corporation Elite—rather than being equally controlled among the common citizens. Are things getting clearer now?

Before I continue with the story, I would like to sidestep to the subject of Operation Paperclip.

The Rockefellers did exactly what they did with the Nazis, they took their "children," the Nazis, back under their wing and gave them refuge within the Military Industrial Complex. By these actions, what you have created is the most powerful government on Earth which is now a Corporate Empire!

While at the same time, you find a safe haven for their top leaders, as promised to them!

At that time, we had some very loyal military leaders, all pro-America who were sworn to defend the land at all cost!

Among them were Secretary of the navy James Forrestal, Admiral Nimitz, Admiral Krusen, and Admiral Byrd.

This loyal group of government people assembled a very large task force and headed South to the Antarctic. The purpose of this task force was to stop the alleged activities of the Aryans or Nazis in Antarctica!

Yes! In one meeting, the word "Aryan" was actually mentioned. No! Not just at any meeting, but at a top secret meeting just before Operation Highjump" was initiated.

As far as the world and America were concerned, Operation Highjump was just an innocent Civilian Expedition!

However, in Admiral Byrd's own words, the mission (code-named "Highjump") was primarily of a military nature. The inside word was out that the task force was sent to eradicate a secret Nazi base in "Queen Maud Land," which the Nazis had renamed "Neuschwabenland" and which had never been explored as profoundly as the rest of Antarctica!

Operation Highjump was a military invasion of Antarctica. On December 2, 1946, three battle groups left from Norfolk, Virginia. They were led by Byrd's command ship, the icebreaker *Northwind*.

*** In my book, this is the operation that stirred up the "Cuckoo's Nest"!

Yes! Roughly as of this date, all hell broke loose in the UFO World. Mass sightings started! The aliens knew that the moment had come that most of the world's civilized population would now finally become aware of their longtime existence. In the modern world, news travels fast! Due to superfast communications, the days of the pony express are over. Our friends, the Nefilim, know that more than well.

The task force included over forty ships, including an aircraft carrier, a submarine, a destroyer, and many support vessels. A British-Norwegian force, an Australian, and a Russian force. All in all, four thousand plus men, aircraft with full firepower!

Yes! This large task force that was assembled was all part of Operation Highjump. Now let me say this: there were rumors, only rumors, that this task force was carrying nuclear weapons!

*** After this operation came to an end, all of the fighting forces were sworn to secrecy! In other words: this *military* operation never took place!

*** We shall soon see why!

Some of the planes that were used for surveillance and for spying in this operation were six (6) R4Ds.

Actually, these planes were converted DC-3s. They were fitted with Jet-Assist takeoff bottles to enable them to take off from the short deck of the Aircraft Carrier *Philippine Sea.*

It was a very powerful task force. The mission was fully equipped and was supposed to last eight (8) months.

However, the expedition was terminated abruptly at the end of February 1947.

What happened? What went wrong?

What happened is that we actually woke up a Semi-Sleeping Giant! And again, we also stirred up the Cuckoo's Nest!

As the task force was on its way down south, to Antarctica, everything was peaceful. As they were approaching the Ross Ice Shelf on their way to Little America, they observed flying discs. Flying saucers flying above them at incredible speeds! Yes, the entire whole four thousand plus men fighting force had seen them! Just about the entire crew of Operation Highjump!

Flying Discs and Flying Saucers, all the same. As some of the flying saucers flew above the fleet and slowed down, the people below on the ship decks observed something very strange.

On the upper portion of the saucer, the so-called upper dome, and under the lower portion of the saucer, the lower dome, something has been spotted. It looked like "Twin 60 mm. rapid fire cannon barrels"!

ADMIAL BYRD DID NOT EXPECT TO SEE THESE FLYING MACHINES IN ANTARCTICA.

They looked like the same twin 60 mm. cannon barrels that were found on top of the newest Panzer battle tanks that were built by the Germans and observed during operation while in battle at the end of WWII, on the Western and Eastern Fronts!

Yes! This weapon system that was very similar to the rapid-fire twin 60 mm cannons, which the German Battle Tanks that were equipped with, performed in a nasty way. Now this weapon system had been known to pierce the 4-inch armor plates that the Allied tanks have been equipped with, and it seems that piercing these armor plates was done with extreme ease!

Except for one thing. During a battle, there are extreme loud and deafening noises, explosions, gunfire, etc. However, these cannons, while they were being fired, were almost noiseless. They never made loud noises of typical cannons while being fired!

After close inspection of Allied damaged vehicles that were hit by these cannons, the Allies knew right away what they were dealing with a weapon, very highly advanced, never seen before!

During the last few legs of the war, America and England agreed not to fire at these special equipped tanks and also not to fire at the Foo Fighters, or so-called flying saucers, that were equipped with such weapons. It seemed that we wanted to capture one (1) so that we would be in a great position to study them further! By the way, believe it or not, Russia also agreed to this, initially!

However, our very close friends, the Russians, shot down one of the flying discs anyway!

It happened in 1945. On this disc, the Russians found the special weapon, made of a set of weird tungsten barrels and ball cascade oscillators. Yes it was a very super, advanced, and unique weapon never seen before! (Could it have been "An Out of This World Design?)

This weapon was so complicated that it took the world's top scientists until only very recently to solve the enigma of this gun system.

This famous double-barrel cannon system was widely known in the Battlefield as the "KSK" Cannon System, the Energy Beam Weapon! Many pictures were taken by the Allied Air Forces over Europe showing UFOs equipped with the same weapon system!

Apparently, this weapon system takes lots of energy to operate and makes the flying saucer very unstable during usage while in flight. This data is only characteristic to the Nazi/German flying saucers, and *not* the ones belonging to the Aliens!

As the attack fleet of Operation Highjump was approaching these so-called Nazi underground bases in Antarctica, everything appeared to be normal, dead calm.

However, as soon as the attack began on those Nazi bases, all hell broke loose! Should I say "Nazi/Alien" bases?

The real fighting didn't even last three weeks!

It seems that the American fleet got its ass kicked pretty bad with all its mighty and powerful armada. It couldn't even make a scratch on the enemy!

It seems that the enemy, the defenders, had such superior firepower that the Americans could not match.

Not only that. It also looked like the weapons that were sent to destroy the enemy, either did not reach their intended targets and/or were blocked by some kind of a barrier, a force field of some kind!

Now! As soon as the Americans stopped firing, the action stopped dead as if on cue, as if by some direct orders given from where—from whom?

The Nazis, the Germans, the Aliens? They did not continue to pursue the attackers further from their home base, under the ice!

With regards to this sort of military action that was taken by the defenders, it seems that the Aliens promised in their original treaty signed with the Germans back in 1936 to give the Nazis the safe haven in Antarctica and to defend them, in sort of a "Defense Mode"! They would help to defend the Nazis to the end, at all cost! Yes, "Defend"!

But as far as to go on the Offense? So far? No! Not yet. But tomorrow, who knows?

This task force was said to also have been equipped with Nuclear weapons! However, they were never used during or after this battle! Why?

My Close Encounters of the "THIRD KIND"

"THE HOLLOW EARTH"

"THE HOLLOW EARTH"

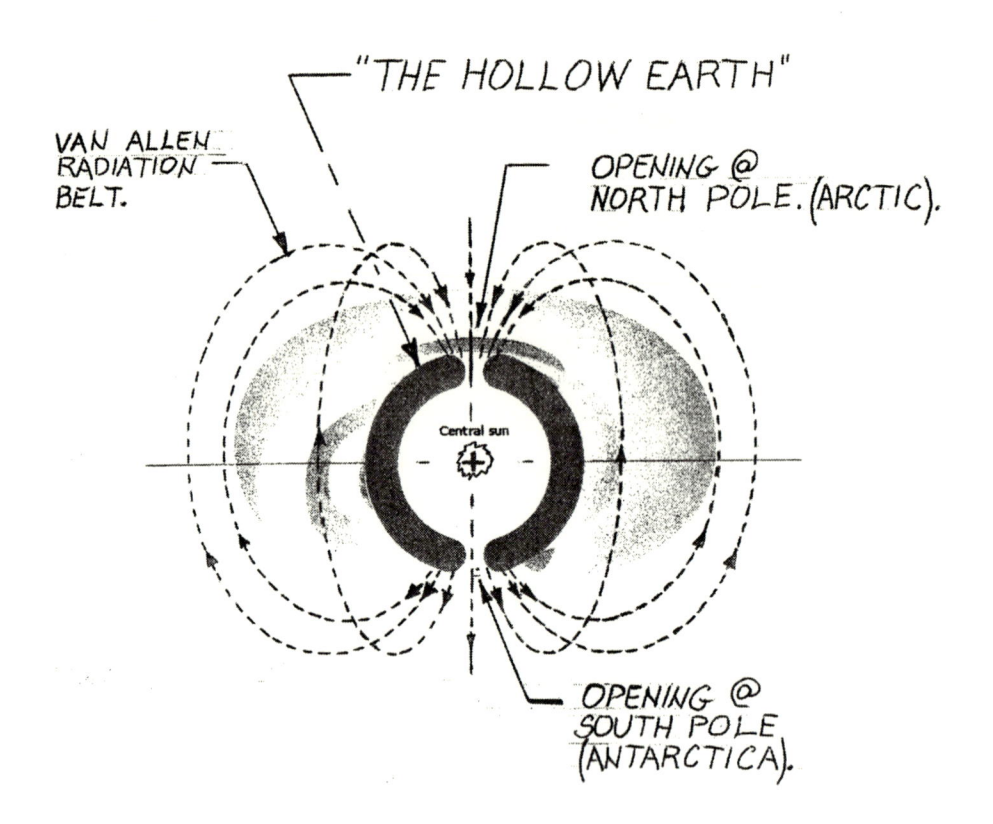

VAN ALLEN RADIATION BELT.

OPENING @ NORTH POLE. (ARCTIC).

Central sun

OPENING @ SOUTH POLE (ANTARCTICA).

IS THIS THE REAL REASON FOR THE STRANGE PATTERN OF THE "VAN ALLEN RADIATION BELT"?

SEE BACK SECTION : "CONCLUSIONS AND CLARIFICATIONS".

ILL."I"

ILL."H" "THE SPHINX

JUST WHAT DOES "OUR" GOVERNMENT KNOW OF WHAT'S BELOW?
SEE BACK SECTION: "CONCLUSIONS AND CLARIFICATIONS".

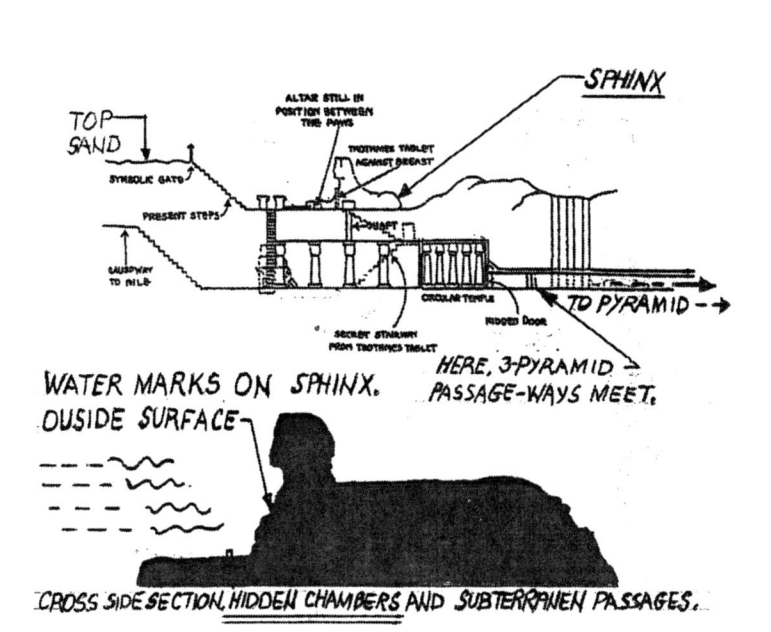

Diagram labels (cross-section, top):
- TOP SAND
- SYMBOLIC GATE
- PRESENT STEPS
- CAUSEWAY TO NILE
- ALTAR STILL IN POSITION BETWEEN THE PAWS
- TROTHMES TABLET AGAINST BREAST
- SHAFT
- SECRET STAIRWAY FROM TROTHMES TABLET
- CIRCULAR TEMPLE
- HIDDEN DOOR
- SPHINX
- TO PYRAMID →
- HERE, 3-PYRAMID PASSAGE-WAYS MEET.

WATER MARKS ON SPHINX. OUSIDE SURFACE

CROSS SIDE SECTION, HIDDEN CHAMBERS AND SUBTERRANEN PASSAGES.

ILL. "F"

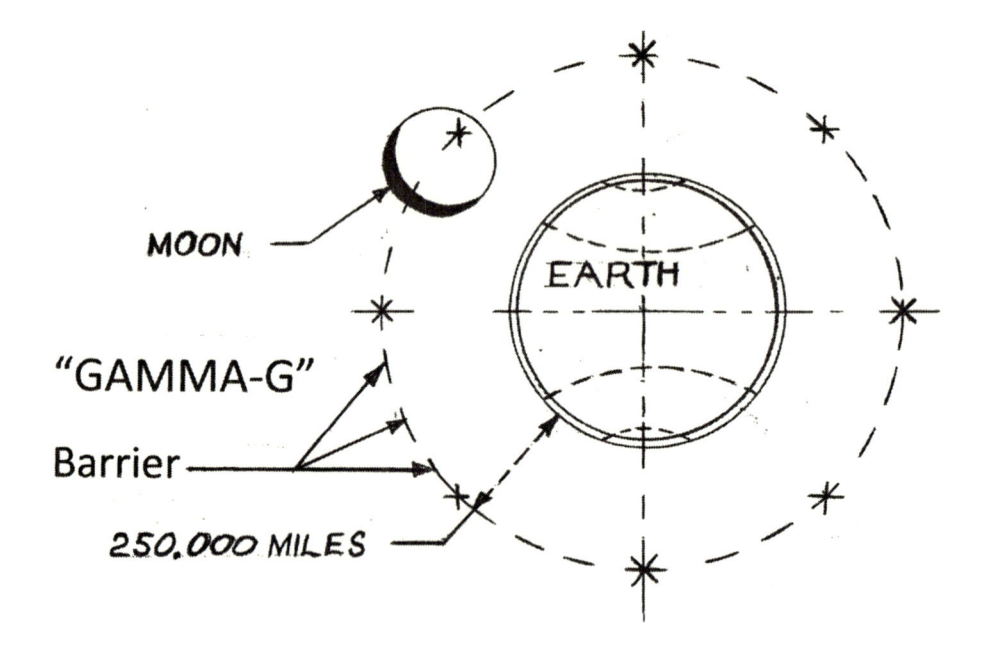

MOON

"GAMMA-G"
Barrier

250,000 MILES

EARTH

"GAMMA-G"
BARRIER

"FOOL'S GOLD". BY CARL SAGAN.

THIS IS THE NEW NAME FOR THIS PICTURE, IT WAS ABOARD PIONEER 10 SPACECRAFT, LAUNCHED ON MARCH 3, 1972.!

WHY? SEE BACK SECTION: "CONCLUSIONS AND CLARIFICATIONS".

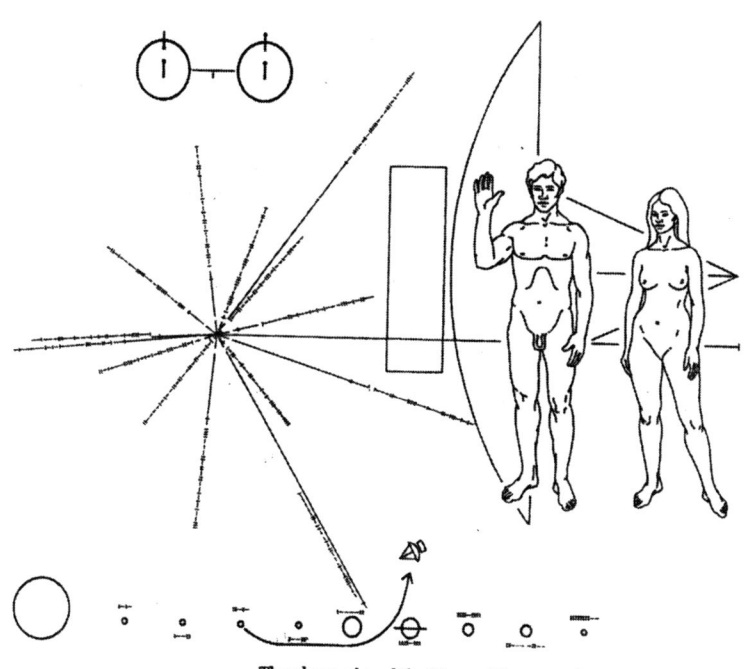

The plaque aboard the *Pioneer 10* spacecraft.

ILL."G"

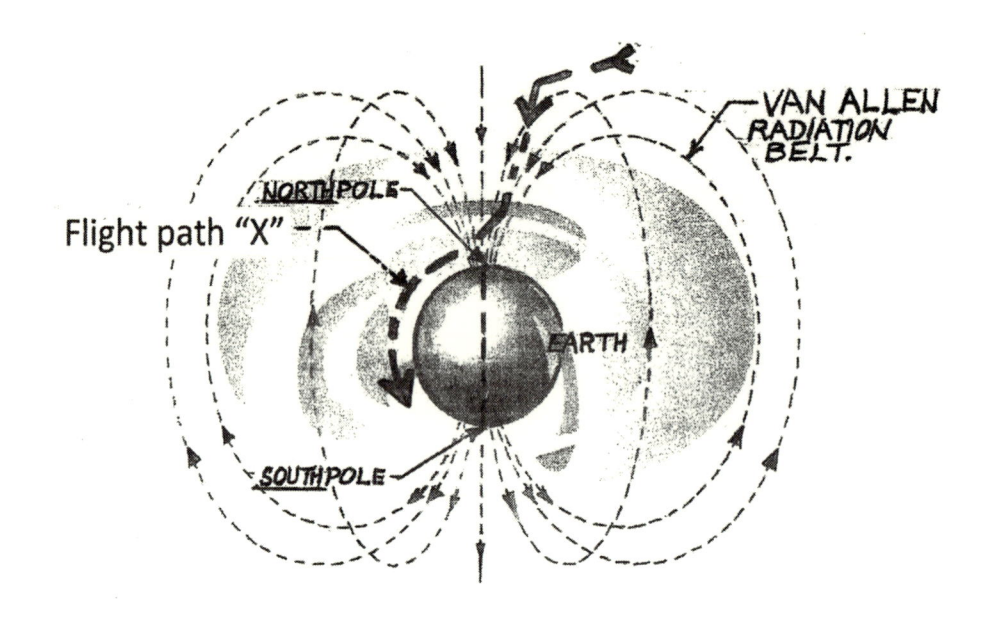

"VAN ALLEN RADIATION BELT"

ILL. "E"

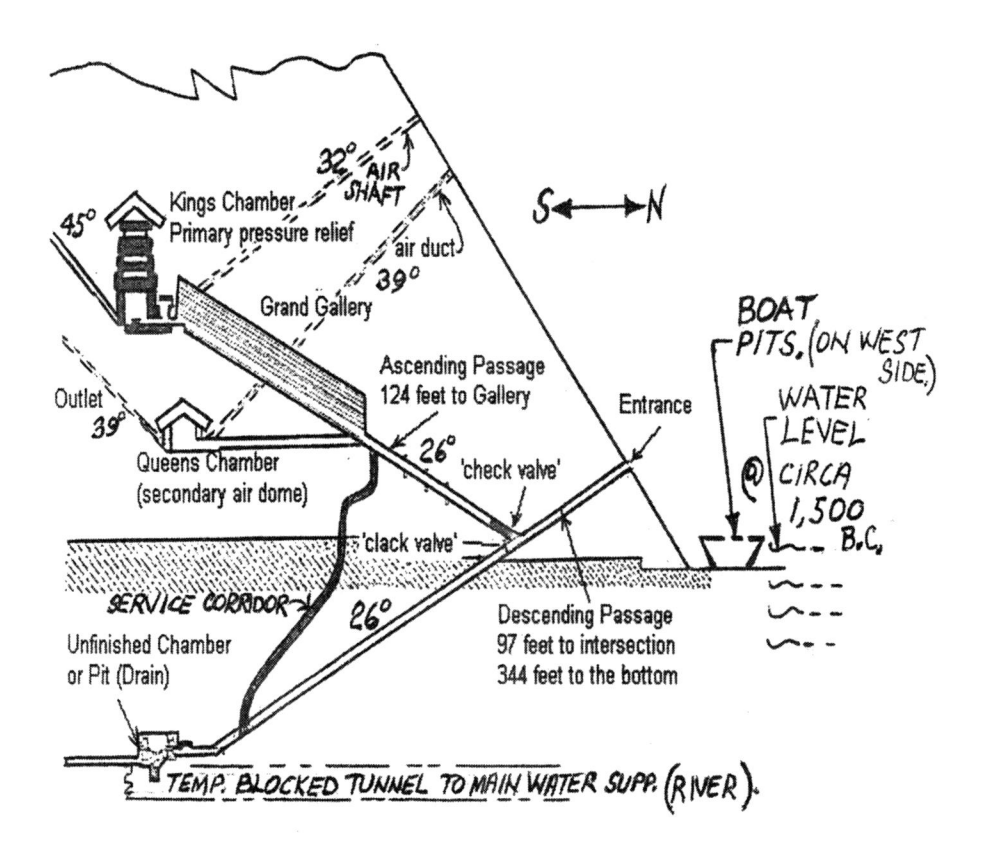

ILL. "B"   "THE PYRAMID"

CHAPTER SEVEN

Operation Highjump, the Black Hole, and Meeting with Aliens

As soon as the action stopped, Admiral Byrd ordered a private mission over the area—a spy mission!

Admiral Byrd ordered three (3) planes, three of the six R4Ds equipped with the supersecret "Trimetricon" spy cameras for an immediate takeoff mission.

The three planes took off; two of them returned on time. However, the third one, the one with Admiral Byrd on board, returned *three hours* late!

The question is, What happened during those *three missing hours*?

The answer could be found in Admiral Byrd's newly discovered Secret Diary!

From all of the information that I could find, these supersecret Trimetricon spy cameras and other photographic equipment on board were set to photograph for over twelve hours nonstop automatically from the very instant that the start button was triggered. This was done for an obvious reason: to make sure that all of the views and sights were photographed without interruption that might occur due to human error during manual operation.

You must remember one very important vital statistic: Back in the years 1945-1947, there was no Internet, no CNN News, no FOX, no MSNBC TV news! There was only what the U.S. Government official news allowed you to read in newspapers or hear over the radio; in other words, by default or by design, we would only know about certain events by very carefully released information from our government. I am not saying that this was good or bad, but it's all there was!

The reason that I just mentioned about the release of information in those days is that people on the streets, the everyday common folks, were told or made to believe that there was no connection between "Roswell," Operation Highjump, and submarine U-977!

Wrong! Wrong! Wrong!

In this day and age, we have great radio programs late at night that discuss everything from UFOs to time travel, paranormal, etc. They are all great shows, and you can learn quite a bit from them. With the right show host, the right guest, you can pick up an enormous amount of true information and data.

However, sometimes it seems that these shows, somehow or another, by design or default, whenever we have what we call an unusual UFO sighting or event, they, the media, always manage to go back to Roswell and try very hard to reinvent Roswell over and over again with the same and old information, but why? Well, by doing so, they take your mind away from what actually caused the Roswell crash. And how it makes a connection to a past event, a previous U.S. military action, especially the one with four thousand plus U.S. Navy personnel as live eyewitnesses!

Now if it's true, if there were four thousand plus navy men who took place in Operation Highjump, with the main prime witness Admiral Byrd, plus I believe two other Admirals, then surely there was at least one UFO, a Flying Saucer, or in the correct Roswell term, a Disc! Yes, a Disc, and not a Weather Balloon!

Actually, our government knew that more than well! So the deal was for every intelligence community in the country to get attention away—even until this day to get attention away from Antarctica, away from the South Pole, away from Operation Highjump, and away from Submarine U-977. And therefore always go back to the good old Roswell, with those great old stories.

Just keep focusing on Roswell; we love Roswell, keep talking about Roswell. Come back y'all! Yes, to Roswell.

Just how many more times are we going to watch Larry King, on *Larry King Live*, stretch out his legs on a beach chair in the sands of Roswell and wait until dawn for a UFO, or should I say Flying Saucer, to appear!

And every so often, the government makes sure that some TV and/or radio station comes up with a program with lots of your favorite experts to discuss Roswell. All of that action is to cause the greatest confusion ever to keep our minds distracted and away from the real thing!

The real thing? Yes! Such as the following:

a. Why did the Flying saucer (disc) crash at Roswell and its nearby area?
b. What happened just a very short time earlier at the South Pole?
c. Yes, the South Pole! The war at the South Pole Antarctica, against the Nazis and their flying saucers.
d. The sightings of the authentic so-called alien flying saucers that belonged to our old friends, the Nefilim (Fallen Angels).
e. And finally, the meeting between Admiral Byrd and the Aryans (the Fallen Angels) seen at that time as "The Tall Blonds," who at times seem to be speaking with a slight German accent.

To hide all of that, the government and/or the famous Illuminati, are taking all your minds away from the South Pole actions and transferring all your thoughts to Roswell and the North Pole; and just remember that it was in the North Pole where Admiral Byrd's secret trip per his diary took place! Oh yeah? What?

A DC-3, (CONVERSION TO AN RD-4). At the South Pole.

AND THE PICTURE BELOW... HERE IS THE FINAL EVIDENCE. ADMIRAL BYRD WAS AT THE SOUTH POLE!

YES ! THIS IS THE REAL THING. AN ACTUAL PICTURE, NOT A FAKE !!!

TAKEN IN THE SOUTH POLE, ANTARCTICA! ON FEBRUARY 16, 1947.

Byrd checking position over the South Pole with sun compass. **February 16, 1947, Operation Highjump.**

Admiral Richard B. Byrd's, Diary Feb 19, 1947

Just keep in mind, you must relate all that you read regarding his secret diary to the **South Pole, Antarctica**! I the author suspect that His diary had been altered by US. govt. agencies! **In Admiral Byrds own words:**

"I must write this diary in secrecy and obscurity. It concerns my Arctic flight of the nineteenth day of February in the year of Nineteen and Forty Seven

There comes a time when the rationality of men must fade into insignificance and one must accept the inevitability of the Truth! I am not at liberty to disclose the following documentation at this writing . . . perhaps it shall never see the light of public scrutiny, but I must do my duty and record here for all to read one day. In a world of greed and exploitation of certain of mankind can no longer suppress that which is truth." **(You, the reader, may find Admiral Byrd's Secret Diary in the rear of the book, under documents and notes).**

No, Suckers! Not on your life, fellow readers! Admiral Byrd's secret flight into the so-called North Pole, meeting with the Aryan aliens—which in my book, as per my research, are nothing but the original two hundred Fallen Angels—did not take place up North! Instead, the meeting took place down South in Antarctica! Yes, at the South Pole!

It seems that all of the actions that took place in the Secret Diary of Admiral Byrd took place inside the South Pole, in Antarctica. All of that took place right after the short military action of Operation Highjump!

Again to clarify a certain item in Operation Highjump, six (6) special spy planes have been built, and or heavily modified for this one time mission. Only six, and each was code-named "R4D" (they were converted DC-3s). All of the six planes were tied by chains and cables to the rear deck of the aircraft carrier *Philippine Sea*; all six planes arrived at the newly set up base Little America IV, in Antarctica. Admiral Byrd was the first one that took off from the carrier's deck and the first to land at Little America IV.

A few pictures exist showing Admiral Byrd with the R4Ds in Antarctica, and one picture actually shows Admiral Byrd inside an R4D, dated February 16, 1947, only forty-eight to seventy-two hours prior to his famous secret flight that took place on February 19, 1947. Takeoff time 0600 Hours as per Admiral Byrd's Secret Diary. It seems that this one lonely innocent picture that was overlooked by the Establishment is stone-cold evidence all by itself that Admiral Byrd was inside the very rare R4D aircraft at the South Pole—yes, in Antarctica!

So yes! the famous flight into the Pole took place inside the South Pole," and *not* in the North Pole!

It seems that "Someone" fudged (modified) the Secret Diary of Admiral Byrd and wanted it to appear as if its actions took place at the North Pole. That someone wanted to divert our attention and our minds away from the South Pole, away from Antarctica, away from the so-called Peaceful and Scientific Expedition named "Highjump"!

Again, ask anybody on the street today the following question: What is, or what was, Operation Highjump? The basic answer that you will probably receive is, "Who's Your What"?

Now you know how successful our government can be when it wants to divert our attention; in this case, the "Seeing Eye Corp.," trying to divert us from the South Pole—Antarctica, Operation Highjump—to the North Pole. Divert our minds away from the Hollow Earth Theory, away from Flying Saucers, and away from Admiral Byrd and his so-called Secret Diaries. Our government never sleeps; it's very clever! It has to be; the security of our nation and citizens should be its top priority!

Now the deliberate confusion regarding "Operation Highjump"? If you would have read all of the books or read on the Internet all of the available data, watch all of the YouTubes, and read all the blogs, they will all give you information and certain dates! So remember what I said earlier in my book, "God" gave you a brain; use it the right way. Gather all information, from all sources, filter them, and come to a conclusion!

In the table of contents, regarding this chapter, I mentioned a Black Hole. Yes, it's a Black Hole, but not the kind that only pertains to time and space; this one is aimed at a very mysterious and sudden lack of movement of the naval fleet of "Operation Highjump."

Now in regard to the fleet movements of Operation Highjump," we are given certain dates; the dates that you read for example is as follows: Ship A leaves port X on day so-and-so. Then ship B leaves port Y on day so-and-so, and ship C leaves port Z on day so-and-so. And then again ship A is going through point so-and-so!

If you read the official information of "Operation Highjump," it would seem that the whole U.S. Navy, taking part in that operation, never disembarked! It is just like an Antarctican vacation! The whole armada got down to the South Pole, to Antarctica, took a great sightseeing cruise, took some Polaroid shots, and then came right back to their home ports after spending only three (3) weeks at Antarctica!

This fleet was fully prepared and equipped in all aspects to fight an all out war, to be out there and engage the enemy for eight (8) months!

Oh yes, the great battle definitely took place!

Now hear this: When the ships returned to their home ports, some of the ships (four or five) of them were damaged so badly, that their captains were ordered to bring them into their home ports under the cover of darkness!

Shortly afterward, these same damaged ships had to be scrapped or, to use a better term, had to be destroyed by a torch!

The actual truth was that they were damaged beyond repair, damaged by secret enemy laser beam weapons—Nazi laser beam weapons, built by the Nazis, for the Nazis, but with Alien guidance! (Remember, these were German weapons, and not the Aryan-Alien weapons.)

PS. I don't think that any of our sea captains with their ships were looking forward to getting hit by the real thing! Because my guess is, if they got hit by the authentic alien weapon, they, with their ships, would have never been seen again.

Right close to the ending of Operation Highjump's main battle against the Nazis, which were protected by the Aliens, the Nefilim, Admiral Byrd took off from his new base Little America IV in Antarctica heading toward the opening of the Pole, the South Pole, right next to the Nazis. (See illustration I.)

As I mentioned earlier, Admiral Byrd's plane returned three hours late to his base camp!

As per Admiral Byrd's secret diary, as he flew into the South Pole, his plane was greeted in midair by two or three Alien flying saucers—yes, the real thing! And just like in the movies, they carried his plane by an invisible energy beam to their deep underground base, inside the Hollow Earth! There, Admiral Bird met with the Alien leader, the leader of the domain of the "Arianni" who was called the "Master," the leader of the Aryan Alien Race. That Alien leader must have heard of Admiral Byrd and his past and therefore respected him for being a scientist-researcher, first, and a military man, second! "Master"? (What happened to the name "Lucifer"?)

As per some UFO, or so-called Alien Investigators, the word is out that other so-called quick-visiting alien races that come here refer to the "Aryans" as the "Banished Ones"! (They know all about them throughout the Universe.)

Now the following statement is of very high importance: While inside the domain of the Arianni, on the way to the leader's chambers, Admiral Byrd saw the Aliens. They were all "Tall Blonds." And they called their own flying machines (saucers) "Flugelrads."

Toward the end of the meeting, the Alien leader, the "Master," told Admiral Byrd basically to tell the outside world that dark days are approaching and to stop using atomic weapons!

After that Meeting, Admiral Byrd, his radioman, and their plane were allowed to leave in a very friendly fashion and returned to their Antarctic base the same way they were guided in, but in reverse order!

At this point of the game, I believe that the aliens, or their so-called "Master," must have tried to use some very clever reverse psychology on Admiral Byrd when he was telling the Admiral about the concern of the usage of Atomic Bomb explosions. (Don't forget! These aliens need the release of extreme energy that can only be produced by exploding Atomic Bombs.) More about that subject later on.

*** WARNING! WARNING! WARNING! Just read the following! What evidence do we have of what took place from the instant the plane took off from its home base in South Pole, Antarctica, during the long flight to the so-called underground alien base inside the Hollow Earth, and then while the aircraft was standing still parked inside the domain of "Arianni," and then the long flight back to home base? What evidence? Think!

Just remember what I have said earlier regarding this "R4D" aircraft. All of these six aircrafts and their Supersecret photographic equipment were all built, modified, for that special Antarctic mission. Each of these aircraft carried more than one camera, as a matter of fact, quite a large number of cameras of all different varieties. All of them were fully loaded and ready to roll. And each aircraft system had built in a foolproof camera trigger device. Once you set the trigger, all of the cameras will keep shooting and taking still and motion pictures for over twelve hours. And as a final note, remember that Admiral Byrd himself was in charge of his own aircraft and managed and maintained his own photographic equipment! He knew his stuff!

Therefore, rest assured that at the instant that this "R4D" spy plane left the ground, all of these super secret cameras were rolling at full speed all the time, nonstop! Yes, taking pictures all that time. Got the picture?

Do you remember in the movie *Contact* when the ball/capsule, with Elli (Jodie Foster) inside, was let go and fell from a great height toward the assigned location? The drop of the capsule only lasted about three to five seconds. However, at the end of the movie we find out that the secret group knew that the tape recorder that was installed inside of that capsule ran and recorded for over eighteen hours!

Until now, if the mission of Admiral Byrd and Operation Highjump was to be so scientific and purely of a Nonmilitary nature, then why is it that until this day, we did not see any of the pictures that were taken by the R4Ds?

Yes, personally, I am interested in the photographs taken by Admiral Byrd on his last flight, or so-called last mission, when his aircraft returned three (3) hours late! An aircraft equipped with the most expensive, supersecret cameras that never fail! Yes, cameras that were running at full capacity during the whole flight. Good Luck!

The U.S. Government used many ways, many means, including some book writers to discredit that famous flight of Admiral Byrd and to confuse the general public as to where the exact location of the so-called Imaginary Adventure of Admiral Byrd took place. They even used the family of the owners of the Bank of America (The "Seeing Eye Corp." People) and the family of the writer F. Amaddeo Giannini who wrote the 1959 book *Worlds Beyond the Poles*.

And then at basically the same time also in 1959 came the case of the missing UFO magazine issue of December 1959. The fiasco in which the editor and writer Ray Palmer was involved. Again, the U.S. Government has ways of confusing you with disinformation to no end. You'll never know whether you are coming or going!

If you read the book *The Hollow Earth* by Dr. R. W. Bernard and as of late, there are many more scientific articles on this topic. You will come to the certain conclusion that there are giant openings in the North Pole and the South Pole! (See illustration I.)

Please! Just look at my sketch in this book in regard to the famous Van Allen radiation belt, and the reason, or my explanation, of why it takes that shape! (See illustration E)

However, satellite pictures are also being modified and "Airbrushed" to hide the openings at the Poles. Astronauts have seen them, Americans and Russians, but they have been sworn to secrecy by any methods required. They all seem to have the earliest cases of Alzheimer's disease I have ever seen.

Oh yes, airbrushing and astronaut brainwashing under the very friendly term called "Debriefings." For more information on that subject, just read the works of Richard C. Hoagland. I believe that he is right on with his theory and proof.

After Operation Highjump, Admiral Byrd stated that he didn't want to frighten anyone undully, but that it was a bitter reality that in case of a new war, the continental United States would be attacked by flying objects, which could fly from Pole to Pole at incredible speeds!

Some time earlier, Admiral Byrd recommended that we build defense bases at the North and South Poles. Admiral Byrd repeated again and again these points of views, resulting from his personal knowledge.

Now it's my opinion that the superfast flying machines that he referred to were the Nazi flying saucers that could fly at incredible speeds, and he did not refer to the Alien flying saucers called "Flugelrads," which are piloted by the Aliens, the Aryans, the Tall Blonds.

Against these aliens' "Flugelrads," Admiral Byrd knew that there could be no real defenses! He also understood by now that until that period in time, the Aliens gave the Nazis full defense capabilities, but no offense capabilities!

Referring again to Admiral Byrd's lost and suddenly found diary from an article in UFO digest, the Original Story of Admiral Byrd's secret diary first came to light during a radio program hosted by Art Bell. Art was apparently interviewing a member of the Byrd family, first cousin, second cousin, whatever, after the remarkable story broke out about the discovery of the lost diary. The initial announcement, members of the Byrd family have come forward to claim that the person interviewed was not in fact a member of the family and that the lost diary did not exist! Oct. 19, 1995.

By the Byrd family statement, it seems that somebody got to them, in one way or another! (The "Seeing Eye Corp."?)

Or was the real diary released with very small changes built in it to confuse the issue!

For example, if you place a bet on a sports team to win or lose, it will take only one (1) key player to be in on the deal and to cause a dropped ball, miss a catch, or fall, etc., and the final score will change drastically.

In this case of the found missing Diary, all somebody had to do is change a location word, such as North Pole versus South Pole, or Arctic versus Antarctic.

In this case, there is irrefutable evidence, beyond any shadow of a doubt, Admiral Byrd was in Antarctica, at the South Pole!

One more possible "Joke"! However, in this case, I will stress again that I last heard from some weather expert regarding the North Pole, named Dr. Pepperoni, who claimed that in the month of February, at the North Pole, it is Dark, Freezing Cold, almost Pitch-black! What would you do with cameras there at that time?

However, in this case, it sure seems that somebody is trying to take attention away from the South Pole, away from Operation Highjump, Nazis, Aliens, Beam weapons, Antarctica, etc., and shift all of the attention toward the North Pole!

So remember, there must never be any connection between the Nazis, the Aliens (Fallen Angles), Submarine U-977, Operation Highjump, and Admiral Byrd's secret flight into the Pole. The South Pole and Roswell! No connection at all!

Not on your life!

Let us check some dates and events. Let us call it how to connect some real dots between known dates and events!

WARNING. After you read the following and digest all the data with correct correlation, you will come upon a *shocker*, the plain truth, and it's right under your noses!

Let us remember one thing, in Operation Highjump, the navy divided the fleet into three (3) groups:

1) The Central Group, which included the aircraft carrier USS *Philippine Sea*, The aircraft carrier had stored on top deck many fighter aircraft; however, all the way to the rear were six (6) specially modified DC-3s aircraft code-named "R4Ds." The aircraft were constructed for this one specific mission. Also the icebreaker, the USS *Northwind*, which served as Admiral Byrd's command ship.
2) The Western Group.
3) The Eastern Group.

For ease of understanding and identifying the movements of the fleet, we will refer to the Central Group and its two main ships.
So let's start to connect some dots.

a. August 6, 1945: Atomic Bomb dropped on Hiroshima.
b. August 9, 1945: Atomic Bomb dropped on Nagasaki.
c. August 17, 1945: Submarine U-977 arrived in Argentina (from?). As of that date—from all information gathered by U.S. intelligences from the crew of the U-977—to early Fall of 1946, plans are drawn up regarding Antarctica! (This submarine finally surrendered to the United States in Boston on November 13, 1945.)
d. August 17, 1945, to August 26, 1946: Plans for the creation of Operation Highjump are drawn up in top secret circles of the U.S. Navy!.
e. August 26, 1946: Admiral Ramsey gave the preliminary orders to start major preparations for Operation Highjump. He stressed that in this action, the U.S. Navy would take full **charge!**
f. Early Fall 1946: All charts and navigational aids to be used for Operation Highjump were assembled at a gathering of minds in Suitland, Maryland. The Ross Sea charts prepared by the British Admiralty seemed to be the most reliable and were subsequently reproduced and dispatched to all ships.
g. Sept 18, 1946: Operation planning was intensified, and an official sailing date of December 2, 1946, was announced.
h. October 1 or October 2, 1946: President Harry Truman tried to stop Operation Highjump after he was briefed on its real military purpose!
i. Nov 12, 1946: Admiral Byrd's comments in his press release states that the purpose of the operation is primarily of military nature. Operation to last eight (8) months.
j. November 25, 1946: USCGC *Northwind* casted off from the Boston Navy Yard, the first to leave its home port!
k. November 28, 1946: USCGC *Northwind* arrived at Norfolk, Virginia and joined the flagship USS *Mount Olympus*.
l. December 3, 1946: All ships at sea. Operation Highjump on its way (first stop, Panama Canal).

m. December 10, 1946: All ships had arrived, crossed the Panama Canal, and started the long journey of many hundreds of miles on their way South.*

n. December 30, 1946: Central group rendezvoused at Scott Island.

o. January 7, 1947:* USS *Philippine Sea* reached Panama Canal Zone.

p. January 10, 1947: USS *Philippine Sea* steamed toward Scott Island.

q. January 15, 1947: The group reached the Bay of Whales.

r. January 16 and 17, 1947: Landing parties went to shore to select a location for Little America IV. (Somewhat north of Little America III, a base built on a previous mission.)

s. January 22, 1947: USS *Philippine Sea* reached 58 Degrees—48' S. Until this period, the skies were clear of any enemy aircraft or of any strange flying machines, and yes, I do mean flying saucers.

t. January 29, 1947: The first two R4Ds took off from the flight deck of USS *Philippine Sea* to their new base at Little America IV.

***Hot note: Admiral Byrd was on the first R4D to take off from the aircraft carrier USS *Philippine Sea*.

u. January 30, 1947: All six (6) R4Ds arrived at Little America IV safely.

*** I mentioned earlier that all six (6) R4D's were tied down to the rear of the flight deck of the aircraft carrier USS *Philippine Sea*. That was the reason and the only reason that the fighter planes could not take off from the flight deck. However, now that the flight deck was cleared, the rest of the fighter aircraft were able to take off!

*** It is at this point in time that the skies opened up! UFOs, Flying Saucers, all over the place, flying above the fleet at will, at incredible high speeds.

---

*   With one exception, USS Philippine Sea, the aircraft carrier loaded with its special cargo, the six (6) R4-D's, and the possibility of (3) nuclear weapons)!

- **v.** February 16, 1947: There is a picture existing showing Admiral Byrd inside an R4D adjusting one of the cameras. That picture is dated February 16, 1947.
- **w.** January 30, 1947 to February 18, 1947: At this point in time, there was virtually no real information in regard to any action or ship movements of the fleet! There was no information at all on any military activities or out of the ordinary naval movements. Very strange, Dead Calm, or Bingo! I have discovered the Holy Grail of this operation, the "Black Hole"!

*** The *shocker* or as I call it the "Black Hole." This was the time period of about two (2) weeks when the main battle (The War) took place between the U.S. Navy and its allies against the Nazis, which were supported by the Aliens, the Aryan race!

Now it seems that the only weapons the Nazis used were their flying saucers armed with the special duel cannon system that I wrote about earlier in the story. By the way, this weapon was causing very devastating damage to our fleet! As the Aliens were just watching and guiding.

- **x.** February 18, 1947: USS *Philippine Sea*, the aircraft carrier, arrived back at Balboa, Canal Zone! The carrier apparently lost many aircraft and also may have suffered battle damage itself.
- **y.** February 19, 1947: This is the start date that Admiral Byrd wrote in his world famous so-called Secret Diary! The Main theme of the diary is as follows: He flew his plane through an opening in the earth, entered through the Pole (I say the South Pole, also at this time of the year the North Pole was very dark, very cold), flew into the Inner Earth, met with an alien race called the "Aryan" race, which consists mainly of Tall Blonds, and he met with their leader called the "Master."

*** Now it is my guess, and it's only a guess, that the aliens contacted Admiral Byrd through mental telepathy and asked him to fly into the pole to meet with them. As his plane flew deep inside the pole, the aliens were all ready for him—they were expecting him! It was a very friendly get-together! Then Admiral Byrd and his plane returned three hours late.

- **z.** February 23, 1947: At Little America IV, all of the R4D aircraft were left behind, due to bad weather. The naval fleet that took part in Operation Highjump is returning to the USA.
- **aa.** March 1, 1947: The Western Group headed back home.
- **ab.** March 4, 1947: The Eastern Group headed back home.
- **ac.** March 5, 1947: On this day, according to *El Mercurio* newspaper of Santiago, Chile, Admiral Byrd was on board the USS *Mount Olympus* This ship served as the communication ship in the Central Group. According to the article, Byrd said the following: "I declare today that it was imperative for the United States to initiate immediate defense measures against hostile regions." The Admiral further stated that he didn't want to frighten anyone unduly, but that it was a bitter reality that in case of a new war in the continental United States, the USA could be attacked by flying objects, which could fly from Pole to Pole at incredible speeds! Admiral Byrd had repeated the above statements and points of view, resulting from his personal knowledge gathered both at the North and South Poles before a news conference held for international news services.
- **ad.** March 11, 1947: As per Admiral Byrd, "I have just attended a staff meeting at the Pentagon. I have stated fully my discovery and the message from the Master. All is duly recorded. The president has been fully advised. I am now detained for several hours [six hours, thirty-nine minutes, to be exact]. I am interviewed intently by top security forces and a medical team. It was an ordeal! I am placed under strict control via the National Security provisions of the United States of America, I am ordered to remain silent in regard to all that I have learned on behalf of humanity! Incredible! I am reminded that I am a military man and I must obey orders."

***The word "Master" refers to the alien leader that Admiral Byrd met with. The leader was mentioned in his secret diary. The leader that asked Admiral Byrd to deliver a message to Washington that they oppose our use of nuclear weapons. Ho, really? Just keep reading on! And again, I got the feeling that some reverse psychology may have been used here by the alien leader.

***Urgent! For the true meaning, for the future of this story, and for the future of all mankind, people on earth, just hear this: When Admiral Byrd met with the aliens, with their leader, the "Master," he very clearly stated in his Secret Diary and on later dates that the Aryan alien race spoke with a "Nordic" or "German" accent. And *no*! He did not meet with the Nazis. The reason for this statement was because in future events, regarding certain UFO abduction cases, some of which were very famous, there were some statements by the abductees that some of the Tall Blonds that occupied the spacecraft spoke with a slight German accent. Immediately, the so-called U.S. government experts tried, and are trying, until this day to make a connection to the Nazis in many instances by publishing UFO magazines that identify with Nazi symbols and insignias, such as swastikas. How convenient! Hey you, yes you! Do not fall for this garbage!

In referring to the leader called Master, is it possible that this entity is in reality Lucifer?

- **ae.** Apr 14, 1947: All ships from Operation Highjump are back at home ports.
- **af.** June 24, 1947: The Kenneth Arnold Sighting.
- **ag.** July 3, 1947: The UFO Crash at Roswell!
  Please, look at the dates and sequence of events above with a very open mind. Now can you make some sort of a connection to Roswell?

*** I bolstered my case, later on in this story, I will focus on the secret unknown events that allegedly occurred between June 24, 1947, and July 3, 1947. Stay tuned!

It is in my opinion, and this will be a repeat statement, that the so-called alleged very fierce military naval action in Antarctica took place between January 30, 1947, and February 18, 1947.

I also mentioned earlier that the Naval fleet during Operation Highjump carried three (3) nuclear weapons. These were never deployed during that operation. However, they may have been buried and/or hidden in Antarctica while the Naval fleet was retreating. For what purpose? Again, read on and stay tuned!

The U.S. Navy, with all its might, together with some Canadian, Australian, and Russian forces tried to penetrate the super heavy/fortified Nazi defenses in Antarctica. Defenses that guarded secret openings to huge underground cities built by the Nazis with the help and guidance of the aliens (yes, the original two hundred Nefilim). Or as they are called allegedly by other alien races, the "Banished Ones"!

Nobody is really sure, but the possibility exists that the German Nazis of today could have a population of over two million (2,000,000) people living underground in Antarctica!

Speaking about the subject with regards to "Possible" government disinformation, please read an excerpt from a well-known Internet site, which was posted only two to three years ago. This posting is a fake and misleading to confuse the issue in connecting Roswell with Operation Highjump. It reads as follows: "Why did the United States Government, in late 1947, only months after the famous Roswell incident, send a naval task force to Antarctica including Admiral Nimitz, Admiral Krusen and Admiral Byrd, called Operation Highjump." Folks, just keep your cool! (Just for a few of you very slow readers who catch on slowly, Operation Highjump took place *first* between December 30, 1946, to February 18, 1947! And then the "Roswell" crash occurred *later* on July 3, 1947.) Just the *reverse*. Thank you! WATCH OUT!

This is only one small example of total disinformation regarding Operation Highjump.

It is also my opinion that the main military action against the alleged Nazi base in Antarctica started as soon as the last R4D aircraft took off from the carrier the *Philippine Sea*. There were a total of six planes of this type involved, and Admiral Byrd was on board behind the controls of the first one to take off, which occurred on or about January 30, 1947, and ended on or about February 18, 1947.

I must repeat this! Before I go on, one very important note: The U.S. military, plus the U.S. Intelligence, plus the U.S. Government, all combined, made sure that all the data that is available to the public regarding Operation Highjump and its real actions and intent down south in Antarctica are either totally misleading or totally false!

Later on, a Rear Admiral (No Name), who was in that invasion and later retired to Texas, said that he was shocked when he read the "Fire From the Sky" report background material (a super top secret military report). He knew there were a lot of aircraft and rocket shoot downs, but did not realize that the situation was so bad.

As I mentioned earlier, the "Highjump" mission that had been expected to last for between six to eight months came to an early and abrupt end. The Chilean press reported that the mission had "run into trouble" and that there had been "many fatalities," that many aircraft and men were lost—the aircraft were operating from the deck of the only aircraft carrier *Philippine Sea*—plus a few other sea planes.

Also, according to the Chilean press, it is known that the "Central Group" of Operation Highjump was evacuated by the Burton Island, an icebreaker, from the Bay of Whales on February 22, 1947. The "Western Group" headed home on March 1, 1947, and the "Eastern Group" did likewise on March 4, 1947, a mere eight (8) weeks after arrival.

It is my guess as to how the Chilean people and their press knew so much about Operation Highjump. This is simple. Did you ever hear of returning wounded soldiers talking while in pain on the way to treatments in nearby Chilean hospitals, or before being dropped off on the way to the USA?

Exactly what was going on is still not a matter of public record; however, it is known that Admiral Byrd was summoned immediately to Washington and was interrogated for over six hours by the security services. All this took place after he was initially welcomed back by the Secretary of War James Forrestal on April 14, 1947. As we now know, James Forrestal, a short time later, committed suicide!

Very strange. It seems that almost all of the high-ranking people, civilian, and military, Admirals and Generals, that were connected to Operation Highjump were sooner or later found to be sort of "Allegedly Insane," put away, and somehow they all committed suicide! Yes, all stone dead, stone-cold dead, from Field Soldiers to Navy Admirals and high Government Officials.

This practice is going on until this day. Let's see. Now let's go back a few years, didn't some ex-Admiral commit suicide with two (2) gunshots? Ho. Ho. Ho. Can you imagine that?

He was Admiral Jeremy Boorda!

Do you remember the Monica Lewinsky story? The Paula Jones story? What a scam! These two names were used as the two of the biggest cover-up stories in the United States to U.S. Navy relationship history!

Admiral Jeremy Boorda was the leader of a group of twenty-four admirals and generals who planned to arrest President Bill Clinton for treason as authorized by the U.S. Uniform Military code! Yes, there were actual plans for a military coup in process against President Bill Clinton.

And per the following partial explanation, you'll see what was almost a "Military Coup"!

Admiral Jeremy Michael Boorda, U.S. Chief of Naval Operations, joined the U.S. Navy as an enlisted sailor and rose through the ranks to become a Four Star Admiral and Chief of Naval Operations—the Navy's most senior military officer and commander of all its active duty and reserve personnel. He hardly appeared to be the kind of man who would commit suicide, yet on the afternoon of May 16, 1996, he went home supposedly for lunch and shot himself (twice, according to some reports). The first explanation for the suicide was that Boorda was embarrassed that he had worn Medal ribbons to which he was not entitled. When it transpired that Boorda was in fact entitled to wear the decorations, a new story emerged: he was suffering from stress about plans for downsizing the Navy. Boorda supposedly left two suicide notes, but neither of these was ever released. In this atmosphere of doubt and implausibility, a bizarre story—never either confirmed or refuted—circulated on the Internet. Boorda was the Leader of twenty-four U.S. Admirals and Generals who planned to arrest Bill Clinton for treason as authorized by the U.S. Uniform Military Code. Clinton had allegedly supplied classified information to the head of the Red Chinese Secret Political Police, but Boorda's death preempted the actions of these senior officers. (The above article that you have just read originated from the *Conspiracy Encyclopedia* by Tom Bennet.)

I have mentioned before that what you have just read is only a partial explanation, and here is the reason why: There may have been two more reasons to bring out the Monica Lewinsky affair.

During the televised Lewinsky controversy, I personally was watching TV and listening to radio programs very frequently; it was very exiting! (The U.S. Government made sure it would be!)

One day, date unknown, I was listening to ABC radio on New York's 770 channel, the *Sean Hannity Show*. His guest at that time was Dick Morris.

Now that guy Dick Morris knew everything about the Clintons, I mean everything! On this particular show, I heard him say the following: "President Clinton knows about real life on Mars, and I don't mean Microbes, not little worms, but actual alien life on the planet Mars and flying saucers, which are used by them for transportation. The real problem for President Clinton is that he does not know how to tell all that to the American people, or the world's population."

So I believe that between the China affair that may have also included sales of certain missile technology to China, the actual possibility of life on Mars and flying saucers, the almost ongoing Military-Naval coup that almost succeeded, it was for that reason the U.S. Intelligence brought out the Paula Jones affair in 1994 and the Monica Lewinsky affair in 1996—all that to brainwash the public with idiotic nonsense to distract from the real thing, life on the planet Mars, and China, in that order!

So now again, let's return to the subject of Antarctica and ask once more, Who were we actually doing battle with? The UFO'S—Nazis or Aliens?

Actually the answer is really simple!

Now let me explain and make sure so you can understand once more what is going on here. In Antarctica, we were doing battle with the Nazis and their flying machines, or flying saucers. However, right next door to the Nazis were the aliens who were assisting the Nazis in building and constructing their underground cities, their flying saucers, and assisted them in battle, especially with regards to the use of those funny-looking little duel cannons that shoot energy beams.

And again, it seems that the Nazi flying saucers were firing at the U.S. Navy fleet and its aircraft as long as the actual attack on their home base was continuing. However, as soon as the actual action of the attack stopped, the Nazi flying saucers stopped firing!

Again, the aliens had their own flying machines, their own flying saucers called "Flugelrads." The aliens promised the Nazis full support and protection only to defend themselves against their enemies. However, that promise did not extend to assist them in any Attack Mode against their enemies. And all that was as a payback by the aliens for the German's assistance in manpower and supplies, per their treaty, in developing the Atomic Bomb during the Second World War. The bomb that is sought by the aliens for many years, for their own needs, as explained earlier.

The domain of the "Arianni" was the name given to the land in the inner world of the Earth that exists between the so-called North Pole and the so-called South Pole and belonging to the alien race called "Aryans" or, as we know them from way back, the Nefilim. Also, the name of the new so-called Nazi homeland in Antarctica was named "Neuschwablenland."

Operation Argus. What was it? Let me explain in very simple terms. As I, the author, mentioned earlier regarding Operation Highjump, the U.S. Navy was equipped with nuclear weapons, three (3) of them, and they were never used at the time against the Germans or the aliens! Most likely, they were hidden in that area of Antarctica for future use.

However, for some mysterious reason, in 1958, three (3) nuclear weapons were exploded in the region of the once held Operation Highjump, and the name for this operation was Operation Argus.

Operation Argus was secretly conducted during August and September of 1958 in the South Atlantic, about 1800 km. (about 1100 miles) southwest of Cape Town, South Africa. It was a very clandestine operation. The name given to the task force involved in this mission was Task 88, which was made of 9 ships. One of these ships was the USS *Norton Sound*, a nuclear missile/rocket carrier.

The USS *Norton Sound* launched 3 rockets! The first on August 27, 1958; the warhead exploded at an altitude of 100 miles. The second on August 30, 1958; the warhead exploded at an altitude of 182 miles. And the third on Sept 6, 1958; the warhead exploded at an altitude of 466 miles. The tests were known as Argus I, Argus II, and Argus III.

These tests were conducted as means to determine the possibility of creating artificial radiation for military purposes and to conduct tests regarding the magnetosphere and the Van Allen radiation belts.

Now here is the possibility of a connection of Operation Argus that took place on August through September of 1958 to the previous Operation Highjump that took place further back in the years 1946 to early 1947. I must repeat, only a possibility of a tie to Operation Argus. The ship, USS *Norton Sound*, sailed from Port Hueneme, California, straight down south, around South America, very, very close to Antarctica. Yes, very close to the same area that previous Operation Highjump took place. Right at the same time as the USS *Norton Sound* was sailing around Antarctica, three nuclear explosions were registered at that area at the time. This ship was also equipped with very high power electronics! Did it set off the three nuclear bombs left behind (planted and hidden for future use?) from Operation Highjump? I don't believe that this was a coincidence. Right afterward, the USS *Norton Sound* continued to the South Atlantic. There were no protests from the Soviet Union!

However, after the three nuclear tests in the South Atlantic, on the return trip back to the home port in Hueneme, California, the USS *Norton Sound* returned via Rio de Janeiro and the Panama Canal. The ship took the shortcut home, but why the same shortcut on the way to the South Atlantic? By now the answer must be obvious.

Yes! The Aryans and the Nazis are still there!

All we know today is that at the top of the world at the North Pole, the Arctic, and at the bottom of the world the South Pole, Antarctica, all of the major Naval fleets of the world are patrolling and encircling the poles, including the opening of the poles, especially the South Pole!

In Operation Argus mentioned above, there was one major surprise, and that was that the three (3) nuclear explosions seemed to hit some kind of protective barrier; no damage was done to the intended target.

Were the aliens aware of the presence of these three nuclear bombs all along? Did they perhaps welcome the nuclear energy release, to enable them to extract more Matter for themselves, to become even more powerful?

Is it possible that the reason the three nuclear weapons did not cause any damage to the enemy base was that the aliens know how to erect a protective dome or force field real quick around any compound, a protective dome that is very similar to the one used to protect the cities on the planet Nibiru?

It's amazing how the aliens, Aryans, the Nefilim, have made a fool out of the human race throughout the centuries through the very careful use of our government officials, acting as our perfect puppet masters. Yes, Boss. No, Boss.

As per what's written in Admiral Byrd's secret diary, the Master, or leader of the alien race, said to Admiral Byrd that they were very concerned about us, the Earthlings, exploding atomic bombs. I do very much believe that aliens were using a game of reverse psychology in their talks with Admiral Byrd.

Do you remember my earlier example? If a hunter or a scientist walk in the woods looking for Bigfoot, and for days he sees nothing, suddenly he sees Bigfoot far away walking in a certain direction to a certain underground cave opening, the immediate reaction of that hunter is to follow Bigfoot in order to catch him. That is a big Mistake! That was the wrong move to make. It seems to me that the so-called Bigfoot is being used as a ploy used by our aliens to divert the attention of the hunter from getting too close to the real mystery, which could be a certain underground cave opening, or a certain parked flying machine, etc. It is very possible that next time you see Bigfoot move in the woods in a certain direction, try to walk back the other way, in the reverse direction that Bigfoot came from. You may actually find something very interesting.

CHAPTER EIGHT

Nuclear Bombs Exploding on Our Mainland, Central USA

That is exactly what happened to us, the American people, in the Nevada desert starting in the year 1951. Yes! We were a bunch of idiots. And here is why.

Just remember, according to Sir John Dee, the so-called Nefilim—the Earth's true "resident aliens" or the two hundred banished ones—will have to extract matter out of energy as a means to an end goal. The only way they can produce it using today's technology is by releasing lots of energy and then, with their scientific capabilities, convert that energy back into matter.

We exploded one or maybe two atomic test bombs before the end of World War II, and then we exploded two more atomic bombs over Japan; lots of energy was released. However, the Nefilim required much, much more to rebuild and restock their fuel and stock supplies in order to provide fuel for their flying machines and, last but not the least, to destroy the Gamma-G Barrier that will permit the original two hundred Nefilim and/or their descendants to leave and escape planet Earth.

Few of the reasons why the aliens chose the USA and North America as their major controlling Corporation centers and Manufacturing facilities after WWII, and of course a test bed are Open Space, Shoulder Room, and a new Transportation System over vast open spaces, Ground, Sea, and Air.

And now the time has come! For what purpose? It is time to produce more energy. How? Very easy. Where?

It is right! At the Nevada test site located in Nye County, Nevada, about 65 miles northwest of the city of Las Vegas. Between January

27, 1951, and the year 1992, there were a total of 928 announced nuclear tests at the Nevada test site. Of these, approximately 828 were exploded underground.

So what did we, the American people, say? Yes, please blow up our country. Yes, please, we love radiation. The more, the better.

Yes! Our leaders who care so much about us, the same leaders who claim that cigarette smoke is bad for us, the people who claim that fats in meats are bad for us. Yes, these same people had the Testicle Fortitude to use our land, our mainland, to explode these nuclear bombs in order to release energy. And, no, our government didn't stop them! More, more, more radiation. It's good for us. Really!

I am just guessing that even if our leaders didn't want to agree to this sort of ridiculous action, they could not help themselves. You don't say *no* to the Seeing Eye Corp.

The Seeing Eye Corp. (the Nefilim) made it happen, one way or another. Now you can really realize on how powerful they are! Nuke our own country? Yes, and with full authorization from the top! How do you like these apples? Can they do this again? Who knows?

In December 1950, President Harry S. Truman approved the establishment of a continental proving ground 65 miles north of Las Vegas, Nevada. Between 1951 and 1992, there were approximately 1,021 nuclear detonations, which also takes into account multiple warheads.

Here comes the clincher. This means that the famous Operation Paperclip extends right to the top of our government! Did the Aliens, Nefilim, Fallen Angels, Aryans, together with the Nazis, have total control of our government? It's getting there, and some of our presidents are fighting them fiercely!

Of course, these Seeing Eye Corp. entities are fighting back against our presidents and leaders by using very clever tools, such as assassination, political scandals, sex scandals, and all sort of false rumors to discredit them.

Sometimes, if the American public eats this crap, then it works. However, if the American public is strong, smart, and looks at the right information by investigating the news stories the correct way, then the enemy can't win!

Modern American history includes catastrophic crimes committed by the government such as when the radioactive fallout from these Nevada tests drifted eastward extending over most of the nation and, of course, the same radiation drifted out into the Atlantic Ocean. There were many related cancer cases. The countless victims of the cancer resulting of these so-called tests had to wait until the 1990s for a formal "apology" and monetary compensation from the U.S. Government. However, by that time, many had already died. A report conducted in 1998 by the National Cancer Institute and Centers for Disease Control and Prevention concluded that nuclear testing had exposed to radiation nearly everyone who has resided in the United States since 1951. Indeed some of the radioactive materials from these atmospheric tests still circulate in the atmosphere at this moment. The report says that at least fifteen thousand Americans died from cancers directly related to these atomic bomb tests.

In the last few years, there are many alleged rumors that some world organizations or governments are planning to reduce the population of the earth. The number flying around is down to around 500,000,000 people (five hundred million people). That means that the Aryans, the Nefilim, have come up with a plan. Yes, the Aryans plan to massively depopulate the earth.

By what methods? Go ahead, pick your choice!

But their most favorite way it seems that was heard over the rumor mill is that they are looking for a large oncoming meteor and to redirect this oncoming meteor into a collision course with earth. As funny as this sounds, don't you think that the rumor mill people realize that the planet Nibiru or Planet X or the Twelfth Planet is heading our way?

In the late 1960s, there were reports in the New York and the New Jersey areas of seeing flying saucers; not only seeing them but also seeing and meeting their alien occupants who happened to speak spoken, broken English with a slight German accent!

Now where did you hear that before? Yavol heir commandant! Or should we say "Yavol heir, Master!" Get it? (Or should it be "Lucifer"?)

Yes, they were the Aryans, the Nefilim speaking with their usual Nordic, German accent.

Oh yes, in New Jersey. Do you remember the famous UFO incident in the mid-1960s with the very famous scientist Dr. Allen J. Hynek, who close to the end of his career turned turncoat. He turned away from what he always believed in and allowed himself to be used as a government propaganda tool. Somebody must have strung a golden carrot in front of his eyes!

How can we forget the "Swamp Gas" incident?

During the end of his investigations, many of Dr. Hynek's cases were sightings involving people seeing the "Tall Blond" aliens who spoke with a German accent!

Now the famous Barney and Betty Hill case. On September 19-20, 1961, during their abduction by an alleged UFO, the Hills were taken by eight to eleven humanoid figures who spoke "broken English" with a German accent. Yes, here we go again.

This is what I call "*awesome*," a real connection to our ancient past.

Is it all starting to come together, Folks?

That is not all, Betty and Barney Hill, while being investigated by the authorities, drew the Star System "Zeta Reticuli" in the Reticulum Constellation.

However, with one major catch, it was six (6) years before astronomers had discovered that same constellation! How about that for you, skeptics!

The following bit of information should be of very great importance to me, the writer, and you, the reader, only because I heard it with my own ears: It was a radio interview that was aired on Tuesday, April 6, 2008, on the *Kevin Smith Show*, which I believe originates in Arizona. I heard it over the Internet. I will repeat what I heard to the best of my recollection. Here it comes. That night he had on a guest named Charles Hall; the show was excellent! Charles Hall served in the USAF during the Vietnam era and was stationed at Indian Springs, a bombing range attached to Nellis AFB, Nevada. He said that while serving there, he discovered that there was a special base there. According to Hall, it was a base for Extraterrestrials whom he met, talked to, and got to know. Actually, that was a major part of his assignment.

Hall is now a computer expert and a nuclear physicist who has worked on secured government projects for many years. He explained why Einstein's theory of relativity is wrong on some key points. Hall also says that these key points are vitally important in understanding how the ET propulsion system works.

Now here is why this story is important. First, all the aliens he met there and spoke to, male and female, were Tall and Blond. Second, they all spoke English with a broken German accent. Third, Hall said that when he questioned the aliens about their spacecraft's propulsion system and where they came from, they answered in the following way: You should not care where we came from because if we told you, it would not matter, it's too far. They also explained that their flying machines can travel from galaxy to galaxy with ease.

Shortly afterward, Charles Hall asked them why does it seem that the area around the propulsion system is partially open? The answer was that during intergalactic space flights, the propulsion system is functioning properly! However, that during flights in Earth's lower atmosphere the propulsion system gets warm and needs extra cooling between flights! WHAT?

What? Z X! Are you kidding?

After traveling for zillions of miles, and maybe many light-years, they need to cool the power plant? It doesn't make sense until we connect the dots.

It seems that the Tall Blonds, just like the Barbie and Ken Dolls, are everywhere. They all speak with a slight Nordic, German accent, and again it looks more and more like they are our old friends, the Nefilim (and/or their offspring), the original two hundred Fallen Angels with one or two Nazis mixed in for effect perhaps.

I have to be very careful with my next statement: I believe that I read a few articles, especially one by Alex Collier, regarding the Tall Blonds as being "Clones"—not only as being Clones, but also that they may have no Soul. Do you now remember the story of Gilgamesh that I wrote about earlier? The possibility that Gilgamesh may have been cloned? Coincidence?

In the Bible, whenever our forefathers saw angels, weren't the angels always described has having long fair hair? Neat, hey?

I, the author of this book, have connected the dots; however, in the defense of Charles Hall, back in 1951, no such information was available to the public. All he knew is what he observed. Aliens who came out of a spaceship!

In 1951, at the famous trial of Julius and Ethel Rosenberg that started on March 6, 1951, the famous "Atomic Espionage" trial, during questioning at one part of the trial, Julius and Ethel Rosenberg spoke of "Warships of Space." Since they had access to top secret information and, at that point, no reason to lie, what was it, exactly, that they meant?

Did they know anything about what happened during Operation Highjump? Did they find out what Admiral Byrd knew about the Aryans? Now remember, they spoke about "Warships of Space." That was back in 1951. Just what files did they see? Did they see any super top secret files regarding the possibility that the United States had at that time some alternative technology? Did they see something they were not supposed to see? And could that be the real reason why their lives came to a brutal and abrupt quick ending at 1953?

Operation Paperclip. What was it, what is it? It was a code name for a 1945 United States Army / CIA (at that time known as Intelligence Objectives Agency, OSS) program to recruit and bring Nazi German scientists' talent into the United States after the allied victory in WWII, despite of any so-called "War Crimes,"* which they were alleged to have committed!

Ernst Zundel, a German scientist turned author, had entered the United States under Operation Paperclip. At the end of the war, he worked at Wright Field, now known as Wright Patterson AFB, where the Roswell debris was eventually housed (allegedly). He also made claims about the nature of the activity in Antarctica.

In his 1970s book, *UFOs, Nazi Secret Weapons?*, Zundel made the claim that at least some Unidentified Flying Objects were German Secret Weapons, which were developed during the Second World War, and that some of them had been shipped out toward the end of the war and hidden at the poles. Publication of the book coincided with a tidal wave of renewed interest in all things paranormal, coming on the heel of what was to be the last major Unidentified Flying Object

---

*   Many records have been whitewashed!

of the Twentieth Century. Zundel was a guest on countless talk shows where he shared his views on spaceships, etc. (He is another German who believed that the Holocaust never took place.)

Now datelinewise, I got to this point in my book to bring the readers up to par of what we, the Human Race, are dealing with and what we are facing. I am also sure that a very small group exists that is trying very hard to make sure that we, the Human Race, survive. However, very, very soon, it may reach an open confrontation. This is not an idea very far-fetched from the Movie *The X-Files*.

And again, remember that it could be very difficult to differentiate between the real Alien Flying Saucers that could be thousands of years old and the new versions built by the Nazis for their own use, or combined use.

In all Unidentified Flying Object cases, the researchers are fully aware of the many reports that concern the sighting of Flying Saucers with strange markings on them, such as Swastikas, what looks like Iron crosses on them, and other strange letters that no one has seen before, also aliens speaking German, etc.

Most have also heard of abductees who have been taken to underground bases with swastika emblems on the walls, or as in the case of noted abductee Alex Christopher who had seen Reptiloids and Nazis working together aboard an antigravity craft or within underground bases in the continental United States.

As I mentioned previously, Barney Hill was apparently not the only one to describe the so-called Nazi connection to Unidentified Flying Object abductions. (Let's be very careful now in the use of the phrase "Nazi Connection" and let's remember the Aliens that are speaking with a Nordic/German Accent.).

However, reports such as Christopher's and Hill's must be taken with a rather large grain of salt. There are far more plausible explanations than the so-called Reptiloids!

***The explanation is simple and is frightening: Just remember what I have told you earlier. These Aliens, Reptiloids, Reptilians, Nefilim, Fallen Angels, Tall Blonds—or by what any other name they would like to be known at the time—are Shape-Shifters. They are

"Super-Shape-Shifters"; they can shape-shift to "*fit*" at an instant! So Watch Out! Make sure you know who your friends are!

Another noted example is the American-born Reinhold Schmidt, a man whose father was born in Germany and who tells in his book *The Kearney Incident* that he was taken on a flying saucer on several occasions. Schmidt states that "the crew spoke German and acted like German soldiers." He also stated that they took him to the "Polar" region."

Now here is my little question: Did they tell him whether they took him to the North Pole or the South Pole? Hummmm?

Now one must admit that if a person were making up such a story, why then would they claim to be taken, of all places, to the Pole? Of course, one must also realize that at the time of Schmidt's comments, the rumors of Secret Nazi Bases at the poles were already very common. After returning, he was allegedly subjected to persecution by the U.S. Government. In his defense, it must be noted that Schmidt's description of the aerial discs, as he called them, matched pictures captured from the Germans in the final days of the Second World War.

In 1959, three large newspapers in Chile reported on front-page articles about Unidentified Flying Object encounters in which the crew members appeared to be German soldiers. This information from the continent of South America matches very closely what I explained to you earlier in the similar reports in the early 1960s in relation to the UFO and Aliens sightings in New York and New Jersey, where the Aliens spoke German or English with a Nordic, German accent.

CHAPTER NINE

Back to Roswell, Silicon Valley, the Death of Countless Microbiologists

Back to Roswell and the "Frightening Conclusion"!

And now we will jump back a few years in time to July 3, 1947, the "Roswell Incident," or the famous "Roswell Crash"! Yes, back to Roswell!

But remember, just about ten days earlier on June 24, 1947, Kenneth Arnold observed nine flying objects flying in formation near Mount Rainer, Washington.

And Now Hear This! That incident was the first known public mass sighting in the USA by a civilian observer. These nine flying discs did not try to hide themselves. The discs flew in formation in the wide open skies as if to say, Here we are!

Now this incident took place only a couple of months after the complete wrap-up of Operation Highjump!

Yes! After Operation Highjump! That operation was totally wrapped up in April of 1947.

This sighting by Kenneth Arnold and the crash at Roswell did not take place right after the bombing of Hiroshima or Nagasaki that took place back in August 6, 1945, and August 9, 1945. Again. The sighting and crash took place right after the final culmination of Operation Highjump in April of 1947.

Now! It is in the opinion of the writer of this book (that's me) that the flying discs or saucers that were seen by Kenneth Arnold and the saucers that crashed at Roswell and/or its vicinity were one of the same!

Yes! The crash at Roswell is a direct result of Operation Highjump. Why? Let's see!

The Aliens knew that it was time to appear in public to the masses after playing low key in the public's eyes; now when the fleet of Operation Highjump approached straight toward them, especially with all of the top admirals on board, including Admiral Byrd, which they had a great respect for as a leader, the Alien leader of the Aryan race, the "Master," had invited and spoke to Admiral Byrd, as per Admiral Byrd's secret Diary.

The flying saucer crashed at Roswell not because of the usage of special radars, and not because of any of the weapons that we may have used, including any superweapons that some people suggested that we may have possessed all the way back in 1947.

Just remember, these aliens, Nefilim, or whatever they are called by any other name, are deeply embedded in our Military Industrial Complex and embedded in our government. Therefore, they would have full knowledge of all of our weapons, our military capability, and all our secrets.

You must now refresh your memory and remember what the aliens were told long ago by Sir John Dee, through Queen Elizabeth I, what they were told regarding extracting their badly needed Matter derived from Energy. Yes, Energy that was to be released by the exploding of Atomic Bombs.

At first, they got that Energy from a few Atomic Bomb tests by the Germans in Europe and then the atomic bomb test at Trinity, USA, and soon afterward, from the two atomic bombs exploding over Japan.

Oh yes. The aliens now extracted the Matter they thought was required for their needs from all these atomic explosions.

And now the aliens were ready! But ready for what?

The aliens knew that the gig is up! Time to make a move, now or never!

A move that the aliens knew they had to make before the infamous date of December 21, 2012.

A move to escape from this planet Earth!

However, remember that the aliens must break through the barrier first, the same Gamma-G Barrier that originates on the moon and that encircles the Earth.

So at this point, the aliens were ready. They had their spaceships fuelled—yes, their Flying Saucers, their Flugelrads—and full of the Energy that they so badly needed.

The Flugelrads took off in a formation of nine (9). Could they perhaps be the same Flying Saucer formation of nine (9) that Kenneth Arnold observed over Mount Rainer, Washington, on June 24, 1947? Also, the first reported mass sighting over the Continental United States!

Dear Fellow Readers, Ladies and Gentlemen, are you finally connecting the *dots* right now?

As the Flying Saucers headed toward the Moon, they approached the invisible chain that was installed around the Earth—yes, the Gamma-G Barrier.

Yes! The Flying Saucers headed toward the Moon! They were on a mission to test and/or destroy the Gamma-G Barrier. However, a very short time later, on July 3, 1947, Flying Saucers seem to come crashing down to Earth around Roswell, New Mexico. At least one that we are now aware of did crash at Roswell. For them and all of us, time may be running short!

This was a test run, the test of the Centuries, and the test of many years of hope by these aliens toward a first step in escaping this planet Earth.

As the flying Saucers approached and hit the invisible barrier, things probably did not go as well as expected. Remember again, this barrier was formed to detect DNA and Genes of the two hundred Nefilim. So the possibility exists that on board their Flying Saucers they brought with them some DNA experiments and samples.

As it seems, the mission, the experiment was a total failure! The occupants of these Flying Saucers, whomever they were, Robots, half Robot, half Alien, Biological Entities, Grays, Small Humanoids, and maybe some actual Aliens.

Whoever they were, these pilots got shocked, or much worse! They were now in a condition that we call "damaged goods."

But as these pilots became stunned, shocked by the Gamma-G Barrier, their spacecrafts, flying saucers, also got damaged, and/or they may have also run very low on fuel during their many attempts to break this barrier.

And again, a very important reminder to my readers, this so-called Gamma-G Barrier around the earth must function as a barrier matching the DNA structure of the Alien's so-called physical body. Now again, this DNA sample could have been in test tubes, and it could also have been injected into the small biological entities, the Grays, etc.

And now the Flying Saucers came crashing down to earth. They crashed at or near Roswell! Ask yourself, why Roswell?

There is only one answer, and that is because the Roswell Air Force Base was there! At the time of the crash, this Roswell Base was known to store nuclear weapons. As a matter of fact, it was the only Air Force base in the USA to possess such weapons. And that is exactly what the flying saucers were heading for, the Atomic Bombs. But why?

I am assuming that the aliens required more fuel and more energy—*immediately*!

And just how the Aliens, Nefilim, with their Flying Saucers planned to use these nuclear bombs, we can only guess.

We understood as explained earlier in this book that the aliens needed to produce energy first, and then convert it with their methods to matter, fuel, etc.

But in the event of an extreme emergency, if the aliens needed matter to fuel their flying saucers, could there be another quick way even though it may be extremely dangerous?

Well, there may indeed be another way. Do remember perhaps when you used to be very young, you may have used to eat or, better, drink raw eggs? How? Well, you take the raw egg, you make a tiny hole at one end and one at the other end, and start sucking the raw egg's substance through the hole at the one end. And I will guarantee you, that within a few seconds, the inner egg will be consumed. Neat trick, Huh?

I am willing to bet that the aliens can perform this trick on Atomic Bombs without disturbing the outer shell. Any time, any place. On the ground, under the ground's surface, in deep missile silos, or in the air, flying next to air force bombers carrying nuclear bombs, or cruise missiles equipped with nuclear bombs? Does this sound more interesting now?

However, in this case, on July 3, 1947, the aliens did not get the chance to prove this theory. Their mission was abruptly over!

After that failed mission that ended up in total disaster for the flying saucers and its occupants, the aliens knew the following:

a. Even though this particular mission failed, they now have the full flying power capability in order to be able to get away from the Earth, into the deep Universe.
b. They now have a proven way and a proven method to fuel their flying saucers.
c. They now must find a way to destroy the invisible barrier around the Earth.
d. And/or the aliens may have to find a way to reinvent themselves, in other words, modify their own internal DNA gene structure to fool and mislead the barrier.
e. If "d" fails, then they must have a plan ready at hand to destroy the origin point of the barrier, totally or partially, the Moon.
f. Now finally, don't forget, as the aliens surely didn't forget, the Deadline: December 21, 2012.
g. And if all that fails, as this deadline approaches, then the aliens will have no choice but to instantly apply and jump into their solution of last resort, which I, the writer, will name the Alternative "ANGEPP."

About this so-called Alternative "ANGEPP," I will discuss its meaning later on in this great epic. Stay Tuned!

So now the aliens must modify their DNA structure. I will repeat that. Now the aliens must modify their DNA structure!

How will they go about it? How will they do it? Well, you must have guessed it by now!

"Abductions." Alien Abductions, or should I call it what it really is? "Human Abductions!"

Abductions of human beings, any type, any shape, any form; also, involving some animals.

Yes! Human Abductions, with our Government's permission as part of the treaties signed between our past U.S. presidents—way back in the 1940s through to the present—and the aliens. I believe that things have gotten out of hand and our leaders are losing all control over this situation regarding human abductions. I also understand from reading other materials that this situation is especially true regarding our very young children, but this subject is not my expertise, and I have not investigated it. Yet I am aware something is happening here, something very sad, something out of the ordinary. Things that I would not dare put in writing involving little children only. You, the readers, are welcome to investigate this subject on your own!

At this stage of the game, our government just can't stop them! You can't stop your overseer! You can't stop your controller!

You also can't stop a "Cornered Rat" that is trying to survive, a rat that will try to destroy you; it will try to tear you apart in its attempt to survive.

The aliens, the Aryans, the Nefilim, are cornered as the date of December 21, 2012, is approaching.

So far the Nefilim have accomplished a great deal. They have rebuilt their flying fleet, and they have gathered all the energy and matter that they needed from the Nevada tests sites mentioned earlier.

It is now time for the next step. They must produce Silicon.

Silicon. What can it be used for? Well, let's see: communication devices, very high tech weapons, high tech power plants, intergalactic transport devices, etc. However, there may be one more use for Silicon, it may be used to integrate biological and artificial tissue in creating certain biological entities, more Grays.

It seems that after the crash at Roswell, about six (6) months to be exact, we managed to built the first Transistor, and the rest is history. We now possess the ability to build any sort of electronics that we desire. Technology to fit any need!

Did you ever hear of Silicon Valley?

By the term "to fit any need," I mean to say that on the same subassembly lines that a certain firm produces certain parts, these parts join other subassembly lines, which are fed to a main assembly line and then could be shipped out part by part to any part of the world with no questions asked, or a complete assembly custom made to fit and be shipped anywhere with no questions asked.

This could very easily be done by the silicon electronic industry for the simple reason that nothing looks like a weapon, or dangerous, especially in the form of subparts.

With today's technology, this method can understandably be applied to any high tech field, mechanical, electrical, or even in the field of agriculture.

It's simple. With today's methods, our old friend, the original two hundred Nefilim, the Seeing Eye Corp. that controls the industry of the world anyway can have any part made and shipped anywhere to assemble who knows what!

Please forgive me, when I refer to as the original two hundred Nefilim, fallen angels, I am also including their so-called offspring. Yes, when you include their offspring, you may be talking about a number that is above two million aliens, (2,000,000 plus). I must also remind you of one more item, the possible existence of some of the tall blonds who may be clones; they may not be able to reproduce.

This number of 2,000,000 plus, is a very important number that will have to be considered toward the Frightening Conclusion of my book.

And now comes into play the name of Bill Gates and his company Microsoft! Do we not remember his name? The name of the one person that even the U.S. Government couldn't touch. They couldn't tell him what to do, and they couldn't prosecute him or his company Microsoft.

Only a few years ago, Silicon Valley could not exist without the name of Microsoft.

Silicon Valley—silicon companies all over, everywhere you looked, every street, every hill, every valley, under every tree, silicon and computer companies.

Yes! It seems that Bill Gates of Microsoft is a very major player in the superupper echelon of the Seeing Eye Corp. He is untouchable!

Yes, of course, the Seeing Eye Corp. is using silicon-based technology very efficiently. They know where every car is located at any time; they know where you are at any time by the usage of your home computer or your Laptop, by you turning on your TV set, or by your cell phone, etc. Yes! They are keeping a very wary and shady eye on the world's population, especially some of its leaders.

However, lately, something changed. Let's go back toward the middle of our story where Sir John Dee told Queen Elizabeth I that the aliens will need to develop Energy, then Matter, then Silicon, and then to work on the DNA factor. I don't believe that neither one of them understood the terms "DNA" or "silicon" in those days; however, they just conveyed the correct message to the Nefilim.

Now here comes the Hot, Very Controversial, Exciting, and perhaps the so-called Dangerous part of the book. This may be Dangerous to some people, pending on their Personal-Biological Situation. (Nothing personal here.)

If you do some real deep research of some of the companies involved in Silicon Valley, you'll find out something very interesting.

Lately, something has changed! Let me explain, or may I make the following statement: Microbiology is in! Silicon is slowly on the way out!

What do I, the writer, mean by that statement? Well, if you do some real research of Silicon Valley, you'll find out that at the time of writing this book, early in 2009, most companies in Silicon Valley are no longer computer-software-only-oriented companies. They are now Microbiology oriented. Yes! The new Microbiology field.

If you have read the newspapers lately, watch the TV news, or listen to radio news, you'll come up with the following conclusion: Microbiology can be harmful to your health!

Why? Because of the simple reason that Microbiologists are dropping dead; they are dying one by one with no end in sight, and they are not dying of natural causes.

Actually, there should be warning signs everywhere, including street signs that state, "A career in Microbiology is dangerous! It's Deadly!"

It seems that the Microbiologists that are being murdered are from all over the modern world—North America, South America, Europe, Israel, and even from a small town called Novosibirsk in Siberia.

These are all the homes of cutting-edge microbiological research centers.

If you read the newspapers, listen to the radio, or watch TV, looking for explanations, even on some special conspiracy Radio stations, you will hear the same stories over and over again.

You will hear about research to fight certain plagues. You will hear about biological weapons, and then you will hear about a group who wants to release a Bio-Plague that will annihilate 90 percent of the world's population. And they* want to take out the scientists that are coming up with a cure—Antidotes!

All of these theories, and I am sure that we will find more theories along these same lines—but are all these theories wrong?

During alien abductions, especially of human females, later on, the women mysteriously get pregnant. And just as mysteriously, they lose their babies. Where did the babies go? Where did they go? No one really knows!

And in almost all cases of human males, the aliens check the sperm and remove a sample of the sperm. Why? Keep reading.

It seems that all abductees get the same *schtick,* the same story: The aliens claim that their planet is dying. Then their race is dying. And they tell their abductees, Stop using nuclear weapons, etc., etc.

Again that is all "Bull"! If you believe so far in what you have read in this book, then you'll believe in the following honest, scary, frightening statement!

Now hear this.

a. Remember, the aliens, the Nefilim, have until December 21, 2012, to get away from this planet Earth.
b. The Nefilim, directly or indirectly, are so far unable to break through the Gamma-G Barrier that exists around the Earth. Why? Because this barrier has built in special sensors that are able to detect immediately, in hyper superspeed, the DNA and Genetic structure of anything that is approaching this barrier, may it be alien or human! I also believe that this so-called invisible barrier may also have a built in so-called Kill System.
c. Just remember, you are dealing with technology way beyond our own. You are talking about technology millions of years ahead of our time.

So our aliens have one, and only one, choice!

---

* (When I used the word "They." I referred to the Seeing Eye Corp itself, the Nefilim. Or one of its independent branches.

They must change or convert their own DNA/Genetic structure in one way or another! Change it completely! So that when each alien/Nefilim goes through the Gamma-G Barrier, the built-in invisible sensors will not be able to detect it and will allow safe passage through. This may be accomplished by genetic manipulation of a certain type of pure human DNA or their embryos. This search is still ongoing!

***Could that be the real reason (please forget what you read or heard from official sources!), I repeat, could that be the real reason why man, a member of the human race, can't go beyond the Moon? Could it be because he or she still has a trace of alien DNA within? A microscopic trace even after thousands of years of interbreeding? Between alien and human females?

So it is possible that by now, all of us, if not almost all of us, are mixed pretty well, a good mixture of alien and human DNA/gene Pool.

How do you like those apples?

***Another special secret! Is that the reason why when NASA is picking men and women, ex-pilots, etc., for training in the astronaut program, many of them, if not all, are now found out to be Masons, or Freemasons, with a special, very special, bloodline? Did you ever think that it is even possible that our Astronauts are being used as alien Guinea Pigs?

And this is one of the main reasons that when our Astronauts return home from a Moon mission, they go through a very long debriefing; and many of them later on seem to be sort of Shaky and incoherent, not focused, brainwashed!

Now! Just think and compare, does Noah's ark look and sound familiar? When I was calling it a giant DNA lab for a special purpose?

Was the real motive of the aliens, the Nefilim, to single out a human that was pure with pure human DNA only to be used in some sinister futuristic motive, such as providing a sample of pure human DNA to be used by the aliens, the Nefilim, in order to assist them in converting their blood and DNA in order to mislead and to fool the Gamma-G Barrier to enable them to escape this planet Earth?

Oh yes! Now do you understand? Now did you get your answer? Now you know what the aliens need! They need, and they are looking for, a *pure human* with *pure human DNA*.

These aliens seem to follow bloodlines very carefully, from generation to generation.

And that is why we are now finding out from certain experts that are using hypnosis on abductees that in almost all of abduction cases, these abductees somehow are all the children and or grandchildren of past abductees.

Do you remember what I mentioned earlier regarding what God told Moses on the mountain in the desert? He told Moses that he knew his forefathers! Were they all abductees?

That would make sense. Slowly, slowly, down the line of each generation, the aliens alter our body structure, in order to create the proper DNA for their own use, and at the same time, it made us smarter.

Remember, they had to make us smarter in the past so we would be able to help and assist them to rebuild and to manufacture what they had lost in the past.

Now I am also sure that somewhere out there is somebody existing, with a body that contains pure human DNA and purely human gene pool.

So if you are abducted, or your children, wife, husband, etc., please don't ask "Why Me?" or ask "Why them?" Now you know why!

Nothing personal! But it's very personal, and it's strictly business!

It's you or them! It's them or you!

Some very high stakes are involved here!

And it seems that they have a firm deadline of December 21, 2012.

Yes, this deadline, December 21, 2012. If you want to connect some more dots, then kindly note, President Obama finally approved on March 9, 2009, a bill that officially approves Stem Cell research!

And that is why the rush with the microbiologists. They are needed for the final step. However, it seems that as soon as they find out exactly what they are working on, Death comes in many ways!

After all, it seems that they control almost—yes, almost everything!

One more terrifying thought, it's going to sound like a nightmare out of the movies. If the moon is hollow, only if, then how about this: if you can't go through the Gamma-G Barrier by deceiving it, then you will have to destroy the barrier!

But you can't destroy it because it's invisible!

So then you must destroy the source! What?

That is right; target Moon! Destroy the moon or the part of the moon that is housing the superdevice from where the invisible Gamma-G Barrier originates.

They have tried, you know; all of these secret space defense weapons: Particle Beam weapons, Space Shuttles firing lasers, even HAARP has been used, aimed at the moon for the last few years, with superhigh voltage power. And that is one of the real reasons why our Ozone layer by now looks like Swiss cheese. "Project HAARP," the High Frequency Active Auroral Research Program, is playing with the fate of all our lives and the very existence of the Earth. This program is conducted by the University of Alaska, Fairbanks, and funded by the U.S. Air Force and Navy. In brief, it is the world largest RF transmitter capable of ELF (Extremely Low Frequency) and VHF (Very High Frequency) transmissions at incredible power.

Did we forget the Star Defense Initiative? All these weapons are 90 percent of the time blasting the Moon.

And the space Shuttles? They may have been assigned a totally different task—a task so secret that many diversions have been created to delude your eyes and mind.

Speaking of connecting the dots, some of the astronauts were trying to get our attention, telling us in their own language of what is really going on. But were we listening? Remember the case of the drunk astronaut? Or the female astronaut who was driving across country with the famous "Diaper Affair" to see her lover? Were you listening? Were you using your brain?

***And now again, with regards to the Moon is hollow.

Do we remember only a few years ago the collapse of the Soviet Union, the old USSR? Did it not happen kind of suddenly and very peacefully? Wasn't it very strange? Not a single shot being fired! That is very rare for the Soviet Union, but it happened!

But here is what you may not have known, or forgot, because it was done so quickly and quietly!

The Russians, very nicely, actually begged us, the Americans, to remove and take back to the United States almost 1,500 nuclear bombs! Yes, one thousand five hundred! And the reason that they, the Russians, gave for this action was to prevent them from falling into the hands of third world countries or terrorist groups.

Can you imagine, we, the USA, received from the Russians 1,500 nuclear bombs, a gift?

A gift for what purpose? For whom?

In the past, the United States had many space shuttle missions that we, the public, were aware of. I am also sure that we had many more of these missions that we were never aware of. Many times, some of us have asked, just what are all these missions for? We always see on TV the same mechanical arm trick. Very hard at work, performing wonders in space, swinging left and right, also picking up a barrel, picking up a fork, picking up a knife, etc. But what were all these secret missions all about really for? What is going on?

What if this whole thing was a prearranged deal, a scam set up by the Seeing Eye Corp., a beautiful picture for public consumption?

This scam may turn out to be a catastrophe for the planet Earth and all of human kind. What if all of these nuclear warheads, atomic bombs, whatever, what if they all found their way to the moon? What if all these bombs found their way aboard space shuttle missions and were transported to the moon?

Did this idiotic idea ever enter your naive little brain?

Isn't it the most perfect way to blow up a portion or the whole Moon without anybody suspecting what is coming? Under our own eyes, under our own noses?

Yes, Folks, in my opinion, this is exactly what is going on, that will go on, until these original Nefilim and their offspring find a way off this Earth.

Right now we, the human race, mean nothing to them. We are only a tool to be used and thrown away, a means to an end.

So how do you feel now? Dear fellow reader. Did you really want to know all of that?

So sleep tight tonight and count your sheep! And one more thing, do you still believe in coincidences?

Believe in coincidences? Of course not, not ever, ever, ever.

***So now it's time for my so-called Grand Finale:

Remember earlier in the story I mentioned the term Alternative "ANGEPP"? So let me suggest a real possibility: I have told you my readers in the beginning of this book that when the original two hundred fallen angels arrived here, they had to Shed their skins in order to be compatible with human form, to be compatible with human females, because they were beautiful.

***However, Shed their skins may have, I repeat may have, one more meaning. Do you remember the story of Gilgamesh? That he may have been cloned? Was he perhaps Tall and Blond?

Now I also told you that by this time, there are over 2,000,000 Aliens and/or their descendants living, existing, on Earth under the South Pole, under Antarctica. I have also told you that right at the same location, next door to the Aliens, is the base of the Nazi Germans. Hello Neighbors! And I have also mentioned that they also numbered over 2,000,000 people.

So now, if all other attempts to escape the Earth fail by the coming date of December 21, 2012, our old friends, the Aliens, will have to perform what is known as the magic act of "Possession"; to put it in simpler terms, to shed their skins in *reverse*!

Usually, in using the method of so-called possession, it works on a one-to-one basis; in other words, each Alien entity will require one human host!

Like I said before, these Aliens are Superclever. They take their time and plan very far in advance for all eventualities. In this case, they used the Nazi/Germans to their advantage in the past. In this present time, the Aliens are protecting the German Nazis as per their original Treaty.

However, the aliens are also protecting them for another reason, preserving their Antarctic neighbors for the future need of their physical bodies! Remember, these Nazi/Germans have been bred underground in Antarctica for over seventy-five years and saved for this one purpose. As a last resort, the Aliens may have to act in a split second and enter their Nazi/German host bodies when the right time arises.

Planet Earth is Hell for the Nefilim! This is their Prison Planet! The right time, there may not be the right time for our old friends, the

Nefilim. Let's see, if the planet Earth totally blows up and the Nefilim are still on it, then if they are in Spirit form, they may survive and/or float in space forever. Or if they are in their human form, they may perish. If a major disaster strikes like the deluge of 13,500 years ago, they may go very deep underground in spirit form and, when it's all over, shape-shift back to human form. However, if it is not possible, then go to the last option called "Alternative ANGEPP." It will be a time of desperation. So remember their neighbors are right there, next door, under a very Protective Dome!

However, by then, for us humans, "No Problemo." We should be all dead!

And now it's time to explain a very important word that popped up toward the end of this story.

ALTERNATIVE "ANGEPP":

"ALIEN NAZI GERMAN EXCELLENT POSSESSION PLAN"

THE END ?

No!

NEXT: Conclusions and Clarifications

Ancient Egyptian Flying Vehicles

These images were found on the ceiling beams of a 3000-year old New Kingdom Temple, located several hundred miles south of Cairo and the Giza Plateau, at Abydos.

These pictures were taken in the year 2000. Look very close at the images! **What do you see?**

CONCLUSIONS AND CLARIFICATIONS

I. DECEMBER 21, 2012: What does this date stand for; where did it come from? During the last 25 years or so, I have read many books and listened to all sorts of information. The most famous date floating around was, and still is, December 21, 2012. This date symbolizes the End of Times and/or the Return of the Gods, referring to the return of the planet Nibiru from its 3,600-year journey through deep space and with it the return of its inhabitants, the race called the Anunnaki. It's bad enough not to be looking forward to this event due to the possible oncoming physical damage between planets that I mentioned earlier, but now we may have the pleasure of seeing and meeting the authentic, famous, and freshly almost-new Anunnaki race! However, I suggest that you see a heart specialist before you take a peek at them. They may be awfully big and very frightening. They may even look a little bit different!

Most experts started with the date of December 21, 2012. However for one reason or another, most of the same experts are now starting to get Amnesia. Lately, it seems to be a disease caused by government arm twisting! Because the year of 2012 is now around the corner, in order to prevent panic, one or two of the so-called top experts in this field have now raised the date to the year 2065 and/or 2085 (yes! AD), the year of the return of the planet Nibiru or the year of end-times. My question now is how can these experts, all famous writers, suddenly as the eleventh hour is approaching, raise their own deadline by about 70 years? If my research is correct, the people of Earth will start seeing the approaching Nibiru very soon. As I mentioned earlier in my story, Major Ed Dames, as he mentioned on the radio show at first, said that after December 21, 2012, he saw nothing, nothing but darkness, blackness! "I believe this one statement" was the first statement that he spoke of very somberly on the radio show that evening!

Some experts and some sources mentioned the same planet, now, possibly being a brown dwarf star and still in a highly Elliptical orbit around the sun (with a very unique orbit of rotating around the earth in a Clockwise motion) with a past known passage occuring 3,600 years ago, and therefore assumed orbital period of about 3,600 to 3,700 years or 3,741 years. These same experts attribute these figures to astronomers of the Maya civilization. However, a brown dwarf with a period of 3,700 years would be clearly evident through infrared and gravitational observation! PS. Just go ahead and ask the Vatican what their superastronomers have seen lately through their Telescopes.

Now remember Quetzalcoatl, the great White God of the Mayan empire, who promised to return on December 21, 2012? Yes! The great White God actually said that he will return on that date, according to the Mayan calendar. So what other verification do we need? That also happens to be the last day of the Mayan calendar! Yes! Straight from the horse's mouth, from the great White God! PS. Again, just as a reminder to my readers, so far, this great Mayan calendar has proven to be deadly accurate! What makes some skeptics think that the accuracy of this date, December 21, 2012, will not be correct?

In a recently published book, titled *2012: Appointment with Marduk*, Turkish writer/researcher Burak Eldem presents a new theory, suggesting a 3,661 years orbital period for the planet Nibiru and claiming a return date in the year AD 2012. According to Eldem's theory, 3,661 is one-seventh of 25,627, which is the total time span of "Five World Ages" according to the Mayan Long Count Calendar system. The last orbital passage of Marduk, he adds, was in 1649 BC and caused great catastrophes on earth! There is no way to stop Nibiru from approaching us. It's coming straight toward us! Just look at the pictures taken by the Infrared Astronomy Satellite Telescope (IRAS). The Images of Nibiru were just bursting within these new photos!

In regard to the planet Nibiru, or Marduk, now also known as Planet X, and/or the Twelfth Planet. (This last title as the Twelfth Planet was given to planet Nibiru, only after the original Twelfth Planet Tiamat exploded, totally destroyed; and as I mentioned earlier, its remains and debris became our asteroid belt.) After very careful research, I can't say with full confidence whether Nibiru is a home planet to its current inhabitants or is being used as a giant way station, or a star gate. (The definition of the word "Inhabitant" is "one that inhabits a place, especially as a permanent resident.)

So just hold on to your hats and remember Richard C. Hoagland's famous saying, "It's going to be a hell of a hair day!"

II. THE HOLLOW EARTH AND THE VAN ALLEN RADIATION BELTS. When I mentioned earlier the trip of Admiral Byrd to the Inner Earth and his flight through the entrance of the South Pole, you must also keep in mind that a similar opening exists at the North Pole. Each opening is circular with a diameter of about 1400 Mi. The thickness of the crust of the earth all around is 800 Mi.

And in the center of this Hollow Earth, there seems to be a Sun, yes, a Sun (800 miles in diameter). And the center of gravity is at the center of the 800-mile Crust. The outer diameter of the Earth is approximately 7,900 mi. This information was provided in a book *The Hollow Earth* by R. Bernard. All that is shown in illustration I. This illustration I also shows the Van Allen Radiation Belts. There are two (2) Belts, an Inner Belt that has the Theo thickness of about 700-10,000 km and the Outer Belt that has the Theo thickness of about 10,000-65,000 km. Please remember the radiation pattern.

Now go and take a look at illustration E. It shows the Earth with Flight Path X. This must be the way that our spaceships (Shuttles) enter and exit the Earth's atmosphere, traveling through the least amount of radiation. (See illustration E)

There are a few theories on why the Van Allen Radiation Belt is shaped the way it is. One unique theory that is possible, only possible, is that at the points of least radiation, at the North Pole and at the South Pole, are the openings, and therefore no landmass; and if there is no landmass or any other solid mass like water, then you can't have a strong radiation source. (Please DO NOT confuse this with the Gamma-G Barrier that was artificially created by an alien race called the Anunnaki.)

III. CLOSE ENCOUNTERS OF THE THIRD (3rd) KIND: (My Experience)! I graduated in Samuel James Tilden High School, Brooklyn, New York, in June 1964. I took me a summer job as a junior councilor at a summer camp very near Dingman Ferry, Pennsylvania. Toward the end of the summer, we the Junior counselors were playing big-time Basketball among the group leaders; the time was approximately 10:00 p.m. Clear skies, I am not sure if there was a full or partial moon. But we could see the outline of the mountains and the mountaintops very easily. Suddenly, behind the first mountain to our front left, drifting very slowly in a right to left movement was the edge of a giant-size pointy bullet that within three to four minutes, we all saw very clearly, against the dark black skies, the outline of a perfect half-side view of the world famous flying-saucer shape! The part that was exposed to us we estimated to be about one-half mile in size! No kidding! We were very scared, concerned. We all knew that this thing didn't belong here! At that moment, the object froze; and within another thirty seconds, it was gone, in a flash, as we stared at it disappear! To all of us, that was a relief; we talked about it for a while and then kept playing. The next morning, we noticed a great deal of military activity in the area and saw at least one military/police roadblock down the road.

IV. THE SPEAR OF DESTINY, AND THE TABLETS OF DESTINIES! These may have been the weapons that destroyed the planet Tiamat. According to all of the information that I have gathered, these two weapons work hand in hand when the need arises. The planet Tiamat was a very large planet; it was mostly a water planet. At first, the Tablets of Destinies were used to charge the planet with some sort of particle beams that somehow broke down the molecular structure of the planet, and then the Spear of Destiny was used to fire a sort of electrical charge at the planet to totally destroy it. Yes, the planet Tiamat was totally destroyed! And it became the Asteroid Belt!

And now the subject of Iraq. I am willing to bet that some of the more realistic reasons for the U.S. invasion of Iraq were to immediately find the hidden ancient weapons such as the Spear of Destiny and the Tablets of Destinies as they may had been hidden anywhere, such as in giant caves in Iraq! And even in Egypt, under the Great Pyramid, or even under the Sphinx.

It was evident that before the start of the war in Iraq on March 20, 2003, U.S. spy satellites have shown abnormal activities near ancient sites that were located in Mesopotamia, Sumer, and especially in Babylon. These activities seemed to include large machineries and a large number of scientists. Again, I must repeat, something was there, something vast and powerful, something that relates to the ancient weapons' family and/or ancient star gates that may began to be activated.

I may be going out on a limb here, but after studying very carefully the performance abilities of the Spear of Destiny and the Tablets of Destinies, it looks like more and more that the Ark of the Covenant and the Magic Rod could be a part of this great weapon system.

Speaking about the Great Pyramid and the Sphinx, do you remember earlier regarding the power beam emanating from the tip of the pyramid toward the planet Nibiru? The beam that was used to divert the planet! Well, time has come again, time to prepare the pyramid for its next mission, which is right around the corner on December 21, 2012.

Now guess who may be chosen to perform this slight cosmetic surgery on the pyramid. It will be probably be none other than the Halliburton Co. The work will be camouflaged as minor construction to renovate parts of the pyramid and the surrounding area. Yes, this evil name from the past will have the honors. Why? Because they are great at what they do! They have the Manpower needed worldwide; they have the engineering know-how, and they have the logistics required for such operations, including urgent military backup, where and when needed on demand. Case closed!

V. CLOSE ENCOUNTERS OF THE FIRST KIND! (My Experience)! I am now going to get to the bottom line and try to elucidate one of the main reasoning behind me writing this book. At the beginning of the book, under the heading of "About the Author," I brought forward some of my background in the Aerospace/Aircraft field so that you would understand that I was writing this book from an engineer's perspective of solving problems, analyzing problems, and listening to many people, some of whom were very high-ranking members of the military and government. And what's more important is that their full trust was placed in me to analyze and solve the problems correctly and promptly.

Somewhere in New York State (the exact situation and location may have been different to protect all parties involved), on one late evening, I was sitting at a famous public restaurant by the bar area, sipping a glass of seltzer, sitting at the far end, all by myself. A short time later, a very tall man, whose height was roughly about 6.8 ft. to 6.10 ft., stood to my right for a few seconds, looked at me, and sat down next to me at the bar. He is the type that the ladies would love, Tall, Handsome, Businesslike, wearing glasses. He opened up with a funny remark that was actually in a response to what I was thinking at that instant. He smiled at me in a friendly way. We started to talk about many subjects, but mostly about aircraft. Remember, this subject is my main background, and after a while, we moved to the subject of Science Fiction. We discussed late-night radio talk shows that cover these subjects, and he was very interested in my knowledge of the subjects, having an open mind and, I guess, keeping very calm in his sort of tricky conversational type of asking me questions. But somehow it seems that we were both on the same wavelength and started to understand and respect each other's line of thinking and points of views. Now here comes the important part of this story, since the start of our conversation, every and each time that I was starting to answer a question or started to ask a question, he stopped me after only the first word out of my mouth, and he completed the rest whether I was asking or answering a question. He chose the exact words and/or sentence that I was going to use! And this was going on for about an hour! After a while, I asked him if he was performing in a Las Vegas magic act of reading minds. He turned around to me in a ninety-degree angle and answered me, smiling, "Oh no, however, I do come from a very, very faraway place, and by now I believe that you and me understand each other. Just keep doing whatever you're doing. You're doing well and keep learning more about the . . ." At this point, he pointed his finger to the sky! At that instant, he dropped a few bills on the bar, smiled, and left very slowly through the main exit. It took me a few minutes to get my head together, took a deep breath, and with a sigh of relief, said to myself, "Holy cow. Thank God!" I knew deep inside of me with whom I just had a conversation with, a very friendly one of them. Yes! An alien being in one form or another. From that day on, I always look around for that same familiar friendly face. Why? Who knows! Perhaps the excitement of knowing that I may at some future date, perhaps, have a chance to discover more about him and the entities whom he may represent!

***Just a footnote, I have been working on the solutions to these problems for quite a few years now. However, only a short time after that strange meeting, I was sitting in my car in a La-Guardia Airport outdoor parking lot, in a very heavy thunder storm, suddenly like a computer, all sort of strange answers came in feeding into my brain, answers that I had been looking for a very long time, they came out of nowhere!

Soon afterwards I started to write this book.

VI. Now, let's have a little fun comparing some real facts with a small mixture of science fiction. In this version, the real facts will come on top!

In 1968, there was a movie titled *The Planet of the Apes* by Pierre Boulle, Rod Serling, and Michael Wilson. The movie carries a great end message, but first, an astronaut crew crash-lands on a planet in the distant future where intelligent talking apes are the dominant species, and humans are the oppressed and enslaved. Throughout the movie, all are warned never to go to and/or enter the Forbidden Zone. The warning came from the Chief Chimpanzee called Dr. Zaius, the elder chimpanzee with the gold hair. At the end, two people escaped, George Taylor, played by Charlton Heston and Nova, played by Linda Harrison. They escaped and rode to the Forbidden Zone, riding on one horse. They come to a stop on the beach, looked up, in dismay, and what did they see? They came face to face with the ruins of the Statue of Liberty, which was buried three-fourth way deep in beach sand. Suddenly, here lies in front of their eyes the evidence about the true origin of the Planet of the Apes. Checkmate! Game over; the secret is out—the secret that the Elders tried to hide for so long, who they really are and where they came from. The Gig is up! Sound familiar? Yes! Somebody is preventing us from entering the Forbidden Zone of knowledge, using all methods available.

In 1984, there was movie titled *2010* written by Arthur C. Clarke. The spacecraft Leonov was on a mission to investigate a giant monolith (the famous black rectangle from the movie *2001: A Space Odyssey*). This monolith was in orbit around the planet Jupiter. As the spacecraft approaches one of Jupiter's moons Europa, the crew received a message, a warning: "Do not approach Europa!" They didn't pay attention and sent a manned probe toward Europa anyway. The probe then glimpses what appears to be foliage beneath the ice, but before it can be photographed, the probe is inexplicably destroyed in a burst of light. While the Russians speculate that it was merely electrostatic buildup, Dr. Floyd is convinced that it was something more, a warning from someone—or something—to stay away from Europa! And now! Reality. In the year 1989, the Russians sent two spacecrafts, Phobos 1 and Phobos 2; the first failed shortly after launch. Phobos 2, the second vessel, succeeded and went into orbit, taking pictures of Mars and one of the large asteroidlike moons, Phobos. Now there are secret reports that a message came over the airwaves for the spacecraft Phobos 2 to stay away from this one moon called Phobos. The Russians didn't listen! The spacecraft was scheduled to send a lander to the twenty-kilometer Martian moon, but it was never released because the ground controllers suddenly and unexpectedly lost all contact with the spacecraft on March 28, 1989. Soon afterward, reports surfaced that the last photograph taken and returned to Earth prior to the failure "contained an object which shouldn't have been there"! The object that was analyzed in "extreme secrecy" by experts seemed to look like a giant cigar about five to seven kilometers in length. Now get this, and this is no joke: they all said that it looked exactly like the space probe in one of the *Star Trek* episodes called "The Doomsday Machine." Now isn't that something! And if that is not enough, there is one more shocking surprise! At the same instant as the one camera on board the spacecraft Phobos 2 was taking pictures of the unidentified flying object, the other camera was pointed and focused on the planet Mars. Suddenly appearing out of nowhere were giant rectangular objects, shapes "embossed" in the Martian surface, arranged in rows parallel to each other. This pattern covered an area of some six hundred square kilometers. (Giant black Monoliths? Couldn't be, could it?) One more memo regarding the movie *2010*. If, but only if, very soon, by early summer or winter of the year 2010, we start seeing a new planet appear in our southern skies, it may start to appear as a dark brown color and very shady at first then get larger and brighter, similar to a second sun; then "Hello Nibiru! Welcome, you all Newcomers!" Or should I say Old Newcomers? And at that instant, you would make sure and look at your calendar and see on what day December 21, 2012 falls because it's going to be "a hell of a hair day!" And in a small closing memo, it is possible that very soon, some of these Newcomers may be arriving a little early using their teleportation system, and arriving to where? Only a small guess. It could be to an area in Iraq called Mesopotamia, where a welcoming committee of well-pretrained U.S. Troops are waiting, where we may have found certain Star Gates.

Binary Sun—two suns blaze in the sky. Could it be the approaching of NIBIRU ? by Don Dixon.

VII. "Fool's Gold." (See illustration G) That is the nickname that I, the author, gave the fantastic picture or this plaque that is made of gold-plated aluminum, which was installed aboard the Pioneer 10 spacecraft launched on March 3, 1972. The plaque contains a message from Earth. (This message, I believe, is used for public consumption.) This is Mankind's first serious attempt to communicate with extraterrestrial civilizations. The Pioneer 10 spacecraft was the first space vehicle designed to explore the environment of the planet Jupiter, and then it will be accelerated by Jupiter's gravity to become the first man-made object to leave our Solar System. The spacecraft will take about 80,000 years to reach the nearest star, about 4.3 light-years away. Now, usually, placing a message aboard Pioneer 10 is very much like trying to locate a dime on a sunny day on a deep sandy shiny beach, or it's like a shipwrecked sailor casting a bottled message into the ocean—an ocean with no end! The message itself intends to communicate the location, nature, biological configuration, and race that refers to the nature of the builders of this spacecraft! Carl Sagan with his wife at the time, artist Linda Salzman Sagan, had an idea on what to put on the plaque and its design. They presented it to NASA, and it was approved! The question is just how much did Carl Sagan know about the so-called extraterrestrial beings? He must have known it all, just like all of the major sci-fi writers—all of his friends, such as Ray Bradbury, Gene Roddenberry, Arthur C. Clarke, Isaac Asimov, and Irving Block. Who is Irving Block? Do you remember the 1956 Movie *Forbidden Planet*, starring Walter Pidgeon and Ann Francis? Just think back on the type of energy sources that this movie showed and spoke about, and then take a trip to Iceland! You will be shocked by what you will find! They use underground thermal heat for their energy sources. Much of the piping and power structures resemble what the movie showed!

So yes, they all knew the real secrets—the secrets of the so-called extraterrestrials, the Aliens, the Anunnaki, and the connection to us, the so-called humans. Oh yes, especially after you take a look at the wall carving at the Temple at Abydos. Case Closed!

One of Carl Sagan's most famous quotes was "Our species need and deserve a citizenship with minds wide awake and a basic understanding of how the world works."

VIII. And now, for a very controversial bit of information that will involve the word's Holocaust and Souls. This closing statement is a concept; it may sound like it came out of a nightmarish science-fiction story. Earlier in a previous chapter, I mentioned that the original two hundred renegade aliens, the Nefilim, are like vampires; they must be invited in on the deal by signing some sort of a treaty. Then they will come in and suck you dry, legally!

Also, I mentioned earlier that when Sir John Dee, as per the instructions of Queen Elizabeth I, contacted a certain angelic race in the so-called Fifth Dimension. They gave him instructions on how to help the trapped two hundred Nefilim renegades how to escape the Earth. I left out one thing, a fee for their service, a payoff, something for something. All over the vast universe, it's all business! In exchange, these so-called Angels demanded Souls! Including your soul. Your soul? Yes. That was not meant to be funny. It may have been part of a deal, part of a very big payoff that may, I repeat, just "may have," partially to do with the Holocaust.

The only way we humans can release our souls is by our death. (That is, if you believe in the existence of a so-called soul.) The more the better. This angelic race that originates in the fifth dimension needs souls! Did you pay attention to the number of deaths that accompanied the wars as of the years 1550 and up? And then came WWII. And the Holocaust. Surprise, surprise! Some of you may ask the question, Why did Sir John Dee obey the Queen and contact the angelic race in the fifth dimension? Well, number one, she was his Queen. Number two, do you remember what Princess Diana said in regards to the Royal family? She called them a bunch of Freakin' Lizards! Well, who then do you think that Queen Elizabeth I was? You don't just say *no* to these creatures! Okay?

According to John Lear, the son of the famous owner of the airplane manufacturing company Lear Jet, and also according to Major Ed Dames, who gave a radio interview on the *Coast to Coast* Radio program on Thursday, April 9, 2009, with George Noory, said that the planet Earth is serving right now as a station and as a center for collecting Souls! For whom? And according to John Lear, the center for this collection location is on the Moon! (That is only if you believe in this theory.) Now according to Richard C. Hoagland, what exactly is going on up there on the Moon? Our Astronauts sure aren't doing any talking! They are scared out of their wits! They are petrified! They also look partially hypnotized.

Well then, if the above has even some truth to it? Then it means that all of the major players during WWII, Pro or Con, including the Church of Peace, were watching and knowing, about the "Holocaust," watching and knowing in silence!

IX. Back in the 1960s and the 1970s, the United States was very proud and famous in having our new ICBMs (Intercontinental Ballistic Missiles) buried deep underground in missile silos, which are actually underground storage chambers for guided missiles on their launch pad ready for firing! When the missile carrying the nuclear warhead reaches its target, it will explode as planned by a certain electronic program.

That explosion is called Nuclear Fusion; this is a nuclear reaction in which atomic nuclei of a lower atomic number fuse together to form a heavier nucleus, accompanied by the release of energy; and for that, the nuclear bomb is composed of many critical elements.

However, if any of these elements are not in place (missing), then there will be no nuclear fusion! No explosion! Back then in the 1960s in some of the Midwestern states in USA, there were stories of UFOs, flying saucers, hovering above some of these silos; and at the same instant, the missiles in these silos were rendered useless for a short time. All the electric power went out for about an hour or so. Soon afterward the electric power was restored and everything went back to normal! Not so!

Maybe cosmetically from the outside shell and from the point of view of electric power supply, everything was okay. But what about the inner guts of the nuclear warhead itself? Was everything okay? Was everything intact? Or were some basic elements missing? Maybe? We never found out, and we will never be told! But I'll bet as usual that some of the elements were not there anymore. Yes, missing. How?

Just keep in mind my earlier comments regarding The Raw Egg Trick! Neat, hey?

Now try to think back about two years ago, the famous incident involving the B-52 Air Force Bomber that flew across our country loaded with six cruise missiles fully armed with nuclear warheads and returning back to their base with the cruise missiles intact! To our joy, we all heard that the cruise missiles were all okay, intact. But again, did anybody ask the question and get an answer to what was the condition of the nuclear warheads aboard these cruise missiles? Were the warheads intact? Were they missing some nuclear elements may be? Did the aircraft and the crew meet a UFO, a flying saucer, in midflight? I certainly was not qualified to see this secret report, if there ever was one. You bet there was!

A short time later, almost immediately, all of the crew members of that flight were dispersed worldwide! No one is talking! No one is to be found! And all the facts, questions, and answers are Gone! Gone! Gone! END OF STORY!

X. Lucifer. Who is he? What is he?

"God" or "god." Who is he? What is he?

Before I get into my last clarification and conclusion, remember one of my opening statements: Speaking of "God," for the sake of my readers, this book is not intended to be a religious book; it is not intended to be used by any religion to promote or demote the name of "God." "God" with capital "G" or little "g" in this book is used strictly as a scientific method to identify, if possible, a certain form or *Entity* in charge or in command of a situation occurring at the time of happening. For the purpose of my reader, it may be the same "God" or "god" that exists today or that existed in the past of old, or may not.

Keeping this in mind, fasten your seat belts, and let's take a trip into the past.

In the vast space of our universe, a large number of spaceships were heading in a certain direction, a direction that would bring them into the neighborhood of the planet Earth. Their occupants were familiar with Earth; they had been there before on previous assignments.

This large number of spaceships were divided into three groups: (1) the Cherubim group on one side, (2) the Ophanim group in the center, and (3) the Seraphim group on the other side.

All of these three groups were on the run. They were being pursued by another group of their own kind, with one exception. The members of this other group, the pursuers, were their superiors. The results of this adventure were already discussed in an earlier chapter. Their leader's name at the time was Lucifer. His loyalty belonged to the Seraphim group. He was one of the Seraphim.

All of these three groups, all of them, were known as the Nefilim. Due to the fact that They fell down to Earth. Two of them originated from the planet Nibiru: the Cherubim and the Seraphim. The third group the Ophanim may have come from a different dimension. It was all a part of a group effort. However, I also explained that when they reached and fell to Earth this time around, they had to transform themselves to look like us. However, there were some humans, including some human leaders, who, for one reason or another, managed to see the Nefilim in their so-called true form, and these descriptions were handed down from generation to generation; they were also described in the Old and the New Testaments.

Just before the deluge some 13,500 years ago, God spoke to Noah and instructed him to build the ark. We now know from the works of great researchers that this so-called god, at least in this instance, was the god Enki who was the leader of all the Nefilim or, in this case, shall I say, the leader of all of the Nibiruites since the word Nephilim, for us, the humans, refers to the original group of about two hundred Nibiruites who fell down to earth.

Enki had a brother named Enlil. These two gods dwelled in heaven, meaning, they lived in spaceships above the Earth. (Oh yes! These two main gods were the original pursuers.) Before I go any further, just to refresh your memory once more. Here on Earth, they, the Nefilim, shed their skins; also remember, they are all great shape-shifters.

1). The Cherubim are described as angels, watchers, and guardians; they also fly the spaceships, and they are winged beings. The biblical prophet Ezekiel described the cherubim as a tetrad of living creatures, each having four faces: a lion, an ox, an eagle, and a man. They are said to have the stature and hands of a man, the feet of a calf, and four wings. Two of the wings extended upward, meeting above and sustaining the throne of God, while the other two stretched downward and covered the creatures themselves. There is also existing a Christian description of a cherub holding a sword in his hand, guarding the entrance to the Garden of Eden.

2) The Ophanim. The word "Ophan" means "wheel" in Hebrew; also, the word "ophnaeem" in Hebrew means bicycle. They were also called "Merkabah Wheels."

Also known as the "Thrones," these angels serve the primary function of being God's chariot. But besides this, they are also noted as being the dispensers of God's judgment, acting with impartialness and humility to bring about the desires of the Lord. Having the most bizarre physical appearance of the celestial host, they are described as great wheels covered with a great many eyes and glowing with light.

In the Jewish Kabbala, this so-called God's chariot is called the "Merkabah." By the way, for your information, about ten years ago, when Israel introduced its latest battle tank, it was named the "Merkabah."

The Ophanim are said to reside in the Sixth and Seventh Heaven or, in a better scientific term, dimension. According to most researchers, the so-called angels of the first, second, third, and fourth dimension need spaceships to travel through space, especially between dimensions. The Ophanim do not!

Yes! These so-called Ophanim angels possess the ability to travel throughout the vast universe on their own. In other words, it seems that this breed of angels, the Opahnim, possess a very unique skill or capability to either travel through universes or dimensions on their own by themselves and/or they have the ability to completely transform themselves into large spaceships (sized to fit as required) in order to transport the other so-called angels including their spaceships between other dimensions and universes. It is also very difficult physically to distinguish between the Cherubim angels and the Ophanim angels in their natural physical state, except that the Ophanim angels are almost never in their natural state; they always perform the function as wheels ("Gallgaleem," which mean "wheels" in Hebrew) and transporters.

3) The Seraphim, whose leader is named Lucifer. Yep! How about that. They are the recorders, record keepers of galactic events, and are the highest ranking and closest to God.

"Seraph" literally means "burning ones" in Hebrew. They emit extreme light, brightness, kind of phosphorescence. The Seraphim are a high-ranking class of celestial beings mentioned in the Old Testament. They are described as having a humanlike form. The only reference to the Seraphim in the Old Testament is found in Isaiah, chapter 6, verses 1 through 3, which details a specific vision this prophet had of these angels. The scripture reads, "In the year that King Uzziah died, I saw the Lord seated on a thrown, high and exalted, and the train of his robe filled the temple. Above him were Seraphs, each with six wings, with two wings they covered their faces, with two they covered their feet, and with two they were flying."

In Orthodox Judaism, the Seraphim are part of a unique and complex angelic hierarchy, where they occupy the fifth rank out of ten ranks of angels. Within Christian theology, the Seraphim occupy the highest rank of angels and are the direct caretakers of God's thrown.

The root of Seraphim comes either from the Hebrew verb "seraph" (to burn) or the Hebrew noun "seraph" (a fiery, flying serpent). It is said that whoever lays eyes on a seraph would instantly be incinerated due to the immense brightness of the Seraph!

Now I just mentioned that Lucifer is the leader of the Seraphim. So after reading this last statement, do you remember the description of Moses in the Old Testament after coming down from Mount Sinai with the second set of the tablets in his hands, the Ten Commandments? "When Moses came down from Mount Sinai with the two tablets of the Testimony in his hands, he was not aware that his face was shone (radiant) because he had spoken with the LORD. When Aaron and all the Israelites saw Moses, his face was shone, and they were afraid to come near him" (Exodus 34:29-30).

The process of natural deduction; what is it? Deductive reasoning should be distinguished from the related concept of *natural deduction*, an approach to *proof theory* that attempts to provide a formal model of logical reasoning as it "naturally" occurs.

Now read the following from the book of Exodus, regarding Moses's testimony:

> And the Lord descended in the cloud, and stood with him there, and proclaimed the name of the Lord. (34:5)

> And the Lord passed by before him, and proclaimed, The Lord, The Lord God, merciful and gracious, longsuffering, and abundant in goodness and truth. (34:6)

> Keeping mercy for thousands, forgiving iniquity and transgression and sin, and that will by no means clear the guilty; visiting the iniquity of the fathers upon the children, and upon the children's children, unto the third and to the fourth generation. (34:7)

> And Moses made haste, and bowed his head toward the earth, and worshipped. (34:8)

> And he said, "If now I have found grace in thy sight, O Lord, let my Lord, I pray thee, go among us; for it is a stiffnecked people; and pardon our iniquity and our sin, and take us for your inheritance." (34:9)

Well, so what do we have here? Moses, on his second trip up Mount Sinai, has spent there forty days and forty nights without any food. Moses came face-to-face with God! Moses saw God in his glory, Moses saw God in his or her natural state, as God is. Yes! Moses saw God face-to-face; he lived, he did not die!

However, as I mentioned earlier in this book, God told Moses that he knew his forefathers: Abraham, Isaac, and Jacob

I also just described the Seraphim angels as the "Burning Ones," who emit extreme light, kind of phosphorescence, and their leader is Lucifer! So who do you think Moses caught the Glow in his face from? I'll give you only one guess—Lucifer.

In the Fatima Prophecy, in the apparition that the little boy saw, the figure of a man who spoke to this little boy said, "You are all my children, you are the children of Lucifer."

At this instant, after reading all that, who do you think God or god is? Yes, Lucifer. He is the God of now!

By that, I mean that he is acting as god now by *default*! And that means that in the absence of the main Gods or gods, "Enlil and Enki," who left the earth some 13,500 years ago, when the flood of Noah arrived, Lucifer became the most powerful angelic entity remaining here in his own prison.

This is also the main reason why right now this planet Earth is in such a shameful condition. What a mess!

Just remember, December 21, 2012, is around the corner.

The "GODS" are returning! WATCH OUT!

Exodus 34:29 It came about when Moses was coming down from Mount Sinai (and the two tablets of the testimony were in Moses' hand as he was coming down from the mountain), that Moses did not know that the skin of his face shone because of his speaking with Him. The LORD.

MOSES COMING DOWN THE MOUNTAIN.
Carrying the second set of Tablets.

DOCUMENTS AND NOTES

1. THE SECRET DIARY OF ADMIRAL BYRD.
2. SECRET JAPANESE PLANS TO BOMB MAINLAND USA.
3. HUMAN FOOT PRINT FOUND NEXT TO DINOSAUR FOOT PRINT

ADMIRAL RICHARD B. BYRD'S DIARY
(EFF: FEB 19 / 1947)

(My Secret Diary)

I must write this diary in secrecy and obscurity. It concerns my Arctic flight of the nineteenth day of February in the year of Nineteen and Forty Seven.

There comes a time when the rationality of men must fade into insignificance and one must accept the inevitability of the Truth! I am not at liberty to disclose the following documentation at this writing . . . perhaps it shall never see the light of public scrutiny, but I must do my duty and record here for all to read one day. In a world of greed and exploitation of certain of mankind can no longer suppress that which is truth.

FLIGHT LOG: BASE CAMP ARCTIC, 2/19/1947

0600 Hours—All preparations are complete for our flight north ward and we are airborne with full fuel tanks at 0610 Hours.

0620 Hours—fuel mixture on starboard engine seems too rich, adjustment made and Pratt Whittneys are running smoothly.

0730 Hours—Radio Check with base camp. All is well and radio reception is normal.

0740 Hours—Note slight oil leak in starboard engine, oil pressure indicator seems normal, however.

0800 Hours—Slight turbulence noted from easterly direction at altitude of 2321 feet, correction to 1700 feet, no further turbulence, but tail wind increases, slight adjustment in throttle controls, aircraft performing very well now.

0815 Hours—Radio Check with base camp, situation normal.

0830 Hours—Turbulence encountered again, increase altitude to 2900 feet, smooth flight conditions again.

0910 Hours—Vast Ice and snow below, note coloration of yellowish nature, and disperse in a linear pattern. Altering course foe a better examination of this color pattern below, note reddish or purple color also. Circle this area two full turns and return to assigned compass heading. Position check made again to base camp, and relay information concerning colorations in the Ice and snow below.

0910 Hours—Both Magnetic and Gyro compasses beginning to gyrate and wobble, we are unable to hold our heading by instrumentation. Take bearing with Sun compass, yet all seems well. The controls are seemingly slow to respond and have sluggish quality, but there is no indication of Icing!

0915 Hours—In the distance is what appears to be mountains.

0949 Hours—29 minutes elapsed flight time from the first sighting of the mountains, it is no illusion. They are mountains and consisting of a small range that I have never seen before!

0955 Hours—Altitude change to 2950 feet, encountering strong turbulence again.

1000 Hours—We are crossing over the small mountain range and still proceeding northward as best as can be ascertained. Beyond the mountain range is what appears to be a valley with a small river or stream running through the center portion. There should be no green valley below! Something is definitely wrong and abnormal here! We should be over Ice and Snow! To the portside are great forests growing on the mountain slopes. Our navigation Instruments are still spinning, the gyroscope is oscillating back and forth!

1005 Hours—I alter altitude to 1400 feet and execute a sharp left turn to better examine the valley below. It is green with either moss or a type of tight knit grass. The Light here seems different. I cannot see the Sun anymore. We make another left turn and we spot what seems to be a large animal of some kind below us. It appears to be an elephant! NO!!! It looks more like a mammoth! This is incredible! Yet, there it is! Decrease altitude to 1000 feet and take binoculars to better examine the animal. It is confirmed—it is definitely a mammoth-like animal! Report this to base camp.

1030 Hours—Encountering more rolling green hills now. The external temperature indicator reads 74 degrees Fahrenheit! Continuing on our heading now. Navigation instruments seem normal now. I am puzzled over their actions. Attempt to contact base camp. Radio is not functioning!

1130 Hours—Countryside below is more level and normal (if I may use that word). Ahead we spot what seems to be a city!!!! This is impossible! Aircraft seems light and oddly buoyant. The controls refuse to respond!! My GOD!!! Off our port and star board wings are a strange type of aircraft. They are closing rapidly alongside! They are disc-shaped and have a radiant quality to them. They are close enough now to see the markings on them. It is a type of Swastika!!! This is fantastic. Where are we! What has happened. I tug at the controls again. They will not respond!!!! We are caught in an invisible vice grip of some type!

1135 Hours—Our radio crackles and a voice comes through in English with what perhaps is a slight Nordic or Germanic accent! The message is: 'Welcome, Admiral, to our domain. We shall land you in exactly seven minutes! Relax, Admiral, you are in good hands.' I note the engines of our plane have stopped running! The aircraft is under some strange control and is now turning itself. The controls are useless.

1140 Hours—Another radio message received. We begin the landing process now, and in moments the plane shudders slightly, and begins a descent as though caught in some great unseen elevator! The downward motion is negligible, and we touch down with only a slight jolt!

1145 Hours—I am making a hasty last entry in the flight log. Several men are approaching on foot toward our aircraft. They are tall with blond hair. In the distance is a large shimmering city pulsating with rainbow hues of color. I do not know what is going to happen now, but I see no signs of weapons on those approaching. I hear now a voice ordering me by name to open the cargo door. I comply. **END LOG**

From this point I write all the following events here from memory. It defies the imagination and would seem all but madness if it had not happened.

The radioman and I are taken from the aircraft and we are received in a most cordial manner. We were then boarded on a small platform-like conveyance with no wheels! It moves us toward the glowing city with great swiftness. As we approach, the city seems to be made of a crystal material. Soon we arrive at a large building that is a type I have never seen before. It appears to be right out of the design board of *Frank Lloyd Wright*, or perhaps more correctly, out of a *Buck Rogers* setting!! We are given some type of warm beverage which tasted like nothing I have ever savored before. It is delicious. After about ten minutes, two of our wondrous appearing hosts come to our quarters and announce that I am to accompany them. I have no choice but to comply. I leave my radioman behind and we walk a short distance and enter into what seems to be an elevator.

We descend downward for some moments, the machine stops, and the door lifts silently upward! We then proceed down a long hallway that is lit by a rose-colored light that seems to be emanating from the very walls themselves! One of the beings motions for us to stop before a great door. Over the door is an inscription that I cannot read. The great door slides noiselessly open and I am beckoned to enter. One of my hosts speaks. '*Have no fear, Admiral, you are to have an audience with the Master...*'

I step inside and my eyes adjust to the beautiful coloration that seems to be filling the room completely. Then I begin to see my surroundings. What greeted my eyes is the most beautiful sight of my entire existence. It is in fact too beautiful and wondrous to describe. It is exquisite and delicate. I do not think there exists a human term that can describe it in any detail with justice! My thoughts are interrupted in a cordial manner by a warm rich voice of melodious quality, '*I bid you welcome to our domain, Admiral.*' I see a man with delicate features and with the etching of years upon his face. He is seated at a long table. He motions me to sit down in one of the chairs. After I am seated, he places his fingertips together and smiles. He speaks softly again, and conveys the following:

> 'We have let you enter here because you are of noble character and well-known on the Surface World, Admiral.'

Surface World, I half-gasp under my breath!

> 'Yes," the Master replies with a smile, 'you are in the domain of the Arianni, the Inner World of the Earth. We shall not long delay your mission, and you will be safely escorted back to the surface and for a distance beyond. But now, Admiral, I shall tell you why you have been summoned here. Our interest rightly begins just after your race exploded the first atomic bombs over Hiroshima and Nagasaki, Japan. It was at that alarming time we sent our flying machines, the "Flugelrads", to your surface world to investigate what your race had done. That is, of course, past history now, my dear Admiral, but I must continue on. You see, we have never interfered before in your race's wars, and barbarity, but now we must, for you have learned to tamper with a certain power that is not for man, namely, that of atomic energy. Our emissaries have already delivered messages to the powers of your world, and yet they do not heed.

Now you have been chosen to be witness here that our world does exist. You see, our Culture and Science is many thousands of years beyond your race, Admiral.'

I interrupted,

'But what does this have to do with me, Sir?'

The Master's eyes seemed to penetrate deeply into my mind, and after studying me for a few moments he replied,

'Your race has now reached the point of no return, for there are those among you who would destroy your very world rather than relinquish their power as they know it . . . ' I nodded, and the Master continued, 'In 1945 and afterward, we tried to contact your race, but our efforts were met with hostility, our Flugelrads were fired upon. Yes, even pursued with malice and animosity by your fighter planes. So, now, I say to you, my son, there is a great storm gathering in your world, a black fury that will not spend itself for many years. There will be no answer in your arms, there will be no safety in your science. It may rage on until every flower of your culture is trampled, and all human things are leveled in vast chaos. Your recent war was only a prelude of what is yet to come for your race. We here see it more clearly with each hour . . . do you say I am mistaken?'

'No,' I answer, 'it happened once before, the dark ages came and they lasted for more than five hundred years.'

'Yes, my son,' replied the Master, 'the dark ages that will come now for your race will cover the Earth like a pall, but I believe that some of your race will live through the storm, beyond that, I cannot say. We see at a great distance a new world stirring from the ruins of your race, seeking its lost and legendary treasures, and they will be here, my son, safe in our keeping. When that time arrives, we shall come forward again to help revive your culture and your race. Perhaps, by then, you will have learned the futility of war and its strife . . . and after that time, certain of your culture and science will be returned for your race to begin anew. You, my son, are to return to the Surface World with this message . . . . '

With these closing words, our meeting seemed at an end. I stood for a moment as in a dream . . . . but, yet, I knew this was reality, and for some strange reason I bowed slightly, either out of respect or humility, I do not know which.

Suddenly, I was again aware that the two beautiful hosts who had brought me here were again at my side. 'This way, Admiral,' motioned one. I turned once more before leaving and looked back toward the Master. A gentle smile was etched on his delicate and ancient face. 'Farewell, my son,' he spoke, then he gestured with a lovely, slender hand a motion of peace and our meeting was truly ended.

Quickly, we walked back through the great door of the Master's chamber and once again entered into the elevator. The door slid silently downward and we were at once going upward. One of my hosts spoke again, 'We must now make haste, Admiral, as the Master desires to delay you no longer on your scheduled timetable and you must return with his message to your race.'

I said nothing. All of this was almost beyond belief, and once again my thoughts were interrupted as we stopped. I entered the room and was again with my radioman. He had an anxious expression on his face. As I approached, I said, 'It is all right, Howie, it is all right.'

The two beings motioned us toward the awaiting conveyance, we boarded, and soon arrived back at the aircraft. The engines were idling and we boarded immediately. The whole atmosphere seemed charged now with a certain air of urgency. After the cargo door was closed the aircraft was immediately lifted by that unseen force until we reached an altitude of 2700 feet. Two of the aircraft were alongside for some distance guiding us on our return way. I must state here, the airspeed indicator registered no reading, yet we were moving along at a very rapid rate.

215 Hours—A radio message comes through. 'We are leaving you now, Admiral, your controls are free. Auf Wiedersehen!!!!' We watched for a moment as the flugelrads disappeared into the pale blue sky.

The aircraft suddenly felt as though caught in a sharp downdraft for a moment. We quickly recovered her control. We do not speak for some time, each man has his thoughts . . . .

ENTRY IN FLIGHT LOG CONTINUES:

220 Hours—We are again over vast areas of ice and snow, and approximately 27 minutes from base camp. We radio them, they respond. We report all conditions normal . . . . normal. Base camp expresses relief at our re-established contact.

300 Hours—We land smoothly at base camp. I have a mission . . . .

END LOG ENTRIES.

March 11, 1947. I have just attended a staff meeting at the Pentagon. I have stated fully my discovery and the message from the Master. All is duly recorded. The President has been advised. I am now detained for several hours (six hours, thirty—nine minutes, to be exact.) I am interviewed intently by **_Top Security Forces_** and a medical team. It was an ordeal!!!! I am placed under strict control via the national security provisions of this United States of America. I am ORDERED TO REMAIN SILENT IN REGARD TO ALL THAT I HAVE LEARNED, ON THE BEHALF OF HUMANITY!!!! Incredible! I am reminded that I am a military man and I must obey orders.

30/12/56: FINAL ENTRY:

These last few years elapsed since 1947 have not been kind . . . I now make my final entry in this singular diary. In closing, I must state that I have faithfully kept this matter secret as directed all these years. It has been completely against my values of moral right. Now, I seem to sense the long night coming on and this secret will not die with me, but as all truth shall, it will triumph and so it shall.

This can be the only hope for mankind. I have seen the truth and it has quickened my spirit and has set me free! I have done my duty toward the monstrous military industrial complex. Now, the long night begins to approach, but there shall be no end. Just as the long night of the Arctic ends, the brilliant sunshine of Truth shall come again . . . . and those who are of darkness shall fall in it's Light. FOR I HAVE SEEN THAT LAND BEYOND THE POLE, THAT CENTER OF THE GREAT UNKNOWN.

Admiral Richard E. Byrd
United States Navy
24 December 1956

END OF ADMIRAL BYRD SECRET DIARY.

SECRET JAPANESE PLANS TO BOMB THE MAINLAND USA. TOWARDS THE VERY END OF WW II, OR EVEN AFTER THE WAR ENDED!

ANOTHER VERY SECRET REASON WHY THE USA RUSHED TO DROP THE ATOMIC BOMB ON JAPAN.

In this book, you have seen a picture with the title "THE FIRST U-BOAT ARRIVES", Portsmouth Naval Shipyard.USA, June 1, 1945. *** HOT FLASH: Aboard this U-BOAT, There were supposedly 2 dead Japanese scientists. Or were they just drugged. Question: what were Japanese scientists doing with the NAZIS? With a U-BOAT full of Uranium!

The usual Assessment . . .

The question arises as to why poison gas was not employed extensively in the World War II as anticipated, especially in the air war. None of the World War II combatant countries, except Japan, employed their stock piles of poison gas in World War II. The only exception was the Japanese who used both poison gas and biological weapons in China. The conventional wisdom is that the combatant countries refrained from using gas because they feared retaliation

BUT . . . *A Planned Bacterial Attack on the United States,* WAS IN THE WORKS!

Proposals included use of these weapons against the United States. They proposed using balloon bombs to carry disease to America and they had a plan in the summer of 1945 to use kamikaze pilots to dump plague infected fleas on San Diego.

Some Japanese generals proposed loading the balloons with weapons of biological warfare, to create epidemics of plague or anthrax in the United States. Other army units wanted to send cattle plague virus to wipe out the American livestock industry or grain smut to wipe out the crops. As it happened, *9,000 balloons* each carried four incendiary and one antipersonnel bomb across the Pacific on the jet stream to create forest fires and terror from Oregon to Michigan.

As the end of the war approached in 1945, Unit 731 embarked on its wildest scheme; codenamed Cherry Blossoms at Night, the plan was to use kamikaze pilots to infest California with the plague.

Toshimi Mizobuchi, who was an instructor for new recruits in Unit 731, said the idea was to use 20 of the 500 new troops who arrived in Harbin in July 1945. A submarine was to take a few of them to the seas off Southern California, and then they were to fly in a plane carried on board the submarine and contaminate San Diego with plague-infected fleas. The target date was to be Sept. 22, 1945. As it happened, the fleet of *submarine seaplane carriers* that assembled was assigned to launch torpedoes at the locks in the Panama canal, but that was changed to attack the US fleet at Ulith just as the war ended.

Unit 731 planned germ warfare against U.S. forces after WW2
kyodo :: 2006-07-22

Imperial Japanese Army's germ warfare unit planned to stage germ attacks against U.S. troops in Japan just after Japan's surrender in World War II in August 1945, according a memorandum left by the unit's commander, Lt. Gen. Shiro Ishii. But the germ warfare team, known as Unit 731, gave up the plan after being told by then top commanders of the Imperial Japanese Army, "Don't die in vain." It is unclear how Ishii planned to carry out the attacks because statements of the memorandum are fragmentary. Unit 731 was known to have made preparations to stage "tokko" suicide germ attacks against U.S. forces just before Japan's surrender.

When America was attacked by *Japanese balloon bombs*, US officials were concerned that these might include some of Japan's infected flea payloads, but no such biological balloon bombs were ever discovered.

In 1944, Japan started launching thousands of bombs, attached to balloons, from their shores to the United States. More than 300 made it to their destination . . .

These paper balloons traveled by jet streams over 4,500 miles, at an altitude of 50,000Ft. They were timed to drop over the United States and Canada. Over 1,000 balloons bombs reached their targets.

Six Americans were killed in Oregon, five children and one adult, they were killed on ;May 5, 1945.

on the History Channel a few days ago. story was about Japan's attempt to develop germ bombs to be carried to America with a 6 engine bomber

***) The Nakajima G10N1 Fugaki, Mt. Fugi bomber (Japan's super-bomber) first mission was scheduled for Sept 22, 1945. It had a new 6-engine (5000 hp each) bomber that could cruise at 32,000 feet and at 423 mph!!! It had a 9000-mile range so it could actually bomb US cities directly from Japan! Where was it scheduled to strike AND what exactly was it's payload ? . . . . It was fuelled, and . . . .

It was scheduled to bomb San Diego, CA and it had a payload of fleas infected with the Bubonic Plague.**("ASSOOO"—FRIENDLY SMILLING JAPANESE)**.

1944-1945 J Plans to attack US
** Fuugaku six-engine planes designed to carry biological weapons to US 1945.09.22 Plan to drop bubonic-plague flea-bombs on San Francisco (designed by Ishii Shiroo)
** Kodama Yoshi (of 'Black Dragons') said to have made fortune supplying such weapons.

END OF SECRET JAPANESE PLAN DOCUMENTS.

HUMAN FOOT PRINT FOUND NEXT TO DINOSAUR FOOT PRINT

"Alvis Delk Cretaceous Footprint"

Abstract:

The Creation Evidence Museum is in possession of a set of Cretaceous footprints discovered by amateur archaeologist Alvis Delk[1] of Stephenville, Texas. This fossil of dense Glen Rose limestone consists of Dinosaur footprint (Acrocanthosaurus) and an eleven-inch human footprint intruded by the dinosaur print.

Introduction:

In early July, 2000 Alvis Delk, assisted by James Bishop (both of Stephenville, Texas), was working in the Cretaceous limestone on the McFall property at the Paluxy River near Glen Rose, Texas and discovered a pristine human footprint intruded by a dinosaur footprint. This discovery was made in the vicinity of McFall I and II Sites where the Creation Evidence Museum team has excavated since the Spring of 1982. The eleven-inch human footprint matches seven other such footprints of the same dimensions in the "Sir George Series," named in honor of His Excellency Governor General Ratu Sir George Cacobau of Fiji.[2]

Scientific Verification of Footprint Authenticity:

The fossil was transported to a professional laboratory where 800 X-rays were performed in a CT Scan procedure. Laboratory technicians verified compression and distribution features clearly seen in both prints, human and dinosaur. This removes any possibility that the prints were carved or altered.

Importance of Discovery:

Professor James Stewart Monroe, writing in *Journal of Geological Education* candidly asserted that "Human footprints in geologically ancient strata would indeed call into doubt many conventional geological concepts."[3] Professor David H. Milne of The Evergreen State College, Olympia, Washington and Professor Steven D. Schafersman of the Department of Geology, Rice University, Houston, Texas made further admissions in writing that "Such an occurrence, if verified, would *seriously disrupt conventional interpretations of biological and geological history* and would *support the doctrines of creationism and catastrophism*."[4]

Professor Steven M. Stanley in *The New Evolutionary Timetable* opined that "any topsy-turvy sequence of fossils would force us to *rethink our theory* . . . As Darwin recognized, a single geographic inconsistency would have *nearly the same power of destruction*."[5]

---

[1] [1] Delk, Alvis has extensive field experience under direct supervision of state certified archaeologists. His personal discoveries range from early Texas Spaniard artifacts to early Texas military maps, etc. This current footprint discovery is in keeping with his tireless pursuit to explore Texas' historical treasures.

[2] Baugh, Carl E., *Academic Justification for Voluntary Inclusion of Scientific Creation in Public Classroom Curricula*, Doctoral Dissertation, Pacific College of Graduate Studies, Melbourne, Australia and Poplar Bluff, Missouri, USA, Fall 1989, p. 196

[3] Monroe, James Stewart, *Journal of Geological Education*, "Creationism, Human Footprints, and Flood Geology", V.35, p.93

[4] Milne, David H., and Schafersman, Steven D., *Journal of Geological Education*, 1983, V.31, p.111

[5] Stanley, Steven M., *The New Evolutionary Timetable*, 1981, p. 171

William E. Dannemeyer of the United States Congress carried the issue to its ultimate conclusion in writing to this researcher, stating that "This is a ***significant breakthrough*** with enormous implications for ***establishing the origin of mankind.***"[1]

Photographic Evidence:

---

[1] Dannemeyer, William E., United States Congress, Personal Correspondence to Carl E. Baugh, 1983

NIBIRU . . . . APPROACHING, by Graig Martin.

THE REAL ROYAL FAMILY? IS IT POSSIBLE?
By, Lucianomorelli.

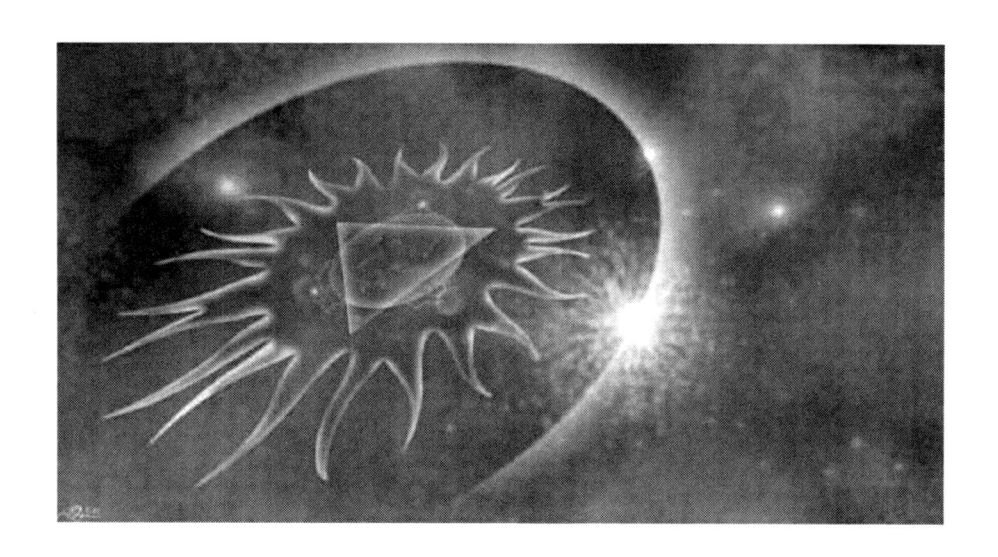

THE OPHANIM, TRANSPORTING THE CHERUBIM AND THE SERAPHIM THROUGH TIME AND SPACE.
By, Tim Odom.

B-29, Superfortress.

INDEX

A

Aaron, 17-18, 57, 59, 61-62, 64-65, 177-78
Adonai, 29-30
Advance Base, 98-99
Agdoleem, 34
alien abductions, 17, 20-23, 149-50, 153
aliens, 16-17, 21-23, 29-31, 49-50, 52-55, 69-70, 93-94, 99-101, 104, 111-12, 120-21, 123-25, 127-30, 133-55, 158-60, 171-72
Alsos, 82-83
Alternative ANGEPP, 150, 158-59, 161
Amalek, 57, 59
American Secret Service, 99-100
am segula, 73-74
ancient artifacts, 43
Andromeda, 66
Antarctica (*see also* South Pole), 49-50, 74-75, 90-91, 95-96, 98-104, 112-14, 116-22, 124-25, 129-31, 133-36, 142-43, 158, 160
antarctic expeditions, 98
Anunnaki, 19-21, 23, 27-31, 49-50, 161-64, 171-72

Apollo 11, 69
Aquarius, 75-76
Arado Ar 234, 90
Arianni, 120-22, 134-35, 187-88
Ark of the Covenant, 57, 59, 61-62, 64-66, 166
Armageddon, 36
Arroway, Elli, 83-84
Aryan, 93, 98, 100, 118, 120-21, 128, 130, 146
Ashem, 29-30
Asimov, Isaac, 171-72
asteroid belt, 27-28, 40-41, 163-65
Ataneeneem, 33-34
Ataneeneem Agdoleem, 34
Atlantis, 30-31, 47-48, 50, 70
atomic bomb, 72, 77-79, 81-83, 85, 87-88, 93, 121, 125, 134, 140, 147
Atomic Espionage trial, 142

B

B-29, 79, 82
B-29 Superfortress, 79, 81-82
B-52, 174
Babylon, 42, 165
Baltic Sea, 77-78
Banda, Lugai, 52

banished ones, 121, 130, 138. *See also* Nefilim
Battle of Waterloo, 43-44
Baumgart, Peter, 89
Bay of Whales, 126-27, 132
BBC News, 77
Bell, Art, 123-24
Bernard, R. W., 123
  Hollow Earth, The, 123
Bilderbergs, 70
Bill & Melinda Gates Foundation, 97
black axiom, 54, 72-73
Black Hole, 112, 119-20, 127-28
Black matter. *See* black axiom
Blitz Bomber. *See* Arado Ar 234
Block, Irving, 171-72
Bocks Car, 81-82
Boettger, Rudolf, 90
Bonaparte, Napoleon, 43-45
Boorda, Jeremy, 132
Born, Max, 78
Boulle, Pierre, 167-68
Bradbury, Ray, 171-72
Braun, Eva, 87-90
Braun, Werner, 68
Burnett, Thom, 133
  Conspiracy Encyclopedia, 132-33
burning bush, 64-65
Burton Island, 132
Bush, George W., 37, 42, 65, 67
Byrd, Richard, Jr., 95-101, 112-14, 116-32, 136-37, 142, 146, 163, 181, 183
Byrnes, Jimmy, 87-88
  Frankly Speaking, 87

C

C-5A, 67
Canaan, 59
cannibalism, 66-67
Captain Kirk, 72-73
Chariots of the Gods (Daniken), 25
cherubim, 175-77, 201-2
chosen people, 30, 74
Christianity, 36-37
Christopher, Alex, 144
Churchill, Winston, 86-88
Church of Peace, 37-38, 173
Clarke, Arthur C., 70-71, 74-75, 168, 171-72
Clinton, Bill, 132-33
Coast to Coast, 75, 173
Collier, Alex, 66-67, 141-42
Communism, 35
Connery, Sean, 35-36
Conspiracy Encyclopedia (Burnett), 133
Contact, 84, 122, *169*
Critical Mass (Hydrick), 82
crop circles, 97
cryogenics, 50, 52
Crystall, Ellen, 66-67
  Silent Invasion, 66-67

D

Dames, Ed, 75-76, 162, 173
Daniken, Erich, 25-26
  Chariots of the Gods, 25
dark energy. *See* black axiom
DC-3, 103, 115, 118, 125

Dead Sea Scrolls, 66
Dee, Sir John, 70-72, 137-38, 146-47, 151-52, 172-73
Deep Impact, 36
deluge, 21-23, 41, 48-49, 52-53, 56, 63-64, 70, 159, 161, 175-76
Diana, Princess, 67-68, 172-73
"diaper affair", 156-57
dinosaurs, 33-34, 181, 183, 196-97
disc. *See* flying saucers
DNA, 22-23, 31, 33-35, 45-49, 65, 69, 71, 74, 147-48, 150, 152, 154-56
Doenitz, Karl, 90-91
Doolittle, James H., 96
"Doomsday Machine, The", 169
Doomsday Seed Bank See Slavard Seed Bank, 97

E

earth, 19-22, 28-31, 33-36, 40-41, 45-50, 52-55, 68-73, 121-23, 127-29, 137-42, 146-50, 153-59, 161-64, 171-76, 178-79, 187-89
Egypt, 13, 15, 44-45, 61, 63-66, 165
Einstein, Albert, 77-78
El Al jumbo jets, 64
Eldem, Burak, 163
  2012: Appointment with Marduk, 163
electromagnetic weapons, 49-50
Elizabeth I (queen), 65-66, 69-72, 146-47, 151-52, 172-73
Enki, 29-30, 73-74, 175-76, 182

Enlil, 29-30, 73-74, 175-76, 182
Enochian, 70-71
Enola Gay, 79, 81-82
Enuma Elish, 27-29
Ethiopian Jews, 64
eugenics, 98
Europa, 168-69
Europe, 36-37, 77, 87-90, 103-4, 146-47, 152-53
extraterrestrial beings, 26, 29, 93, 141, 172. *See also* aliens

F

fallen angels. *See* Nefilim
Fat Man (bomb), 78-79
Ferini, Enrico, 79-80
fifth dimension, 71, 172-73
floyd bennett, 96
Flugelrads, 93-94, 120-21, 123-24, 134, 146-47, 187-89. *See also* flying saucers
flying saucers, 19-20, 23-25, 34-35, 69-70, 93-97, 101, 103-4, 113-14, 116-17, 119, 124, 126-28, 133-34, 139-40, 143-49, 173-74
Fokker trimotor, 98
foo fighters, 93-94, 103-4
Forbidden Planet, 172
forbidden zone, 167-68
Ford, Edsel, 95-96
Forrestal, James, 100, 131-32
Foster, Judy, 84, 122
fourth prophecy, 36
Francis, Ann, 171-72
Frankly Speaking, 87

Freemasons, 69-70, 154-55
fusion weapons, 49-50

G

galactic alignment, 54, 72-73
gamma G barrier, 45, 47
Gates, Bill, 151-52
Geeboreem, 46-47, 66-67
genetic engineering, 20, 25-26
genetic manipulation, 29-31, 33, 154
genetics, 22-23, 25, 45-46, 50, 52, 98
geological surveys, 99
German Workers' Party, 92
ghost rockets, 96
Giannini, F. Amaddeo, 123
Worlds Beyond the Poles, 123
giants, 33-34, 46-48, 52-53, 74, 169, 171
Gilgamesh, 52-53, 141-42, 158
goblins, 53
grays, 20-21, 53-54, 147-48, 150-51
Great Pyramid of Giza, 56, 62
great sea creatures, 33-34
great white god. *See* Quetzalcoatl
Grenada, 50, 52

H

HAARP, 156-57
Hadden, S. R., 84
Hall, Charles, 140-42
Harrison, Linda, 167-68
Haunebu, 93-94. *See also* flying saucers

Hawass, Zahi, 56
hayeor, 59, 61
heavy water, 76-78
Hebrew, 17, 22, 26, 28, 34, 46-47, 59, 61, 176-78
Hercules C-130s, 64
Heron, Patric, 17-18
Heston, Charlton, 168
High Frequency Active Auroral Research Program. *See* HAARP
Hill, Barney, 141
Hill, Betty, 141
Hindenburg, Paul Von, 93
Hiroshima, 17-18, 23-25, 76-79, 81-83, 85-87, 125, 146, 187-88
Hitler, Adolf, 76-78, 86-95, 97-98
Mein Kampf, 92
Hoagland, Richard C., 46, 52, 123, 163, 173
hollow earth, 119, 121-22, 163-64
Hollow Earth, The (Bernard), 123
hollow earth theory, 119
Holocaust, 94-95, 143, 172-73
Homo erectus, 28-29
Homo sapiens, 29
human evolution, 25
humpback whale, 73
Hussein, Saddam, 42-43, 87
Hydrick, Carter, 82
Critical Mass, 82
Hynek, Allen J., 140

I

ICBM, 173
Illuminati, 69-71, 97-98, 114, 117

Inanna, 52-53
Infrared Astronomy Satellite Telescope. See IRAS
intelligence information, 19
Intercontinental Ballistic Missiles. See ICBM
Intruders, 67-68
Iraq war, 21-22, 41-43
IRAS, 27-28, 162-63
Iron Cross, 143-44
Ishtar, 51-53
Israel, 15, 17, 26, 37-38, 59, 61, 64-65, 74, 152-53, 176-77
Israelites, 56-59, 61, 63-66, 177-78

J

Japan, 9-10, 17-18, 76-79, 82-88, 137-38, 146-47, 187-88, 192-96
Jewish Democrats, 37
Jews, 36-37, 64, 91-92, 94-95
John Paul II (pope), 35-36
Jones, Paula, 132-34
Jordan River, 57, 59
Joshua, 57, 59
Jupiter, 27-28, 68, 168, 171
Jurassic Park, 53

K

Kabbala, 177
Kearney Incident, The (Schmidt), 145
Kenneth Arnold, 23-25, 130, 146-47
Kevin Smith Show, 140-41
KGB, 76-78

Kilgallen, Dorothy, 96-97
Kimball, Glenn, 17-18
King, Larry, 115
King's Chamber, 56-57, 62, 64
King James Bible, 65-66
Krusen (Admiral), 100, 131

L

Larry King Live, 113, 115
Lear, John, 172-73
Lewinsky, Monica, 132-34
Lindbergh, Charles, 98
Little America, 98-99, 101, 103, 118-19, 121, 126-28
Little America IV, 119, 121, 127-28
Little Boy (bomb), 37, 78-79, 81-82, 85-87, 182
Lucifer, 34-38, 54, 120-21, 130, 139-40, 174-75, 177-79, 181-82
Luftwaffe troops, 89-90

M

Mack, John E., 67-68
magic rod. *See* rod
Mamelukes, 43-44
Manhattan project, 78-81, 83
Marcel, Jesse A., 23-24, 75-76
Marduk, 38, 40, 162-63
Mars, 27-28, 133-34, 168-69, 171
Marzulli, Lynn, 17-18
Masons, 47, 69-70, 154-55
Mattern (German writer), 91
Maya civilization, 162
Medal of Honor, 95-96

Mein Kampf (Hitler), 92
Merkabah, 176-77
Mesopotamia, 28-29, 165, 169, 171
meteor, 36, 140
microbiologists, 22-23, 152-53, 155-56
microbiology, 71, 152-53
Microsoft, 151-52
Middle East, 23, 25-26
Midian, 64-65
military conflict, 18-19
mini ice age, 29, 50
monolith, 70-71, 168
moon, 28, 33-34, 45-47, 67-70, 75-76, 146-47, 149-50, 154-58, 164, 168-69, 172-73
Morris, Dick, 133
Moses, 17-18, 56-57, 59-66, 155, 177-80, 182-83
Mount Sinai, 177-80, 182
Mueller, Heinrich, 88-90

N

Nagasaki, 17-18, 23-25, 76-79, 81-83, 85-86, 125, 145-46, 187-88
NASA, 35-36, 66, 154-55, 171-72
National Socialists German Workers' Party, 92
Nazi Germany, 54, 77-78, 86, 98-100
Near East, 26
Nebuchadnezzar, King, 29
Nefilim, 17, 22-23, 30-31, 33-34, 37-38, 44-50, 52-54, 65-67, 69-73, 83-87, 93-94, 117-18, 134-44, 146-55, 157-59, 175-76

Neuschwabenland, 99-101
New Testament, 18-19, 26, 33-34, 59, 61, 65-66, 175-76
New York Times, 68, 95-96
Nibiru, 20, 27-31, 33, 35-36, 40, 49, 54-55, 59, 61-65, 72-75, 98, 137, 140, 161-63, 166, 169-71
Nile River, 55-56, 59, 61, 64-65
Nimitz, Chester, 100, 130-31
Nimrod, 52-53
Ninsun, Rimat, 52
Noah, 18, 23, 29, 47-49, 52-53, 56, 64, 155, 175-76, 179, 182
Noah's ark, 18, 23, 155
Noah's flood. *See* deluge
Nordic, 53, 66, 129-30, 139-42, 144-45, 185-86
North Pole, 95-98, 114, 117-19, 122-25, 127-28, 134-36, 144-45, 163-64
NSDAP. *See* National Socialists German Workers' Party
nuclear bomb, 23, 79, 174
nuclear calendar, 85-86
nuclear fusion, 78, 173-74

O

Old Testament, 18-19, 26-28, 33-34, 46-49, 53, 59, 61, 177-78
Operation Argus, 134-36
Operation Highjump, 99-101, 103-4, 112-14, 116, 118-20, 122-26, 128-32, 134-36, 142, 145-46
Operation Paperclip, 99-100, 138-39, 142-43

Operation Solomon, 64
Operation Urgent Fury, 50, 52
Ophan, 176
Ophanim, 175-77, 201-2
Oppenheimer, J. Robert, 78
Order out of Chaos, 42, 93

P

Panama canal, 126, 136, 193-94
Phobos (Jupiter's moon), 169
Phobos 1 (spacecraft), 169
phobos 2 (spacecraft), 169, 171
Pidgeon, Walter, 172
Pioneer 10, 171
Piper, Roddy, 33
Planet of the Apes, The, 168
planet x, 27-28, 31, 36, 140, 163
plutonium bomb, 81
point of parity, 69
possession, 48, 158-59, 161, 196-97
Potsdam Conference, 86
Project Clementine, 68
Promised Land, 64-65

Q

Queen Maud Land. *See* Neuschwabenland
Quetzalcoatl, 29-30, 73-74, 95, 162-63

R

R4D, 118-19, 122, 126-28, 131
Ramsey, Bertram, 125-26
Red Sea, 57, 59
Renaissance, 67, 72
reptilians, 53, 65-69, 143-44
Reptiloids, 143-44
Republican Guard, 42
Reticulum constellation, 140-41
Rockefeller, John D., Jr., 96
Rockefeller Foundation, 97-98
rod, 56-57, 59, 61-65, 166, 168
Roddenberry, Gene, 74-75, 171-72
Rosenberg, Ethel, 142
Rosenberg, Julius, 142
Rosetta Stone, 44-45
Ross Ice Shelf, 98-99, 101, 103
Roswell, 17, 22-25, 113-14, 116-17, 125, 129-31, 143, 145-48, 150-51
Roswell crash, 25, 113-14, 130-31, 146
Rumsfeld, Donald, 22-23

S

Sagan, Carl, 83-84, 171-72
Sagan, Linda Salzman, 172
Schmidt, Reinhold, 145
  Kearney Incident, The, 145
Schreter, Heinz, 91
Schwarzkopf, Norman, 52
science fiction, 72-73, 166-68
Scorpio, 75-76
Sean Hannity Show, 133
Second World War. *See* World War II
Secret Diary of Admiral Byrd, 113, 118-19, 121, 124, 128-29, 137, 146, 181, 183, 191, 193

Seeing Eye Corp., 83-85, 88, 94-95, 97-98, 118-19, 122-24, 138-39, 151-54, 157-58
Seraphim, 175, 177-78, 181, 201-2
Serling, Rod, 167-68
shape-shifters. *See* aliens
Shoemaker, Gene, 68
Shoemaker-Levy 9, 68
Silent Invasion (Crystall), 67
silicon, 71, 146, 150-53
Silicon Valley, 145-46, 150-53
Sitchin, Zecariah
 12th Planet, The, 19, 26, 30, 53
Sitchin, Zecharia, 17-19, 21-23, 25-27, 29-31, 37-38, 40, 43, 65-66, 74-75
Slavs, 91-92
solar system, 19-22, 25, 27, 171
South Pole, 95-96, 98-99, 113-25, 127-28, 134-36, 144-45, 158, 163-64
Soviet Union, 35-36, 76-77, 135-36, 156-57
spaceship, 53, 142
Spanish Inquisition, 36-37
Spear of Destiny, 38, 40, 164-65
Sphinx, 44-45, 165-66
Spitsbergen, 95-97
Stalin, Joseph, 86-88
star defense initiative, 156-57
star gates, 41-43, 163, 165, 169, 171
Star Trek IV: The Voyage Home, 73
stem cell research, 155-56
Sumer, 28-29, 165
Sumerian language, 19, 26-27
Svalbard archipelago, 95-96
Svalbard Seed Bank, 97-98
Swastika, 144

T

TABLETS of DESTINIES, 40, 164-66
Tall Blonds, 21, 93, 117, 120-21, 123-24, 127-30, 141-44, 151-52
Taylor, George, 167-68
ten plagues, 61-62, 64, 66
 blood, 61-62
 boils, 61-63
 darkness, 61, 64
 death of the firstborn, 61, 64
 disease to livestock, 61, 63
 flies, 61, 63
 frogs, 61, 63
 hail, 61-63
 lice, 61-63
 locusts, 61, 63
terraforming, 33-34
Thermonuclear Hybrid bomb, 77-78
They Live, 33
Tiamat, 27-28, 31, 37-38, 40-41, 45, 163, 165
time gates, 43
Tinian Island, 79
trimetricon spy cameras, 112-13
Trinity bomb, 78-79
Truman, Harry S., 86-88, 139
Tsarion, Michael, 17-18, 22-23, 30-31, 37-38, 65-66
12th Planet, The (Sitchin), 19, 26, 30, 53
2010, 75, 168, 171

2012: Appointment with Marduk (Eldem), 163
2001: A Space Odyssey, 70, 168
two hundred renegades. *See* Nefilim

U

U-234, 82-83, 85-86, 90-91
U-530, 90-91
U-853, 90-91
U-977, 90-91, 99, 113-14, 125
UFO, 23, 25, 53, 96-97, 101, 114, 116, 121, 123-24, 130, 134, 140, 145, 174
UFOs, Nazi Secret Weapons? (Zundel), 143
Uncle Sam, 43, 74-75. *See also* U.S. government
Unidentified Flying Objects, 142-45, 168, 171
Ur, 28-29
uranium-235, 76-82
uranium bomb, 81
Uruk, 52-53
U.S. government, 27, 30-31, 113, 122-23, 130-31, 133, 139, 145, 152
USS *Mount Olympus*, 126, 128
USS *Northwind*, 101, 125-26
USS *Norton Sound*, 135-36
USS *Philippine Sea*, 103, 118, 124-28, 130-32
Uzziah, King, 177-78

V

vampires, 93-94, 172

Van Allen belt, 45-46, 123, 135, 163-64
Vatican, 34-37, 44-45, 65-66, 71, 74-75, 162
Veil's Machines, 94. *See also* flying saucers
Virgin Mary, 35, 69

W

Walls of Jericho, 57, 59
water schnorchel, 91
weapons of mass destruction. *See* WMD
White House, 74
Wilson, Michael, 167-68
WMD, 42
Worlds Beyond the Poles (Giannini), 123
World War II, 18, 37, 79, 94, 99, 103, 134, 138, 143, 145, 173
WWII. *See* World War II

X

X-Files, The, 143

Y

Yahweh, 29-30
Yalta Conference, 87-88
Yeor, 59, 61-62, 64-65
YouTube, 30, 68

Z

Zagami, Leo, 70-71

BACK COVER PAINTING "BLUE SAUCER".

BY: Andrew Leipzig. zig@planetzig.com

AGE: 51. GENDER: MALE. INDUSTRY: ART.
OCCUPATION: ARTIST. LOCATION: EASTERN LONG ISLAND: NEW YORK: UNITED STATES.

77 GARFIELD AVENUE, SAYVILLE, LONG ISLAND NEW YORK 11782 • (631) 567-0919

About Me

Artist—Artrepreneur. Surrealist visions rich in color and imagination fill the artwork of Andrew 'ZIG' Leipzig. Freelancer, Former Graphic Specialist For Grumman Space Systems, Performed drawing live as the 'Artificer' in 'Artmosphere',—Artist Laureate Visit www.planetzig.com.

Surrealist visions rich in color and imagination fill the artwork of Andrew Leipzig. As A Graphic Specialist For Grumman/Northrop Grumman Space and Electronics Systems, his computer graphic work has been on display in the White House and the Kremlin, work for two Presidents with ground breaking graphics in computer modeling simulation for NASA, the Navy's B-2, EA6-B, E-2C flight trainers and marketing. Andrew has recently shown his fine art in the Hamptons and NYC as well as the Islip Art Museum in their curator select show 'Free Play'. Awards include 1st Place Long Island Tourist and Information Bureau Contest to promote tourism, International award of excellence and many best in shows. Performed drawing live as the 'Artificer' in 'Artmosphere' at the Tilles Center. His artwork captures original thought and vision *computer graphics* in an array of media in a style that is unique to art

Deep Analysis: Frightening Conclusion

NEED ARTWORK CALL
(631) 567-0919 TODAY OR *EMAIL US* FOR A QUOTE OR SIMPLY TO DISCUSS YOUR COMPANY, PROJECT, PRODUCT OR VENTURE

ZIGS 3D GALLERY

VISIT OUR ALL NEW 3D TILT GALLERY

Andy Leipzig, Zig Studios brings you the finest art available, commercial and private ventures, we've been professionally freelancing for the past 30 years, we're where the artists and ad agencies go for quality work at a fair price. if you need anything from a website to full blown Trade show. we specialize in getting your product and company off the ground with a million dollar look while understanding your budget. Give us a call 631-567-0919

Visit www.planetzig.com.